PRAISE FOR
VIPERS RUN

"Tyler opens the throttle on this fast-moving biker-themed erotic romance. . . . Tyler brings her polished style to this red-hot page-turner."   —*Publishers Weekly*

"Think *Sons of Anarchy* with a lot more romance. No one can write a gritty bad boy like Tyler, and here she pulls out all the stops. Readers will find a lot of steamy sex and a raw, dark edginess they've never encountered before. An exciting beginning to a new series."
                                                  —*RT Book Reviews*

"An exciting and very hot story . . . a very hot, steamy romance . . . filled with suspense, excitement, heated sexual scenes, a great couple, and a well-written story."
                                                  —The Reading Cafe

PRAISE FOR THE NOVELS
OF STEPHANIE TYLER

"A raw, sexy world."
          —*New York Times* bestselling author Maya Banks

"Kept me on the edge of my seat . . . breathtaking danger, sizzling romance, and unexpected twists."
          —*New York Times* bestselling author Alexandra Ivy

continued . . .

"Fresh and sexy . . . a great read with smoking-hot scenes."   —Nocturne Romance Reads

"Unforgettable."
          —*New York Times* bestselling author Cherry Adair

"Red-hot romance. White-knuckle suspense."
          —*New York Times* bestselling author Lara Adrian

"Sexy and witty."   —Fresh Fiction

"Stephanie Tyler is a master."   —Romance Junkies

Also by Stephanie Tyler

The Eternal Wolf Clan Series
Dire Warning
(A Penguin Special)
Dire Needs
Dire Wants
Dire Desires

Lonely Is the Night
(A Penguin Special)

The Section 8 Novels
Surrender
Unbreakable
Fragmented

The Skulls Creek Novels
Vipers Run

VIPERS RULE

A Skulls Creek Novel

Stephanie Tyler

A SIGNET ECLIPSE BOOK

SIGNET ECLIPSE
Published by the Penguin Group
Penguin Group (USA) LLC, 375 Hudson Street,
New York, New York 10014

USA | Canada | UK | Ireland | Australia | New Zealand | India | South Africa | China
penguin.com
A Penguin Random House Company

First published by Signet Eclipse, an imprint of New American Library,
a division of Penguin Group (USA) LLC

First Printing, July 2015

ISBN 978-0-451-47047-8

Printed in the United States of America
10 9 8 7 6 5 4 3 2 1

For my MC-loving readers . . .

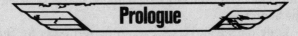

Prologue

Heavy metal music blasted through the speakers of the sweet, cherry red Ford Mustang as Tals took the ramp to the parkway in a swift motion and then really let her loose on the open road.

It was nearly one in the morning. Maddie wouldn't notice the car was missing. She might see that the odometer was higher and her gas tank was almost empty, but he had a feeling she didn't notice things like that. She was surrounded by people who did things for her.

He was mostly pissed she wouldn't let him in to be one of those people. But at sixteen, he knew he was too young to feel that strongly about any girl—though that didn't stop him from knowing something about him and Maddie was just "right."

Obviously he was thinking about Maddie too much to notice the police car silently trailing him. He did notice when the lights flashed and the sirens wailed, and instinctively, he sped the hell up . . . but there was a cop waiting at the next mile marker, blocking the road.

Fuck me.

His heart was still racing hours later when Maddie

came into the police station, alone. She made eye contact with him while he was handcuffed to the bench with a few drunk and disorderlies.

He smirked. Because hey, she'd definitely noticed him, and she'd been working damned hard to pretend she hadn't.

Long dark hair. Hazel eyes. A perfect body for the flowing hippie shirts she always wore with ripped-up jeans. It was summertime, and her flip-flops showed her toenails, which were painted with blue polish.

She was so fucking perfect, it made him ache. It was worse when she looked at him, and she did look at him, all the time, when he was supposed to not notice. But it was the oldest story in the book—bad boy from the wrong side of the tracks falls for rich girl who can't be with him.

But she wanted to. And who said the story had to end badly?

"Are you pressing charges?" one of the policemen asked Maddie, and she had the damned nerve to consider it. That was the flaw in his plan—he'd never figured she'd make that move.

Shit.

She shook her head no, a tight expression on her face. She had to sign some papers, and she kept her back to him while she was at the desk. When she walked out, she didn't make eye contact.

She hadn't sent in her grandmother—or her father. It could've been worse. Way worse. Not that getting arrested was ever good.

Dad would be proud, though.

"Christ," he muttered out loud as he waited for his ride home.

His one phone call had, of course, been to Tenn,

who'd been at work and unable to get any messages—or leave the job—until he was finished filming. So Tals had hung out outside the police station, sitting on another bench, watching the faces of the men and women who entered. Prisoners were brought around the back, so these people were here to see loved ones—they had that frazzled look, because they were justifiably worried and had no clue what they'd find beyond those doors. He was familiar with being on both sides, thanks to his father, who regularly put him, his mother and his brother through nights like this.

Tals had managed to stay clean until now. That wasn't to say he hadn't done things to warrant being inside, but he'd been really good about not getting caught.

"Seriously, Tals?"

Tals looked up at his brother. They were fraternal twins, although there was no denying they were brothers. Tenn was a little taller, and his eyes were brown instead of blue like Tals's were. But they had the same facial features that garnered plenty of attention. "Yeah, seriously."

Tenn sighed and together they walked across the parking lot to their mom's car, an ancient station wagon that she was convinced was too unsafe to drive. She took cabs back and forth to work, and Tals was convinced she had no clue that he and Tenn drove the thing on a regular basis.

She had no clue about a lot of things, but hell, talking about her was one of the few things that could get him and Tenn fighting. "Anyway, thanks for coming to get me."

"No problem." Tenn put the key in the ignition, and both said a silent prayer that the thing would start. After a tense few moments, it did, and they were headed through town, passing the exclusive community called Jessamine, where all the shit had started. "But all that over a girl?"

"Over a car," Tals corrected.

"You can bullshit a lot of people, *Talon*. Pretty much everyone but me."

Tals stewed over that for a minute. "She's different, *Tenn*."

It was Tenn's turn to correct him. "She's rich. She's trouble."

"You're not wrong," was all Tals could manage. "Don't tell Preach."

"Which part?"

"All of it."

Chapter 1

Fifteen years later

Axl Rose's screaming falsetto screeched through the speakers as Tals drove the rebuilt 1974 Pontiac Firebird Trans Am SD455 nose to nose with the equally hot-rodded 1968 Ford Mustang GT500KR. The cars were important, but the drivers were the real part of this race, and Tals had the lack of fear and love of speed that always gave him the advantage.

Miles from home, in a stolen car in an illegal street race was the perfect end to the year. Smoke billowed from his exhaust as the car roared under him. His hands gripped the wheel so tightly he knew they'd ache tomorrow, and the engine alternately purred and rumbled as he took the tight corners on this stretch of now-deserted road.

He was never as free as he was during these moments. Treating the streets like a racetrack. These illegal street races were run on a dime, with an eye toward protecting its participants.

He wasn't supposed to be racing like this. Or stealing cars for Havoc. But now that Cage was back as the MC's XO, the second in charge, Tals was freed up from some of the heavier MC responsibilities and had more free time on his hands. He was back to being enforcer of Vipers, something he excelled at. His rep preceded him, so not too many guys wanted to deal with him flexing his muscles.

A bored Tals was a really bad thing. Especially for all the people set to lose major money tonight when he won.

Which he would.

The course laid out for the race would take no more than ten minutes—ten minutes that would alternately feel like a lifetime and fly by, the last mile stretching straight out in front of him.

Although he could never shake off his status as an MC member—never wanted to, either, since he'd fought damned hard for it—tonight he wasn't Tals from Vipers MC, an enforcer, repo man or ex-Army. Tonight he was completely free.

Tonight he was also winning the fucking race, which he accomplished with a heavy foot on the gas, a tight swerve into the final stretch and balls of steel to take on the residential street at 110 mph.

His body still shook from the adrenaline when he eased the car to a stop about a hundred feet past the actual finish line. He took a few deep breaths, head back, eyes closed, trying to convince himself the car had stopped moving.

It took about that long for the crowds to reach him. When he finally pushed out of the car, he found himself surrounded by the men and women who'd parked their cars along the sides of the finish line—at least forty cars and far more people, all feeling the vibe of the race and feeding off it. Music blasted, women danced on cars . . . and it would all continue until the police got wind of it.

Tals gave it twenty minutes and planned to be gone in fifteen. He headed to find Bear, pocketing his winnings along the way and handing the keys back to Mel, who'd been the one to steal the car Tals had raced.

"Good job, man." Mel clapped him on the shoulder.

"Always a blast. You taking her back home?"

Mel sighed. "Maybe. I'm going to take her for another ride myself before I do, but I knew she'd like you better."

Tals ran his hand along the nearest car's bumper. "They always do."

"Things good at home?" Mel asked.

Tals smiled. "Living the dream."

Mel snorted. "Give my best to Preacher—don't tell him about the car."

Tals had no intention of doing that, although he didn't doubt Preach would get wind of tonight's race. Guy had radar for this shit, especially where Tals was involved.

Thankfully, though, things were back to normal at Vipers. And when things were this quiet, it meant more time for him to get into trouble, which was really the kind of shit he lived for. And that's why he hadn't been able to think of any better way to ring in the New Year than a fast car, fast cash and heading back to Vipers to share in the celebration.

He finally found his fellow MC member—and Bear was having a blast in that way only a red-blooded American male could—without reservations. Unabashed, with no limits.

Hell, Tals had been like that once.

No, he'd appeared to be like that, and probably most still saw him that way. Except for the MC members he was closest to. Preach, Cage, Rocco and Bear? They all saw through him like he was fucking paper.

And although he'd never discussed it with any of them, especially not Bear, the guy still knew. He took care of Tals as much as Tals took care of him. And Tals pretended not to notice . . . and Bear seemed to prefer it that way.

"Tals, you got a call from Sal," Bear told him, handing him his phone. Tals never wanted any distractions while he drove, but now, with his adrenaline roaring, a little repo would work out just fine.

"Time to go to work." But hell, work wasn't really work to him, and he had several jobs, most of which fell under the Vipers MC umbrella. Repo'ing was one of them, although his main work for the club involved enforcing. Keeping order, imposing rules and justice.

He liked that role a lot.

"No one else will take this motherfucking job," Sal was grousing in his ear. "You know anything about that?"

"Nope," Tals said, not bothering to try for innocent— didn't work, even when he was. "I'll keep trying."

"Find her."

"Hey, I'm better than nothing."

"Not by much." Sal hung up in his ear, and Tals sighed.

"Where're we going?" Bear asked.

Tals looked down at the money roll, then over at Mel. "You stay and have fun. I'll take this one—an easy job."

"You sure?" Bear asked, even as he was allowing two women to pull him back into the street-side celebration.

Tals grinned, shook his head. "Yeah, I'm sure."

The job was several hours outside his usual territory. He'd initially been tagged for it when he was doing a difficult repo close by. Sal said taking Cathy's car would be an easy reward.

There was nothing easy about taking a single mother's only mode of transportation. And so he'd warned her, had initially walked away from the job, reporting to Sal that the address he had was bad. He'd done that once more, buying her several months, but, like she'd told him, she couldn't create money from air.

"Where the fuck's your old man?" he'd asked, motioning to the three kids playing on the patch of grass outside the motel room.

She'd rolled her eyes. "Prison. Again. Sometimes I think he likes it better in there than out here. You know how that goes."

Yeah, Tals knew that all too well. It was easier for most of them on the inside. And even though he got it, this time he would need to take the car back—she was too far behind in payments and he couldn't keep other guys off her ass forever. Tals could only threaten so many of them before one of them would ignore him. He'd make them regret it, of course, but she'd be stuck.

He knocked on the door softly, because it was so late. And she opened it, in pajamas, her eyes tired. There'd been no New Year's celebration for her.

He gave her credit for opening the door for him. "Gotta take it this time, Cathy."

Her eyes watered, but she refused to let the tears fall. "You bought me a lot of time. I can't be mad at you." But she was—and he was on his way to becoming just another in a long line of men who'd disappointed her. She reached to the chair next to the door and handed him the keys. "I'm sure you know where it's parked."

"Show me. And you've got to empty it anyway."

She sighed as she stepped out of the motel room,

shutting the door behind her. "I never leave anything in it, since I've been waiting for this to happen."

It was parked a few doors down. Tals looked it over, started it up easily and then got out.

"Are we all set?" Cathy asked, eyeing the door to the room where the kids slept.

"One more thing." He handed her a set of keys and an envelope. And then he pointed to the car he'd released from the flatbed and parked right in front of her door. It was nothing special to look at, needed a paint job that Mel was supposed to do, but the engine purred like a baby. It was a good, strong car.

"Tals, I can't afford—"

"It's yours. First month's insurance is paid—it's registered under your name."

"Tals . . ."

"For the kids," he said roughly. "Don't fuck it up."

She smiled gently, then touched his cheek like a mother would. Like his mother used to. "You're a good boy, Tals. Now try to take your own advice."

He couldn't help it—he laughed.

He had another three-hour ride back to Skulls Creek— he'd miss the party at the clubhouse, but hell, he didn't care. Every night could be a party for him, if he wanted it to be.

But it was a new year, and things felt different. He wasn't really sure why. Maybe because Cage was back with Vipers, but nothing had changed within the South Carolina city itself.

He dialed his brother's number now, then pulled the flatbed onto the highway as it rang.

He and Tenn had grown up on what was most definitely the wrong side of the tracks in Skulls. But now there really wasn't a wrong side—just an MC side. Skulls was thriving. There wasn't violence or squalor, in no small part due to Preacher taking over Vipers. Still, they worked hard to keep out of trouble, mainly in the form of drug-pushing MCs, and Tals knew most of the Skulls community didn't fully understand or appreciate the Vipers' role in that.

Preach always said he didn't give a shit, but being treated like he was a criminal definitely got to him.

Tals had been looked on as one for as long as he could remember, but he'd also always gotten a lot of interest from the women of Skulls. And the Army. And Vipers. Havoc too. And Havoc allowed him to indulge in stealing and racing cars without bringing the law into Skulls or on Vipers.

Vipers relied on vigilante justice. Old-fashioned, but very effective.

"Happy New Year, brother." Tenn's voice sounded muffled . . . and slightly drunk. And Tenn rarely drank, so Tals wasn't sure if this was a good sign or not. "You out celebrating?"

"I was. Then I caught a job."

"Never ends, right?" Tenn went quiet, but there was obviously a party going on in the background.

"How'd you spend your night?"

"Threw a party for the guys who weren't working," Tenn said. "They invited some friends—it got bigger than I thought. Sometimes I forget how young these guys are."

"Not too young for you," Tals said.

"Yeah." Tenn's voice had that far-off quality to it, but true to form, he shook himself out of it before he got too maudlin. "Love you, bro. Be safe."

"Love you, Tenn—be safe."

It was the same every time. Just because they didn't live in the same house anymore didn't mean they weren't as close. It'd been painful when Tenn moved away—Tals swore he felt it physically. Having Cage gone for months had left Tals hanging in the wind, and even though Bear had been there to steady him, it hadn't been easy.

No matter how much he tried to fill the space, it never worked.

"I'll change that this year." He wasn't sure how. Maybe he'd give more women a chance—fuck the one-night stands. Try to open his horizons and look for a real old lady.

The whole one-night-stand shit hadn't ever been that easy for him—the mechanics were, because orgasms were never bad, as was finding willing women. But if he added up all the one-night stands—and fuck, that could take a long time—he'd realize something was missing.

Hell, he didn't even have to add them up to know that. It was a space he'd never filled, a hole in his heart that never healed. As much as he tried to wall it up, compartmentalize it, he could never separate it for long.

New Year's Eve always made him think of Maddie . . . no matter what he did since then, what country he was in, whether he was partying, stone-cold sober, in the desert, fighting another MC member or stealing a car, Tals could no more not think about Maddie on New Year's Eve than he could stop breathing.

Chapter 2

The battle cry of "Happy New Year!" echoed all around her, ringing through the air amid the clink of champagne glasses and cheers. Maddie held up her glass of champagne and forced a smile.

Maddie Wells had done that so much tonight her face hurt, but at this point it was plastered on. Still was when her husband—Hugh Montgomery—sidled up to her and announced, "Maddie, life of the party—and the most gorgeous woman in the room, as usual."

In actuality, she wasn't the life of the party, and Hugh always threw in the part about her looks. At this point, it rang hollow. She smiled at him, noted the attention they were receiving, aware of the flashbulbs popping in their faces.

Hugh posed, the way he always did.

She couldn't wait to kick her heels off and get out of this room, this building. She was far more comfortable behind the scenes. She never needed the credit. It wasn't about that. But lately she'd begun to overshadow the work.

Maybe she should've expected it, since she married

a man who owned the company where she'd been climbing the ladder for ten years. But Hugh had been pulling her into the spotlight, no matter how much she protested.

Tonight was another example. Suddenly, she was the subject of photographs and nonstop speculation. The more Hugh paraded her out to the press, so seemingly proud . . . the wider the chasm grew between them. She hadn't realized that it was irreparably broken, or at least had refused to admit it to herself until last month . . .

She left a charity dinner hours early to meet him upstate— eschewing the car he'd sent for her in favor of a rental. It wasn't what she'd pick for herself but rather a staid sedan, but she was in control and alone. Wind in her hair, singing, tank top and jeans—she was in high school again. Not the happiest of times and yet, somehow, at her worst moments, she came back again and again to that time. Mistakes. Regrets. Recriminations.

She opened the door, prepared to have a nice dinner with Hugh . . . and ended up surprising him and his other woman. One of them, anyway.

On paper they were the perfect couple, the up-and-coming marketing exec—who did everything from picking the new lines to meeting with buyers—falls in love with the CFO of the entire company. Obviously, real life had nothing on paper; real life trumped paper. In fact, real life was a tall, thin redheaded model who trampled over it with her stilettos. And a blonde who fit the same pattern. And, Maddie was sure, if she did some digging, she'd find more—all, of course, of the "she didn't mean anything to me" variety, according to Hugh. Which was bullshit.

"It meant something to me!" she'd told him quietly, and then she'd taken off her ring calmly, surprising herself with her restraint. She'd placed it on the small table between them.

And then she'd picked up a vase of flowers and thrown it at his head. When he managed to duck—just in time—she picked up anything else she could find and continued blindly throwing until she was tired and he'd locked himself in his bathroom.

Then she'd packed, thrown what she could into large wheeled bags, emptied out her makeup and jewelry (only pieces she'd bought herself) and then she'd called for her own car.

"I don't want anything from you," she'd told him before she'd moved herself into a hotel.

He stared at her oddly, the hurt in his voice apparent when he said, "You never did."

You never did.

God, that truth hit her right between the eyes. She had to take some of the blame for this failed relationship, and her part in it had her far more upset than his part. Which was, of course, a symptom of the larger problem surrounding their marriage.

Maybe I'm not meant to be married. Or in a relationship. Because she was very much married to her work . . . or at least, she had been, until she'd started feeling restless and unfulfilled last year, in a way she hadn't been able to articulate or explain. It hung over her like a cloud, until it began to weigh her down.

She'd actually begun to call in sick to work, something she hadn't done in . . .

Something she hadn't *ever* done, not even when she *had* been sick. And that's when the rumors started. No matter how often she denied them to well-meaning friends, no matter how many times she and Hugh stepped out together over the past month in their just-for-show moments—because he'd asked her to stay in

New York through the end of the season and this New Year's Eve Charity Ball the company hosted every year, and she'd complied. She'd put her wedding ring back on. She'd even moved back into their penthouse, and he'd moved into the guest bedroom, or else people would definitely talk. In the meantime, Hugh promised the divorce wouldn't be contentious. It would remain private, and they'd issue a joint statement.

He'd had no idea she'd already been planning on resigning.

"I've done more than my share for charity," she murmured to Hugh now, pretended to brush his lapel when really, she was dropping her wedding ring in the pocket with his boutonniere. "Don't call, don't write, unless it's through your lawyer."

On the way out, Maddie passed by Lettie, a woman who, if not exactly a friend, was someone she'd come up alongside in this company. She knew, better than anyone, that Maddie hadn't slept her way to the top. She was trustworthy. Maddie felt guilty for not telling her that, effective tonight, she was resigning from the company, but at the moment, Lettie's focus was firmly elsewhere.

"Who's that?" Maddie couldn't help but ask, since Lettie had locked eyes with a handsome man decidedly underdressed for the occasion—and looking damned good making that statement in a leather jacket and jeans.

"Who cares?" Lettie murmured, not tearing her gaze from the man. He smiled at her, motioned to the balcony. In return, she nodded and began walking his way.

Maddie pulled her back. "You can't be serious."

"I'm very serious. And very single. Don't worry— I'll keep it PG on the balcony. These corporate stiffs couldn't handle it."

"Last time I looked, you were corporate."

"Thanks for not calling me a stiff." Lettie glanced at her, slightly flushed with alcohol. "What's the problem? You never had a bad-boy phase?"

She said, "No," quickly. Too quickly, since her mind had already gone straight to Tals, as it had more than ever this past month, like she knew her fate was sealed and she was actively avoiding thinking about it until the very last moment.

For them it had always been about fate.

"You should never, ever play poker. I don't know how you made it so far in the corporate world, the way you let all your emotions show on your face."

"I do not," Maddie protested. In truth, she always had, but she'd been better at it before last month. Now she found herself unable to care about the career—the life—she'd so carefully built for herself. Around herself, like impenetrable walls. She'd escaped the family gates, but she'd gated herself in, just the same.

Lettie seemed to have forgotten about her own bad boy and was now firmly focused on Maddie. "And you're lying about the bad-boy phase."

"I never acted on it. Big difference." Another partial lie about that long-ago New Year's celebration.

"And that's the problem. You're with all these high-powered guys who're too selfish to care about anything in the bedroom but themselves," Lettie pointed out.

Instead of reminding Lettie that she was married (and wasn't that the biggest irony, that she couldn't even get the words out any longer?), Maddie asked, "And bad boys don't do that?'

"Oh honey, no, they don't."

She thought about Tals . . . the way the girls in school used to preen when he came around on his bike. The way she used to as well—secretly, though. Because she wasn't going to give him the satisfaction. "Go for it, Lettie. Have fun for both of us."

"You don't have to tell me twice." Lettie made her way to the balcony, and Maddie watched her as the elevator doors closed, effectively cutting her off from the world that had been hers for ten years, and coveted by her for many before that.

Her car was already waiting at the valet station. She'd left instructions for it to be pulled around at 12:30 a.m. sharp. It was packed and ready, and she got in, ball gown and all, kicked her heels off and took off in her Mustang GT.

She always bought Mustangs, and they were always some variation on cherry red, like the one Tals had stolen. She hadn't liked the color much when she'd gotten it. After Tals had driven it, though, she swore something happened to the damned car. It was almost supercharged, like it remembered him and wanted to be driven the way he'd driven it.

Which was ridiculous. And didn't stop her thinking it every single time.

And didn't stop her from buying this car again. Vintage model, though. Like that would make it so different.

"Time to turn the brain off, Maddie," she told herself out loud as she cranked the radio up and barreled onto the highway, the car revving, like it was telling her to get her shit together and enjoy the ride.

She gripped the wheel with her buttery-soft leather fingerless racing gloves—in bright red—and she systematically unpinned her hair so it hung loosely, tumbling over her shoulders. It got warmer the farther south she drove, and she opened the windows at one point so her hair whipped around her shoulders as she pushed the speed limits.

When she'd first planned on quitting her job and moving out—and on from Hugh—she hadn't been sure of her destination. Not at first. But then "Stop Draggin' My Heart Around" came on the radio when she was on the way to their house upstate after leaving the New Year's Eve party . . . and she promptly turned the car around and headed to Jessamine—aka Skulls Creek, South Carolina.

If anyone had told her before now that she'd be escaping back to her family home, she'd have laughed. Now she couldn't think of a better place to go, although it was less about her family and more about the man the song reminded her of: Tals Garrity.

You don't even know if he's still in Skulls Creek.

No, that wasn't true at all. She did know. Grams had brought him up in their last few conversations, almost like she might've predicted this would happen. Like she somehow knew that, no matter how hard she tried to not follow in her mother's footsteps, Maddie had some of that flightiness, that irresponsibility in her that she'd fought so hard to banish. And maybe she did somehow know that her soon-to-be ex-husband was cheating on her.

Because Maddie herself had no goddamned clue. Then again, she'd been working so hard over the past years, it was a wonder she knew his name. So was her marriage everything she'd thought it would be? Definitely not. Had she thought Hugh would cheat on her?

Never. She knew he was in the company of young, beautiful women all the time, but for her, marriage was forever. She'd told him that when he'd proposed, and as a child of divorce himself, he'd agreed.

So much for that.

She hadn't smiled like this in at least a month, starting with the day she'd discovered her ex was sleeping around with everybody in his path. She wasn't sure if it would've been better had it been one woman for an extended period of time instead of the constant stream of women, all younger than she'd been when they'd first met.

She was five years older and wiser . . . and obviously wilder, if taking off like this was any indication. And ten hours later, she was almost . . . home.

Her childhood home. Right now she was homeless, almost a guest in her own life.

She turned the radio up in response, a Stevie Nicks song coming on when she needed it most. She sang along with it, her voice a throaty rasp into the wind. She wasn't the best singer, but music had always brought her more comfort than anything.

She was free, and it was New Year's. If that wasn't fate, she didn't know what was.

Chapter 3

It was close to four in the morning and Tals was on the
final stretch to Skulls Creek. As he rounded a sharp turn
on the highway, he saw taillights in front of him—
taillights to a Ford Mustang GT he'd always been partial to. When he saw the back tire rock, his hands tightened, because he knew what was about to happen, and
he watched helplessly as the tire blew, making the car
fishtail like crazy.

It was lucky it happened on a quiet highway. Also
lucky that whoever was behind the wheel knew how to
handle the car, because it quickly stabilized, slowed
and pulled to the side of the road.

Tals followed, drove past the car slowly in order to
pull ahead of it, in case it needed to be loaded onto the
flatbed. He glanced at the disabled car as he went past.
"Lookin' for Love" came on the radio as he recognized
the driver. He braked—hard. Stared. Cursed his luck
and wondered if the gods were up there laughing their
asses off at him.

Because talk about all the wrong places.

Because Maddie Wells. Of all the women he could

possibly run across—and there could be a hell of a lot of them, and many of them would no doubt want to hit him with the tire iron, even though he'd never made any of them promises—why did it have to be the only one who'd ever had his heart?

She'd had it, and he wasn't even sure she'd realized it. What he did know was that she'd never wanted it, and one-sided relationships were the worst. Especially those that had been going on in his head and were still painfully fresh memories in his mind some thirteen years later.

He chalked it up to youth. Hormones. The fact that teenagers were dramatic as fuck.

So what was his excuse now, when his heart was beating out of his chest and his dick had started to harden.

I wonder if she smells the same . . . like citrus and gardenias? Like heaven?

He wasn't getting close enough to her—or to heaven—to find out.

What got him out of the car was what usually did—he had nothing to lose. Nothing he hadn't already lost. But before he could walk toward her, he noted the text from Bear, asking where he was.

He texted back, 10 miles out from Skulls, on highway. Stopped to fix a flat for someone.

Bear's response was immediate. Line of Heathens headed your way in about fifteen.

Shit. I'll be done before that.

Just what he needed—his MC's biggest enemy running into him and Maddie on a dark, deserted road.

Fuck fate. Fuck it hard.

"Tals? Is that . . . ?"

Maddie's voice sounded the same, that slightly raspy drawl that made her sound sexy, even as a teenager. It ran like lightning up his spine, and he forced himself to look in her direction, all the while hoping that what he'd seen through the car window was an optical illusion . . .

No dice—she looked the same.

No. She looked even better, and better still when she got out of the car and walked toward him. She'd left a teenager and she was all woman now, softly curved, her skin glowing with health and what looked like very little makeup. She'd never needed it. Her long dark hair was loose, and it was over one shoulder. She made no move to fuss with it.

She looked good. Expensive, in a full-length black gown that seemed to glitter, her feet shoved into impossibly high heels that she walked in elegantly.

And just like that, his New Year's went from great to gut-clenching. Although he couldn't deny that he was happy to see her, the way he'd always been. Even though she'd had him arrested more than once . . . and almost sent him to prison for assault by keeping her mouth closed.

Twice.

Fuck.

Just change her goddamned tire and end this.

"What are you doing here?" he asked, his tone sounding more like a demand.

"Visiting my grandmother."

"At five in the morning on New Year's Day?"

She nodded, then blurted out, "I'm getting a divorce."

Small-town gossip was unavoidable, and soon everyone would be talking about this. Some would be happy to see Maddie cut down to size.

Tals wasn't one of them. Hell, all she did was have a career and marry a rich guy. He didn't see a parallel between the two—she'd always worked hard, been serious. She'd gotten out, and for that alone, a lot of her old Jessamine "friends" would no doubt be particularly happy when they discovered she was being humiliated by her husband.

She was married . . . and now she was getting divorced. And she was standing in front of him, no wedding ring in sight. On New Year's Day.

And no, he wasn't going to get any of his hopes up. She'd be gone soon enough, and then he'd shove this to the back of his mind with all the other old memories that hurt too much to deal with.

As the famous saying went, there really were no coincidences. At least none worth ignoring, and there'd never truly been a way for her to ignore Tals.

Happening upon him was a regular occurrence growing up, but she'd never taken it as a sign of anything beyond that's what happened in a relatively small city. After all, they'd gone to the same high school—it was inevitable they'd cross paths.

Although, not really. They lived on opposite ends of town. Hung out with separate crowds. He grew up within a motorcycle gang—and then officially joined the Vipers MC.

"Are you okay, Maddie?" he asked, concern in his low, rough voice.

"Fine," she managed. "A little shaken." But she was a good driver, and the roads were thankfully dry. "I don't know what happened."

God, he looked good. Even with only the side glow from the headlights, she could see that he'd aged well, from bad boy to all man. He put the man in the leather jacket and jeans back at the charity ball to shame. His blond hair was mostly tucked under a bandanna, but she could see it was still curled around the back of his neck. He wore a tight-fitting dark thermal Henley, jeans, and black motorcycle boots, his Vipers cut no doubt lying on the seat next to him in the truck marked VIPERS TOWING.

"You're staring, Maddie. You used to be a lot more subtle about it."

Before she could get embarrassed, she shot back, "You never were."

He gave her that wolfish half grin that had gotten sexier over time. "Wasn't trying to be."

She'd told him about the divorce because she had no doubt he'd see the news reports, Then again, maybe he didn't check Page Six and the like. Maybe he didn't concern himself with the gossip, even if it pertained to local families. She'd lived in New York for so long, been such a part of the social scene, that there was a certain amount of ego involved, where she'd begun to feel like every day was a photo op, a chance to sell herself—and her business, by extension. That was the name of the game today, and whether she liked it or not (for the record, she found it exhausting), that was the way the fashion business worked. She was an extension of the brands she curated.

She hadn't realized she'd been drowning until she'd crossed the state line and drew what felt like her first deep breath in years.

And now Tals was so close. Too close.

And he certainly didn't seem happy to see her. If anything, there was an air of annoyance as he stalked by her and stared at her back tire while shaking his head. "Ridiculous. These tires are the most expensive pieces of shit."

She almost laughed at that, but she didn't. Mainly because she was afraid it would come out as a sob. "I can just call Triple A," she started, but he ignored her. He was moving fast, grabbing tools from his truck.

And here she was, a helpless girl with a flat. And she hated being helpless. "I'm okay. I can . . ."

"You don't know how to change a tire." Tals's voice was a growl that covered her, part reassuring and part dangerous as anything.

"How do you know?"

He gave her a sideways glance before grabbing the tire iron and began to take the flat off.

"Can you show me how to do this for myself?" she asked.

He took in her dress and her heels. "You'll get filthy."

"I'll live."

"I don't like to let women do heavy lifting when I'm around." He moved past her and knelt on the ground in front of the tire.

It was less sexist than protective, but it still rankled her and her reinvigorated quest for independence. "You won't always be here."

He acknowledged that with a long look, starting at her legs and raking up her body. "That's a shame."

She was ready to agree. Instead she kicked off her heels and crouched down next to him.

He smelled so damned good. Clean. Masculine . . . very much like the adventures she sought.

"You ready?" he asked.

"More than you know," she murmured.

"Back up before you get hurt," he told her, in probably the most fitting statement ever, before he took off the blown tire. In what seemed like minutes, he'd put on the full-sized one Hugh had insisted she carry around in her trunk.

Tals hauled the heavy tire like it weighed nothing, and when the new one was on, he put the blown one back in the trunk. He'd moved all her bags out of the way . . . and he hadn't commented on why she had so much with her for a visit. He simply put them all back, closed her trunk, then put his tools back in the truck. And started to get in, calling, "You're all set. Better get back on the road."

"Tals, I'd like to take you to dinner."

"There's no charge for this, Maddie."

"I'm not—thank you—but that's not why I'd like to take you to dinner." She bit her bottom lip—an old habit that she seemed to revert to only around him. Mainly because he stared at her lips every time she did it, and she liked him staring at her, the way he used to. "Maybe tomorrow night?"

"Are you seriously asking me out on a date?"

"Why's that so hard to believe?"

He snorted. His only answer to that being, "I think you should head back to New York."

"I'm not going back there. Not for a while," she told him. "I'm staying in Skulls Creek."

"In Jessamine," he corrected, like mentioning the split within the city borders would remind her of the split that kept them apart. "Too much water under the bridge. Glad I was here to help with the tire."

"This wasn't where I wanted to do this," she blurted out, and by doing so, stopped him from getting into the truck.

"But you'd planned on doing this?" He turned to her, his eyebrows raised.

"Yes."

He shook his head in disapproval—of her, of her plan . . . she didn't know which. Maybe both. "You left."

"I'm back," she said simply.

"And that's supposed to mean something nine years later?" With that, he ground his jaw and started walking away.

It had never stopped mattering—she'd simply forced

herself to bury it deeply, and even so, she hadn't been able to give herself completely to Hugh. And then, when she hadn't been looking, the sands had shifted, and the reminder of what she could've had shook her into clarity.

Because of that she followed him, her bare feet soundless on the tarred highway. Before she could reach out and touch his shoulder, he whirled around, faster than she could've ever expected, and caught her by her biceps.

"Don't," he warned.

"I wasn't going to—"

"You don't ever try to walk up behind a man like me."

She didn't want to ask, but it slipped out before she could stop it. "What kind of man is that?"

"The kind you never wanted to know."

The truth hit her squarely in the chest. All she'd missed out on. All she refused to miss out on in the future. "I want to move past the old, Tals. And see if we can get to something new."

"But we have old business, Maddie. None of this is new."

When he said that, she reached out and traced the bottom of the rose tattoo that peeked out from his short sleeve . . . the same way she'd traced it after the first time they'd slept together. "It feels new. It needs to be new."

Tals smiled at her, not unkindly, but certainly not the way she wanted him to. "Get to your grandmother's safely, Maddie. Happy New Year."

This time she let him get into his truck. But, she noted, he didn't move until she got into her car and pulled onto the highway.

It was only when she did so that she noticed a line of motorcycles come up over the horizon line behind her. Behind Tals too, since he was now following her closely.

Was that why he was rushing? Was that another MC who wanted to hurt him? Grams had told her there'd been some trouble in town but that the Vipers were working hard to keep drugs and other bad news out of Skulls Creek.

She kept her hands on the wheel, driving faster.

Vipers MC had always been a part of Skulls Creek—some said for better and some for worse, but for her they were a fixture. A symbol. Not, however, bad boys to chase, as many of her friends and classmates had felt.

At that point, Tals hadn't been a member of Vipers. He wasn't hanging out with the MC. He was close with his brother, Tenn. And his best friend, Cage, a former Heathen MC member.

To her they were all to be avoided. Time wasters. Heartbreakers. She'd been lectured her whole life about not going down that path.

When she got off the highway, with Tals still on her tail, she noted that the bikes had remained on the highway. And still Tals followed her home, pulling away once she got inside the gates.

His rejection had only strengthened her resolve. She'd rejected him dozens of times in high school—turnabout was fair play. Tals had never played fair, and she intended to follow his lead.

She only wished she'd been able to figure out how effectively he'd reeled her in, almost from day one . . .

Fifteen years earlier, and she hadn't expected to find Tals lying in the shade on the grass in the secluded area that was only ten minutes from the main building but on the side of campus no one ever hung out on.

Except for her. And, apparently, Tals, who was on his back, one arm thrown over his forehead and the other extended and holding a tattered paperback book. His leather jacket was tossed casually next to him, and he wore a faded T-shirt and equally beat-up jeans, with thick, steel-toed boots.

He looked more like a man than any guy in school she could think of, with the exception of his twin brother. All her Jessamine friends agreed with that assessment, even though she'd never actually discussed it with them.

The last time she'd been this close to him had been two weeks ago at the police station. Since then she'd seen him from a distance, but she'd managed to avoid a confrontation like the one she was about to have.

"I know you're standing there," he said finally. "Are you just going to stare, or is there a purpose to your creepy stalking/Peeping Tom act?"

"I'm not—" she started with an angry huff, then refused to justify herself to him. "I'm here because this is my spot." She felt stupid the second the words came out of her mouth, but that didn't stop her from pointing to the tree she always sat under during her free periods, as if that would prove something.

He drew out a sarcastic "Ohhhh," and he rolled onto his side. "So what're you gonna do, Maddie? Have me arrested? Again?"

"You stole my car," she pointed out. "People get arrested when they do illegal things like that."

"I borrowed your car," he corrected. "I had every intention of bringing it back. Besides, I asked if I could take her for a spin and you refused."

Because you slept with a girl who was supposed to be one of my best friends, she wanted to tell him. "I have every right to refuse to let you drive my car."

"And I have every right to stay in my spot," Tals told her with a satisfied smile, and she tried not to let him see how upset she was getting at the thought of having her daily refuge taken from her. "Also, I was here before you."

She crossed her arms over her chest. "How do you know that? I come here every day."

"So do I," Tals said defiantly, then added, "Guess we come here at different times."

It was the start of a new quarter, and schedules had changed a bit, so that made sense. But still, she'd been coming here for a year and a half and she'd never seen another person. Until now.

She sighed. "So what now?"

Tals shrugged and lay back on the grass in a fluid motion, head propped on his hand. "Now I'm going back to reading."

She opened her mouth, then closed it. "I'm not leaving."

"Good for you. Didn't say you had to. You were the one acting like I was trespassing on your private property."

Okay, that was true. "What are you reading?" she asked, because she didn't know what else to say.

He put down the book and looked at her, like talking to her was a great bother. Which was crap, because he was the one who was always talking to her in the halls, at parties . . .

Talking, not flirting. That he reserved for other girls in her circle, who most willingly flirted back. With her, it was simple talk, albeit sarcastic jabs back and forth, mainly initiated by her.

Finally, he shifted, and she noted that there was a pencil stuck inside the book. She could see that he'd underlined passages and even written what looked like notes in the margins. And then he flipped the book so she could see the cover. Shakespeare's *Taming of the Shrew*, which wasn't on their junior year's curriculum.

She must've been frowning because he said, "I liked *Macbeth*, so I just kept reading the other plays."

"Oh. I've read most of them too. Do you like that one?" God, why was she doing this? Guilty conscience because of the arrest?

"Yeah, I do. I like how Kate builds walls around herself to keep everyone out until she finds someone strong enough to break through them."

She felt her throat tighten. "He doesn't make it easy for her."

"Definitely not. But the challenge is part of the fun." He paused. "Guess it goes to show you that first impressions are pretty on target."

"How do you figure? They hated each other. Or at least, Kate couldn't stand him."

"Yeah, right. That's what she showed the world, but she knew."

She shrugged, like it didn't matter. "If that's what you think . . ."

"It is. So, Maddie, what was your first impression of me?"

"You're not serious."

"Completely."

She stared into his blue eyes, swallowed hard, then blurted out, "I thought you were a delinquent. And a jerk."

"And I knew you were a snob," he countered with a nod, like he'd proven his point. Then he flipped onto his back again and started to read.

Except . . .

Dammit. "Tals."

He glanced over at her. "Yeah?"

"I lied."

He put his book down. "I thought you were beautiful . . . I thought, she doesn't fit in with those Jessamine people. At all."

That made her smile. "I thought you were handsome. Dangerous." She paused. "But not happy."

He blinked. She put a hand to her throat as it tightened with emotion. He was the first person in her life she'd ever been completely honest with, and she hadn't had to say a word.

He'd read her, but obviously, she'd read him too.

"So," he started. "I guess we can coexist peacefully."

"If our schedules match," she added quickly.

"Right. If." He glanced at her before he got up, stuffing the book into his back pocket. "I guess I'll see you when I see you."

He sauntered away, and she tried not to watch him, but she snuck a few glances in his direction.

He didn't look back . . . At least she didn't catch him.

And the next day he was back. Still reading *Taming*. So she set her bag down and reached into it, walked over and handed him the movie she'd brought.

He looked at the Elizabeth Taylor/Richard Burton version of the play and then up at her. "What, I'm too stupid to actually be reading, so you thought I needed the movie?"

"What? No! It's just . . . you seemed so into it." God, she was scrambling. This was a stupid idea—they weren't friends, and the fact that he was insulted proved how far she'd overstepped. "The way you talked about it . . . and first impressions. And I saw you had written in the book. Underlining things, and I do that when I'm really into something. The movie is great," she finished lamely, pulling it back.

He took it from her before she could. "Thanks. I'll return it."

She nodded, then went back to the tree, sat and rummaged in her bag like none of it mattered. He went back to reading, and she attempted to settle in and do some of her own work. But it was hard to concentrate on anything with Tals this close.

Finally, she heard the distant bell that signaled the change of class. She got up and noted he didn't. "Don't you have class?"

He glanced up. "Don't worry about it."

"I'm not." It was no skin off her back if he cut class, got detention, got suspended. Missed their daily meetings . . .

"Have a good one," he told her absently, his concentration on the book. She walked away, not turning back to see if he was watching her go.

In her recollections—in her dreams—he always was.

Chapter 4

Maddie slept well past noon, then pulled on a robe and joined her grandmother in the dining room for an early supper. If she'd had her way, she'd have slept straight through till the next morning, but she had to make an appearance. Or rather, had to put on an appearance. She might be hiding from her present by running toward her past, but in this house, she'd never admit that.

Right before she headed downstairs, she made a quick call, because while she slept, the next part of her plan for Tals had formed.

She was still smiling a little about that as she went into the dining room.

"Maddie, I was hoping you'd make it down." Her grandmother looked the same, a little older but no less dignified. Maddie bent down for a hug and a kiss on the cheek.

"I was later than I thought. I had a flat outside of town." Grams had known she was coming in late, so Maddie didn't feel that guilty. At least, not about that.

But she wasn't going to mention Vipers Towing. Or Tals.

"I suppose Hugh's not joining us?" Grams asked after Maddie sat down.

The question immediately took away any appetite she might've had. "No, Grams, he's not. We're getting a divorce. I've moved out."

"How are you going to work from here?"

"I'm not. I quit. There was no way to stay in that company. The divorce would stir up too much controversy." As it was, this might bring some bad press to Hugh's business, but he'd done that himself.

With a little help from you, the harsh voice of her toughest inner critic reminded her.

Behind these gated walls there was a mess that no one knew about. Until Tals. In one night he'd slammed the walls down—and she'd let him—and then she'd known she had to get out. Escape from the gates and from Tals.

He is still here. Her hands rubbed along her jean-clad thighs as she thought about him.

You're putting too much on him.

But she'd never been able to shake thoughts of him. Probably, she hadn't been meant to shake his touch.

It had been tolerable when he'd been states away and she hadn't seen him. She'd known that laying eyes on him would change everything.

She'd been right—it had. All those aching feelings had rushed back. Time hadn't stood still, but she'd been made wiser. She could only hope it wasn't too late.

Grams pointed to the chair next to her. "Your friends will be happy to see you."

Maddie gave a small smile and poured herself some coffee before settling into her chair. She'd given scant thought to her high school friends and their reaction to her return—her focus had been more on her happiness than her old life.

Many she'd gone to school with had stayed close to home, married men with family money in the good old Southern tradition of the small, wealthy enclave. She'd escaped, and even though she'd married wealth, she hadn't gotten a lot of approval from her grandmother, who'd wanted her to stay in Jessamine. There would be many who'd welcome her back with open arms, but there would be just as many who would be thrilled that she'd failed. But she didn't care about any of that. She certainly wasn't coming back to Skulls Creek for them, or for her family.

Her childhood had been a lonely one. She'd been raised by Grams, which meant she'd seen more of the staff than anyone, and had been basically ignored by her parents. Dad was supersuccessful and her mom had been flighty. At least that's what Maddie had been told—she had few memories of Margaret Wells, who'd left when Maddie was five. All Maddie knew was that one morning Margaret Wells left the house and never came back. Grams had looked for her, utilizing private detectives, with no luck.

It made her father more driven than he'd been, if that were possible.

"Have you spoken with your father?" Grams asked, and now Maddie's appetite was officially gone. Maddie and her dad talked once a week, mainly about Maddie's work. Her father was the most driven man she knew, and she'd definitely inherited that trait. Or, at the very least, imbibed it.

"We spoke a few days ago—he's in Japan." And Maddie had yet to tell him about her and Hugh.

"He still comes home once a month for dinner." Grams looked over the tops of her reading glasses at Maddie, a not-so-subtle condemnation of how little Maddie had been home since leaving for college. So few and far between—she'd go directly to the house, drive behind the gates and not leave until she could get back on the highway. All in case Tals had been around.

She couldn't risk seeing him then, hadn't wanted to be pulled to him—it was the most helpless she'd ever felt. Not that he'd made her feel bad. No, in fact, it was just the opposite.

Maddie didn't have to leave Skulls Creek to escape. She'd actually been running herself right into another prison when she'd had Tals—and her freedom—less than five miles from her childhood home.

She was lucky she hadn't wasted more time. And she refused to believe it was too late. Tals might be a player and have a million women after him . . . but he'd always viewed her differently. She was counting on that to still be true.

Tals watched the gates swallow Maddie's car up—the same goddamned model she'd driven in high school—thinking about how he'd always known this was as far as he'd get with Maddie. He'd always known she was almost as walled in as her family's house was.

Hindsight made him realize she was actually more so. And he'd tried his best to find a way in without breaking her walls down completely, but obviously, he hadn't been successful.

He'd gotten close though during junior and senior year, when he'd discovered they both preferred the quiet spot on the west side of the school.

She was always smart as hell. Funny too, although he was pretty sure a lot of her friends didn't see that side of her. That was fine by him, because he liked knowing things about her that others didn't.

He had a feeling she liked it too. He told himself she

did, while Tenn grumbled about "rich girls" even as he proceeded to screw the closeted rich boys . . . and other men around town.

After a while Tenn stopped answering Tals when asked about his love life, and Tals stopped asking him.

Maddie was such a pretty girl, even at an age when many of them were gangly or awkward. Maddie always stood out, and from the second Tals saw her, she was burned into his brain.

"Girls like that don't mix with guys like us," Tenn would tell him—not unkindly, though. It was a simple truth, one meant to protect Tals from the possible issues of dealing with a woman who had no idea what the MC lifestyle was all about.

Maybe it was wishful thinking, but still, Tals could see Maddie fitting in. She wanted to fit in somewhere, and it certainly wasn't with her friends and family.

She was an outsider in a way he'd never been. He'd always had an extended family to go along with his immediate one.

Who did she turn to when she had a problem? Is that why she always looked haunted to him?

He'd talked to her every chance he'd gotten. She'd acted exasperated, huffed a little . . . but she'd always answered him. Grudgingly, but it would be easier if she simply ignored him, walked the other way.

And now she was back. Asking him out on a date.

He turned his truck around, went back to the Skulls side of town, to Vipers clubhouse, where he made himself breakfast.

Everyone else had come in hours earlier, so he'd gotten several hours of quiet before the men were up and moving.

Most Vipers business ventures were nighttime ones—

the tattoo shop, the bar, and although the car shop was open during the day, Tals dealt with the night shift. Never mind actual MC business.

Tals was going to head to his room to try to sleep around lunchtime—he knew it wouldn't happen, but it never hurt to try—when Rocco walked in with an odd look on his face. Maybe because he was carrying a dozen red roses. Long-stemmed. Expensive as fuck.

That made Tals's gut tighten and the tattoo on his arm tingle, the way it had from the goddamned second she'd touched it. Of course she'd pick roses—anything else wouldn't make him suddenly feel nostalgic as fuck and angry as hell all at once.

"Aren't you sweet? But you're not getting lucky tonight," Cage called, and Rocco rolled his eyes.

"You wish, asshole. They're for you." Rocco plunked the vase down in front of Tals, obviously delighting in this shit.

Tals stared up at him. "Sorry, but I already have plans tonight."

Bear came into the room and looked between Tals and the roses. Narrowed his eyes but didn't say anything. Thankfully.

"Aren't you going to read the card and put us out of our misery?" Cage prompted.

"And put yourself into a ton more?" Rocco added, plucking the card out from the arrangement and holding it out to Tals.

Tals grabbed it after a beat. He could lie, of course, about whom they were from, but these guys would find out soon enough.

He made no move to hide the card as Cage circled behind him. "Maddie. I knew it."

Tals growled, "You did not know it," through clenched teeth.

"Maddie Wells?" Preacher had picked that moment to come downstairs. Dammit.

"She's back in town," Bear jumped in to explain before Tals could. "Tals was helping her."

"She had a flat tire. Heathens were riding through, circling her. That's all," Tals explained.

"This is more than a thank-you," Preacher noted, pointing to the roses. "And here I thought she couldn't stand you."

Tals shrugged. "You know women. Who the fuck knows why any of them change their minds?"

"Must've done something more than just change a flat," Rocco pressed on. "I mean, I've seen you change a tire and I've never wanted to send you flowers."

Tals shot him the finger. "Maybe you're not looking from the right angle."

That got the men laughing, jostling one another and, for the moment, took the focus off Tals. He was eternally grateful that Cage hadn't announced anything else that was written on the card—his best friend had always been good about not making someone feel like shit about their past.

Tals slid it into the envelope and put it into his pocket, the handwritten contents echoing over and over in his brain.

Tonight. Eight p.m. I'll pick you up.

For the love of all that was good and holy . . .

"Think Holly could use some flowers?" he asked Preacher abruptly.

"Not sure what she could use these days," Preacher said roughly. "Plus, they're secondhand. Women are funny about that shit."

Tals grumbled, picked up the heavy vase and headed

to Holly's room. She took a while to respond to his knock, and when she did, she opened the door slowly. Ever since she'd been shot in her tattoo shop while defending Calla and Cage's youngest brother, she'd been closed off. Well, more closed off than normal, and bitchier, which was no mean feat.

"What?" was all she asked, her tone clipped and cool.

"Want these flowers? Some chick gave them to me and I don't want them."

She narrowed her eyes.

"They're too pretty to just throw out," he continued when she didn't say anything. The door edged open a bit more, and she took the vase, backed up and closed the door in his face. "You're welcome," he muttered.

Because *women*.

Preacher had been watching the whole thing from down the hall. "How'd you know she'd take the flowers?"

"Haven't you ever looked through her tattoo portfolio? Roses are her specialty." Tals slapped a hand on Preacher's shoulder before he left. Poor bastard had fallen hard for her, probably from the first day Vipers had taken her in. She was some kind of MC political prisoner, and it wasn't a secret that the No'Ones would've outright killed her already if Preacher hadn't claimed her.

Saying he'd claimed her was one thing . . . but the reality was, they'd never actually been a couple. Holly was really fucked-up when she'd come here.

Still was.

Chapter 5

Giving Holly the roses did something, because she texted him afterward that she had an opening late that evening. She'd been working on a piece on his side for a while, plus adding to his sleeve, which he'd started when he'd been sixteen.

She was also teaching him to use the guns. He'd started out apprenticing in this shop a long time ago, but quickly realized that, even though he appreciated the art form, sitting that still for long periods of time wasn't his thing.

Until the Army had taught him patience he never thought he possessed. They'd made it all about will, about survival, and that brought it home to Tals.

The shop was crowded already, but it would get more so as the hours passed. Holly never minded a good show—having a half-naked man or woman on her table after midnight ensured that the shop would get more crowded, bringing out the party atmosphere she preferred. The looser people got, the more money they dropped on tattoos. And the more Vipers who were hanging out, the more women from town would show to try to get their attention.

"Let's go, Tals. I haven't got all night." Holly's voice was sharp like a whip, but she was nowhere near as icy and reserved as she came off. That was all a protective shell around her six feet of stunning beauty, and there'd been times over the last years that Tals had wanted to kick Preacher's ass for the way he circled her but never touched.

He was pretty sure Holly felt the same.

But hell, none of that was his problem, and stripping his shirt and getting his ink was the perfect refuge, since he wasn't waiting around for Maddie to pick him up for their date.

He'd called her, left her a voice mail message—he'd had to dig for her phone number since she'd conveniently left it off the card, no doubt purposely so he couldn't cancel—telling her he thought it was better if they kept their distance.

Preacher hadn't said anything more about it to him, but toward the middle of the session, Tals looked up and saw Preacher standing against the wall, looking decidedly unhappy. Which was odd, considering how packed this place was.

Which also meant odds were that Preach was pissed about the possibility of Tals hanging out with Maddie.

Holly's gloved hand ran along his side as she stared down at her work. She glanced up at him. "What's wrong? Too much at once?"

He lowered his voice. "Preach looks like he wants to kill someone. Probably me."

She gave him a brief smile. "Why's that? The woman behind the flowers?"

"Yeah."

"I think he's looking at you like that because you're

all goddamned alike," she said crisply as Calla saun- tered over. "All want what you can't have."

But there was no reason for Preacher not to have Holly—it seemed so much less complicated than what he was dealing with. Or avoiding. "Sometimes you can't have what you want," he corrected. "Trust me."

Holly shook her head. "No matter which way you slice it, for me the chase is always better than the catch."

"Not always," Calla corrected her. The bar was closed that night, and she often hung out here with Holly.

"Go away before I kick your sunny little ass," Holly grumbled haughtily . . . and lovingly, for her. She and Calla had gotten close, and it was good to see. Because this wasn't an easy life for any woman.

Calla was obviously the right one for Cage, because she made it look pretty damned effortless. Especially so because Tals knew how bad things had been for them to get to this point—between Cage's battles with the Heathens, the MC he'd been born into, and Calla's near-death experience at the hands of a guy who'd been stalking her since high school, the couple had had more than their share of tribulations.

Then again, they didn't have a history with each other, a past that would make it near to impossible to be together. Never mind other obstacles, like zero trust.

"Fuck," he muttered, buried his head in his arm.

"Try to melt into it," Holly soothed as the needle be- gan to buzz again. "Close your eyes. This shouldn't be stressful. Turn your goddamned mind off."

Easier said than done, but he did close his eyes and attempt to enjoy the high he always got from the nee- dle's buzz.

Until Rocco called out, "Special delivery for Tals."

"Fuck. If these are more flowers . . ."

"I'll take them," Holly said brightly.

But they weren't. It was a basket of chocolate. He looked up at Rocco, Cage, Calla and Bear. "It took all of you to deliver this?"

"It was heavy," Rocco explained with a smile.

"What is she doing?" Bear asked with a frown.

"She's, ah, coming on strong," Cage said diplomatically as he stared at it, even as Rocco and Bear began rifling through.

"She knows you," Calla added. "Oh, is that milk chocolate?"

"Christ." Tals ran a hand through his hair. This wasn't ever how he courted a woman. If he liked her, he said so to her. Asked her out. Kissed her.

That's exactly why she was doing this. Her way of telling him she remembered their discussions. A late-night talk he'd never forgotten either.

Apparently, Maddie wanted to make sure he never did.

It had been a long night, and Preacher didn't have to hang out at the shop watching Holly. Everyone knew she was his, even the guys from town who stopped in regularly to flirt with her.

Granted, Holly always flirted back when he was around—he wondered what happened when he wasn't, and decided he didn't want to know.

Most men kept a respectful distance, but it was a fine line. She wasn't his old lady, but being claimed by the club's president meant she had a certain amount of respect and to ignore her flirting was considered disrespectful. Of course, some men—mainly those from town who weren't associated with Vipers, and sometimes men from other MCs—didn't give a shit. They'd push and she'd let them (unless they put their hands on her—that, she never tolerated) until Preacher marched over and effectively scared them away.

Tals had finally finished his tattoo, and he managed to avoid Preacher when he left. Smart move, since Preacher could tell this Maddie shit was going to be trouble. Maddie Wells always brought Tals trouble—and Preacher would've thought that by now Tals would be smarter about that shit.

None of these guys were smart when it came to women. None of them. And he'd have to include himself in that pile.

The guy hanging on Holly was tall and lanky, with heavily tattooed arms. He looked like an artist or a singer. Definitely not MC, but Holly was standing really close to him as they pored over the tattoo book together. She was smiling—flirting—and since she had no idea Preacher was watching, it wasn't any kind of act to make him jealous.

Which was why it was so effective in making him jealous. Enough to want to throw the fucking artist/singer poser through the wall.

These days, he told himself he was hanging around to make sure she didn't overdo it, since she wasn't fully healed from the gunshot she'd taken months earlier, right in this shop. She hadn't gone to many of the PT sessions Preacher had set up for her, but he often caught her stretching her leg while doing yoga poses.

She wasn't limping at all, didn't seem to be in any obvious pain at the moment, although he knew from experience that gunshot wounds tended to ache with certain weather . . . and that would never fade.

Unconsciously, he rubbed his thigh, the way he did lately every time he thought about Holly. Which was becoming disproportionately more and more frequent . . . and driving him up a goddamned wall.

Now that Cage was back in place as XO, Tals was much happier to move back into his head enforcer role.

Preacher had the time to step back from the situation and focus on other things.

Like Holly. "Closing time," he announced, causing Holly and Poser-Guy to look up from the book. He pointed to the clock, which read three in the morning. Nothing good ever happened after three a.m.

Gigi and Calla were helping to clear the space, although once Preacher spoke, most tended to listen.

Except Holly. "I have to do another sketch."

"He can make an appointment for another day," Preacher informed her.

Poser-Guy stared him down, and then his gaze traveled to the pocket on Preacher's cut. He paled slightly, looked back at Holly and said, "I'll call for that appointment."

And then he left. Quickly. Maybe he wasn't as stupid as Preacher initially thought.

"Are you going to stand there nightly and scare away all my customers?" Holly asked.

"Until you take care of yourself, yes."

"I'm fine, Preacher." But even as she spoke, he could see the slight clench of her teeth as she walked out from behind the desk. "Gigi, you'll lock up? Money's already in the safe."

"I'll hang out and make sure she's okay," Calla said. "Just tell Cage I'll be over in a few."

Preacher nodded, locked the front door before walking with Holly through the back door, across the alleyway and into the Vipers clubhouse from the side entrance.

Rocco and Cage were there, heads together. "What's wrong?" Preacher asked.

Rocco jerked his head toward the table. "More roses. For Holly," he added.

"Maddie again?" Preacher asked, even though he

didn't need to. When Cage nodded, he asked, "Where's Tals?"

"Went for a ride," Rocco confirmed. "Not to see Maddie."

"Who's Maddie?" Holly asked.

"Tals's past," Preacher answered, aware of how grim his tone sounded.

Rocco sighed. "Doesn't sound like a good thing."

Cage broke in with, "It's not," a frown creasing his forehead.

"Do we need to keep them apart?" Rocco looked concerned now as well.

"I can do that just fine on my own, but thanks." Tals's sarcastic drawl ripped through the air, creating instant tension.

Preacher glanced at him but didn't apologize. Why would he? "Was a time when you needed looking after."

Tals acknowledged that with a nod, his expression softening. "I've never not been grateful for you taking out the trash and turning Vipers around."

Truth was, Preacher had looked after Tals and Tenn from the time the two delinquents broke into this very clubhouse and announced they were ready to become a part of this charter.

Cage, who'd already been staying at the clubhouse with some regularity, had watched the twins with quiet interest. He was almost the same age as the twins, dealing with his own rocky road to young adulthood.

Preacher remembered looking at the blond boys and telling them, "I'm not running a fucking babysitting service."

Tenn's eyes had shot with quiet fire, but it had been Tals who'd stepped squarely in front of Preacher. "I don't see any motherfucking babies here."

The haunting truth of those words had stung Preacher way more deeply than he'd ever admit. Because those two and Cage? They'd never had a childhood. Hadn't been Preacher's fault, but he'd been breaking his ass, trying to figure out a way to stop the vicious cycle. To put choice—and pride—back into the MC.

At that time, he'd met Sweet, the newest head of Havoc MC, and he'd made Preacher see things differently. Or at least gave him hope that things could be different, no matter how bad Vipers had gotten.

"I heard you killed Dale," Tals had continued, referencing Vipers' old president.

"How the fuck is that your business?"

Tals glanced back at Tenn, not so much for strength as for permission. Tenn gave Preacher a long look before saying, "Your reach hasn't extended to the other Viper charters."

The way he spoke—it wasn't an accusation, but rather a stated fact. Before he could say anything, Cage informed them, "Preach had to clean house here first. How do you know so much about it?"

Great, now Preacher had a twelve-year-old defending him, and another two waiting for him to invite them in. He could tell despite their cocky attitudes that they were hurting. It was only later he'd learn what charter the twins had come from—they'd actually run from it, and their mother.

He'd put a hand on Cage's shoulder. "Why don't you come in, have something to eat and tell me what's going on?" He paused. "Anyone going to be looking for you?"

"Our mom. We have to check in, but she told us to come to you."

Great. Just fucking great, Preacher remembered thinking. Now he asked Tals, "You're not seeing Maddie again, right?"

"Gonna be hard to avoid, considering she's moving back here," Tals said.

"Fuck." They'd have to discuss this later, and preferably not in front of Holly, who stood there waiting for him . . . and looking decidedly too interested in the conversation. "Let's get you to bed."

"I'm not a child."

"You don't take care of your leg, I'll treat you like one," Preacher retorted roughly and, with a hand on her back, led her away from the men and up the stairs to her room. It was down the hall from his.

When she went inside and sat on her bed, the relief was evident. She rubbed a hand down her thigh, then looked at him guiltily before retorting, "It's the snow that's coming. You said yourself I'll always feel it."

Instead of answering her, he grabbed her some Advil and opened a water. She took both gratefully, then stripped down easily in front of him, until she just wore a short T-shirt and a pink thong. Holly's figure just made everything she wore look dirty and hot . . . in a way that made his cock ache. "Get some sleep."

"Are you coming back?"

"Later." Long after she was asleep.

"Is it true?" Holly called as he went to shut the door behind him.

"Gonna have to be a little more specific, darlin'," Preacher drawled, knowing full well she was referring to the rumor that he'd killed the previous president of Vipers and wrestled control away, because she'd been there for his walk down memory lane. Sometimes he told her because he needed to remember exactly what this MC was built on and why. To remind himself that what he'd done mattered.

He'd never had the luxury of going into the military—he'd considered it, but during the time he would've enlisted, it became obvious to him that leaving Vipers at that point would've put his plans back for far too long. Based on what'd been happening inside the MC, there wasn't a moment to waste.

He'd gone from foster care to MC life, becoming a young probie at fifteen. This was the violent and dangerous life he knew, although he wanted better. He didn't want to live on the Jessamine side of Skulls, but he was tired of feeling dirty all the time.

He could never stomach the violence Vipers stood for, but he'd realized it was his best chance to learn another way. He had no skills but criminal ones, and working with Vipers allowed him access to things— and cash—and he began to envision his empire.

He'd bided his time until he was strong enough— and feared enough—and then he'd made his moves.

"Did you kill the old Vipers president?" Holly prompted now.

"You've been here for years. Why ask now?"

"I think you might actually tell me. You know there are a lot of rumors about you."

He did. And he rarely thought about the old days, except when he felt the need to pull himself back from the edge. "You of all people should know not to believe everything you hear."

"But I can see it, Preacher."

He didn't bother answering, or denying. She didn't really need one, and yeah, he'd been a crazy motherfucker. After a while he was no longer sure where playing that role ended and his real personality began. He supposed, in the end, it hadn't mattered. Both of those sides made up the leader he was, and he answered Holly's original question with a "Yes."

She studied him for a long moment. "Why get rid of him? You were young for a power grab. You weren't a legacy. Supposedly," she added quickly.

He wanted to ask her if she didn't know him better than that, but hell, he was never really forthcoming. Holly had good intuition, and still, her question bothered the hell out of him . . . but any anger he had toward it was pointed directly back at him. He simply stared at her steadily as he answered, telling her, "He was molesting his stepdaughter. A man like that deserves to be put down, no questions asked. She was eight years old. A lot of MC members knew about it, but none of them did anything. So I killed him and I gave the men who'd known what he'd been doing the option of getting the fuck out of my sight or getting killed too."

It was Holly's turn to stare at him. "How many of them took you up on the first offer?"

"None of them. And yes, I kept my promise." With that the conversation effectively ended. He shut the door in case it hadn't.

Chapter 6

Tals hadn't shown. Not that she'd been surprised. Upset, insulted and angry, yes. All of which she really didn't have any right to be.

She wasn't going to be good at this rejection thing. Was he out with someone else? She knew she had no right to ask that, but she was back to being sixteen and seventeen and jealous as hell.

At least he'd called. How he'd gotten her number, she had no idea, but again, that wasn't a surprise. The Tals she'd known had always been resourceful.

She was going to need the element of surprise. Until she figured out what that should be, she'd court him with the flowers. She hoped he'd understand—remember—why red roses, especially after she'd touched his tattoo last night, but it had been a long time.

"Can I get you anything else?" the waitress asked. She was too young to remember Maddie, but she did give her a longer once-over than usual.

"I'm good—just the check, please." Maddie had excused herself from one of her grandmother's dinners, saying she already had plans. She'd rather eat alone than deal with the questions.

Grams had tried to head them off, explaining to her friends that Maddie had come home to regroup after leaving Hugh. She hadn't given details, bless her, but news of Hugh's cheating had spread pretty quickly. Although it was humiliating to have people learn the most intimate details of her life, it forced her to admit that she'd left the relationship years earlier. Now her focus was firmly on the past. On righting wrongs. On fixing things.

She refused to worry about what might happen if she was too late.

She looked around the streets as she sat at the window and watched the slow late-evening bustle that defined Skulls Creek. She wore a black slouchy beanie, a little makeup and glasses. And although she felt exposed, she was relieved to go unnoticed for quite a while. She ate lunch as she noted the cute new shops that lined the streets. She'd known this part of town had gone through a bad time when she was young, but this was always the way she remembered it—fresh and brimming with life. Some of the business names had changed, the signs looked refreshed, but Skulls Creek was alive as ever, and for the smallish-sized city, that was a compliment.

Real estate agents could still call this place a haven to potential customers—they didn't have to give the hard sell. A ride through town was enough to showcase the cozy yet cosmopolitan feeling.

What used to be the bad side of town had changed. Rumor had it that Vipers bought up property here as it became available, fixed it up. Sold some of the properties and kept some. There was still a distinct feel be-

tween the two sides of town, but not in the good/bad
way. This side was considered more artsy and modern
as opposed to the more old-fashioned feel of the gated
communities.

There was room for both, an acceptance of the two
sides of the city, even if Vipers MC wasn't completely
embraced.

They'd never admit it, but Vipers would probably
hate it if that happened.

She paid the check, left the restaurant and window-
shopped. It was close to ten at night, and several of the
shops remained open, taking advantage of the post–
holiday season shoppers. Across the way, Vipers Ink
glowed softly. The shop was open, but it looked oddly
empty. It was probably a bit early.

Maybe they had time for a walk-in. She rubbed her
side unconsciously as she began to walk across the street.
She'd been promising herself she'd do this forever.

The young man behind the desk wore a sleeveless
T-shirt, despite the season, his arms covered in ink.
"Can I help you?"

"Do you take walk-ins?"

"Depends on what you want and if Holly's got the
time." He motioned to the tall blond woman sitting in
the back corner of the shop. She was sketching something, and the shop was empty, save for one young
woman getting a tattoo on her ankle. And whining like
she was being tortured. "Hey, Holly—got some time?"

Holly looked up, her eyes a piercing green, and took
her time walking over to where Maddie stood. She gave
Maddie the once-over, although Maddie couldn't deny
that she did the same thing, though she hoped she was
more subtle.

Holly eyed her, then said to the younger guy, "Another one," without taking her eyes from Maddie's.

"Another what?" Maddie asked sharply, in no mood for bullshit.

"Just tell me what kind of tattoo you want—a little heart or butterfly? Make sure it's hidden under your bikini line?"

"Oh please. And I won't bitch and moan like that one." Maddie jerked her head toward the young woman who was now crying. Her tattoo was literally the size of a nickel. Holly raised a brow and let Maddie continue. "I was thinking of a dream catcher—here." She pointed to her side. "Not sure of the exact placement. I was considering my arm, but . . ."

"Too thin," Holly said, suddenly interested enough to abandon the crying woman—and also pulling up Maddie's shirt to stare at her side. "Come in the back and take your shirt off. I need to see you before I decide."

Maddie followed her into a private room that was both comfortable and functional. There were photos displayed of women who'd had their mastectomy scars covered with tattoos, along with reconstructed breasts that had tattooed nipples. "Did you do all of these?"

"Yes," Holly said. "Sometimes they'll do it up front, but most of the time, they're more comfortable back here. Now, shirt off."

Maddie stripped easily as she heard the young woman whine, "Aren't you going to finish mine?" through the open door.

Holly backed up, called out, "No," then turned to her, and her eyes held a challenge. "Bra too—I'll need to check the whole area."

Maddie unhooked her bra, meeting the challenge, and raised her arm for Holly to check out the area.

Holly ran her hands there, murmuring about perfect contours and the ribs will hurt like a bitch, but mainly

Maddie couldn't make out what she said. "Good. Give me a few minutes to sketch. Don't get dressed—wrap in the blanket if you're cold."

Maddie wasn't. Instead, she turned to peruse more of the pictures. Some of the tattoos were silly; some were beautiful. Some had roses, prominently displayed.

Suddenly, she said, "I'd like roses instead." When she was met with silence, she looked over her shoulder. "Sorry—is that a problem?"

"Better you figure it now. It's not coming off." Holly stared at her. "Roses are my specialty. What are you looking for?"

Maddie laughed, but there was little humor behind it. Holly was up again, touching her shoulder and back. "We'll have to move the placement. I've got an idea."

At least one of them did.

As Holly's pencil scratched the paper, Maddie began to leaf through a book of tattoo photographs on the table absently. Until she ran across one that looked really familiar. She traced the skull and crossbones, noting that the next picture was an after. She couldn't resist asking, "Is this Tals?"

Holly glanced up for a second, and if she was surprised, she didn't show it. "Yes. How do you know him?"

Another loaded question. "We went to high school together."

Holly nodded slowly, then went back to drawing. Finally, she took the sketch and went to the copy machine. Maddie remained topless, waiting.

When she came back over, she lifted Maddie's arm over her head. "Hold it just like that."

Then she applied the paper, took it off and stood back for a few minutes, nodding. "That's it. Take a look."

Maddie did.

It was far more extensive than she'd imagined, with the first rose beginning almost along the front of her hip, flowers and vines rising up and branching out along her shoulder. "It's so perfect."

"I know," Holly said without so much as a smile. "How much color?"

"Muted, but I definitely want color."

Holly showed her a few pictures and they agreed on colors. And a price.

"This will take hours," Holly warned.

"Good. I'm in no rush."

"We might even have to split it over two sessions. I'd rather it heal well than rush it." Holly was definitely a perfectionist. "You can wear these—I'd rather work outside."

Holly handed her a poncholike wrap—it was gorgeous and silky. "God, I love this. Who's it from?"

"Me," Holly said as Maddie pulled it on. It was specially made to cover her breasts while allowing her side and back to be exposed at will.

"Do you sell them?"

Holly's brows raised. "I make them for friends."

"So you never give them out," Maddie countered.

Holly was obviously fighting a smile. "So, you're a bitch, just like the other rich girls from Skulls. Heard your grandparents started the exclusive community so they didn't have to use the name Skulls Creek."

So Holly had known exactly who she was from the moment she'd walked in. And Holly was right—Maddie's grandfather had come up with the name Jessamine, after the state flower, and that exclusive community had been created to give the illusion of separation between the rich and the rest of the town. "Vipers wasn't exactly the upstanding institution it is now."

Holly's voice was haughty. "Still isn't. They just hide it better than most."

"My grandmother used to date a Viper," Maddie told her.

"Everybody dates a Viper," Holly answered. "They fool around with rich girls, but none of you is right for them in the long term."

Maddie didn't know how to answer that. She wasn't even sure she wanted to. Anything insinuating Tals wasn't right for her, or that she wasn't right for Tals, was enough to make her palms itch and her anger heat. She'd never wanted to physically fight someone in her life—save for the punch she'd thrown at her ex—but the urge to do so was strong now.

And Holly knew it, knew she'd gotten under Maddie's skin.

"Your girlfriend's getting a tattoo," was all Holly's voice mail message said in her clipped tones.

"She's not my girlfriend," Tals bit out to the phone as though Holly were actually on the line. He texted Holly. How do you know who she is?

A minute later Holly texted back, She recognized your tattoo in the book. Asked about you. She's a walk-in. She'll be here a while.

Dammit. Maybe he should go in and end this once and for all. Before he could stop himself, or call Cage to talk him out of it, Tals found himself on his bike, heading toward Vipers Ink.

It wasn't as crowded as a weekend night, but word had spread of a pretty woman on the table . . . and Holly was doing her famous roses.

Maddie was half naked on the damned table, in front of the entire room.

Turning and walking away would be the smart thing. Obviously, he was pretty much a dumbass, since he moved forward, approaching the table.

"Nice of you to join us, Tals," Holly said.

Maddie's head was facing the other direction—Tals could see the tension in her bare shoulder—but she didn't move.

Tals stared at the beginnings of the tattoo. Along Maddie's perfect skin, the outline of the twining roses was really fucking perfect. So were Maddie's curves, even better than he remembered.

Holly prodded him, and he cursed her under his breath. He walked around the table and stared down at Maddie. She was definitely experiencing a tattoo high—her cheeks were flushed and her eyes held that faraway glaze. Her lips parted . . . and her flush deepened when she looked up at him.

"Hey," she said softly.

He didn't want to be nice to her, didn't want to encourage this at all. "Hey," he managed back. Barely. Because suddenly his throat was tight. If he'd ever thought all those years ago that she'd be getting a tattoo in a Vipers shop, and looking damned comfortable doing so . . .

No. He wasn't going there. The past had cost him, although not as much as it could've. And no thanks to her. "How long are you staying in town?"

"I have no plans to leave, Tals."

"Maddie, we can't . . ." He stopped. "I can't do this."

"You haven't even tried."

"You can't just come back here and paint a pretty picture over the past, act like we were some kind of happy couple."

"I feel like we could've been. For a while we pretended we were . . . and I wasn't pretending," she admitted, then added, "But I don't want things the way they were. I want them better. I have to talk to you about what happened."

"I don't want to revisit it."

Holly had stopped working in favor of listening to the conversation. In fact, somehow everyone was watching, like they were some kind of goddamned reality show.

Cage was there—Calla too. People from town. Gigi, who worked for Holly. Rocco and Bear.

"Don't you all have anything better to fucking do?" he asked them all gruffly.

"No," Cage answered simply.

Rocco shook his head in unison with Bear and said, "Don't let us interrupt you. Pretty roses, Maddie."

"Thanks," Maddie told him.

"Don't encourage her," Tals bit out.

"Why not?" Maddie asked. "Do you have a girl-friend?"

A lightbulb went off in Tals's mind. "What if I said yes?"

"You'd be lying," Calla said brightly.

He glanced at Holly, looking for support. "Shouldn't you be . . . using that or something?" He waved to the gun.

Holly responded by putting it down and rubbing the outline with the antibiotic ointment, which made the tattoo—and Maddie's skin—look good. Too good.

He cleared his throat and looked away.

"Come back next week and I'll do the color," Holly told her.

"Can I keep this cape?" Maddie asked as Holly helped her sit up and drink a soda.

Holly rolled her eyes. "Christ, you're a pain in the ass. Fine. Keep it. Your clothes are in the back."

Maddie smiled and headed to where Holly pointed. Then she turned to him. "Tals, let me take you out to dinner. Please. I'm going to be here indefinitely. If nothing else, I'd like to make things up to you. I'd like to be your friend."

There was silence, like the whole room was waiting on his answer. He took a deep breath and said, "Maddie—"

And somehow, in her mind, that was a yes. "Tomorrow night. I'll pick you up. I know where you live."

After she walked away, without waiting for a response—with all of them watching, and they were not subtle about it—Tals sighed. "Fuck me."

"I think she's trying," Rocco said mildly. "What the hell did you do to her in high school?"

"Chased her, exactly the way she's chasing me," Tals admitted, glancing over to where Holly and Calla had their heads together. At least they were pretending to give him space.

"Any luck?" Cage asked.

In the end it hadn't been about luck at all, but Tals wasn't ready to talk about that. "No."

Bear was studying him.

"What?"

"You want to go out with her."

"I want to do a lot of things that aren't good for me," Tals muttered.

"And you usually do them," Bear offered. "And you have a lot of fun in the process."

"Go away," Tals muttered irritably, then turned to Cage. "Not a word to Tenn about this," Tals warned.

Cage sighed. "Yeah, you two keeping secrets from each other always works out so fucking well."

"This time it's not a secret. It's just a bump in the road Tenn doesn't need to know about. I don't tell him about the women I date. Much."

Cage's brows rose. "Now you and Maddie are dating?"

"Wrong choice of words. Come on, don't screw with me. Go back and play house with Calla and forget all about this."

"You'd better hope Calla doesn't say anything to Tenn—you know how close they've gotten," Cage reminded him.

"You keep your woman under control." Tals was only half kidding. Less than a quarter kidding.

"Yeah, right."

"What happened to women obeying?"

"Preacher seems to have outlawed it, among other archaic practices," Holly said, without a trace of irony. Calla laughed.

"Women," both men muttered at the same time.

"Speaking of, Maddie's taking a long time," Holly commented.

"I'll go check," Tals said. As he went toward the back, he took the Coke can Holly held out to him.

"There's candy back there too," she called. "And plenty of privacy."

He held up his middle finger to her—to all of them who laughed after Holly spoke—and pushed into the curtained areas. "Hey, Maddie? You all right?"

He heard a weak, "I've been better," and found her sitting on the bench in one of the changing areas, head between her legs. She still wore the wrap, and he could see inside the sides of the poncho.

Probably not the right time to remind himself of what he'd been missing, but fuck, he wasn't a saint.

"It's okay—you'll be fine. Hang on." He grabbed a straw—there were several of them in a cup next to the candy, as this happened all the time. "Take a sip."

She did.

"Come on. Sit up slowly," he urged.

She did that too. She looked pale. A bit unsteady, but it was nothing sugar wouldn't cure. "I was fine. And then . . . I don't know . . . I got dizzy."

"It happens to just about everyone. The adrenaline crash."

She was nodding and drinking. He opened a pack of M&M's and she took a few, munched on them. Her color was getting better. "Thanks."

"You need to get off your feet and rest. A good night's sleep will help."

"Right." She moved to grab her bag and rifle for her keys, attempting to stand.

And failed. "Whoa." He caught her, a hand on the bare skin of her waist. She sucked in a quick breath and grabbed at his biceps. For a long moment, they just stared at each other . . . It would be really easy to kiss her. To pull the poncho off.

Her cheeks flushed, like she knew what he was thinking, but even so, she smiled. "Thanks."

"I'll drive you home."

She didn't fight that. He had her, grabbed her bag and her clothes and walked her out with the poncho, his hand still under it.

Which the whole group saw, because he knew they'd never leave now.

Holly approached Maddie, murmured to her, while he asked Rocco, "Pick me up at Maddie's place?"

Rocco's brows raised, but all he said was, "Not a problem."

They walked out, with his hand still rubbing the warm skin on her side and back, the spot that hadn't gotten ink. Ink he couldn't wait to see again, to study . . .

Yeah, so much for just being friends.

But he told himself his only goal tonight was getting her home safely. To that end, he made sure she got into the passenger's side all right—she was definitely unsteady but markedly improved. She took a few big breaths and said, "I'm all right. The air helped."

It was January, and it wasn't the warmest night, but it wasn't the coldest either. He ran his hand along the roof before getting in, which she noticed.

"You really want air?"

She looked at him, a flash in her eyes. And nodded.

"Look what you're wearing, Maddie."

She raised her chin at him. "I know exactly what I'm wearing. I have to protect the ink."

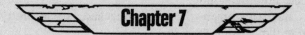

Chapter 7

The wind whipped around him. The air was frosty and snow was on its way, but Tals had an appointment to keep. He pulled into the lot of the building just on the outskirts of town, one Vipers used for special meetings and to house visiting charter members in the upstairs apartments.

The first floor housed a big gymlike area. Tonight the building was locked up tight and alarmed. Tals had mentioned he'd go check on it, since Preacher liked someone to do so several times a day to make sure no one was fucking with it.

Tals could think of very few who'd dare, but that didn't mean it couldn't happen. Preacher was smart, not paranoid.

But Tals had a more specific purpose in mind tonight—he was doing more than coming to check on the place. He got out of his truck and began a slow walk over to the lone other car in the lot.

The woman named Giselle was huddled inside behind the wheel and was waiting for him . . . and looking like she was ready to peal out of the lot. Running him over in the process, of course.

He moved toward her window, hands up in a wave; then he stuck them in his pockets in an attempt to appear nonthreatening.

But to a woman who'd been attacked, he was pretty sure that wasn't possible.

She rolled down her window a millimeter, and he said, "Giselle, I'm Tals. I know Ryker sent you." Then he said, "Lila Rose," which let her know she was safe and in the right place. Lila Rose was the name of the woman who'd put them together.

She nodded. He pulled keys out of his pockets and pointed to the building, then walked away, opened the building and turned on the lights.

Then he waited.

Finally, she got out of the car. She was carrying—he was warned of that ahead of time. How proficient she was was another story. And after what seemed like another eternity, she started to walk toward him, trying to cover her six and watch him at the same time.

He made a mental note to teach her how to do just that first thing.

He let her go past, trying not to stare at her at all, but noting the bruise that was still visible on her cheek. Which meant there were more, no doubt, under the baggy sweats she wore. Based on the way she moved, she was sore. He'd have to take a verbal assessment so he didn't injure her further, but the fact that she trusted him enough to come here to train was a good sign.

A couple of hours later, Tals determined that Giselle knew what she was doing with the gun, at least safety-wise. She could load and unload, and she also packed a pretty good punch.

It was a start.

"So tomorrow?" she asked eagerly.

He was busy as fuck, but didn't have the heart to say no. As he nodded, he noticed a tall blonde out of the corner of his eye. Holly.

Giselle looked over her shoulder. "Someone else you're helping?"

"Looks like it. Tomorrow. Same time. I'll walk you out."

"No. I can do it." She smiled. "But watch me, okay?"

He would. Holly smiled at her as they passed, and there was silence as he waited until Giselle got in her car and drove off. Then he turned his attention to Holly.

Like she hadn't caused enough trouble last night.

"Hope I didn't interrupt the session with Giselle," she started. And she actually sounded . . . nervous. It was the first time he could ever remember hearing it in her voice.

He stared at her steadily. "You didn't. How long have you known?"

Holly shrugged. "Women talk about these things."

"To their men?"

"Not this, no."

He hoped not. A lot of these guys got proprietary with their women, and he touched their women. But he knew, too, that the women talked, or none of them would find him through Ryker. "Preach will have my ass."

"Well, at least one of us would be getting something, because he's not touching mine."

Tals put his head back against the wall, closed his eyes. "That is so much more than I wanted to know."

Holly gave a soft, slightly evil laugh. "Let's go, then."

"Kill me."

"I could take you up on that."

"Then you don't need me." He stared at her. "And you don't, Holly, so what's going on?"

She shrugged. Pointed to her leg. "It hurts, but it's not about that. Ever since that night . . ."

That night when Eli, Cage's stepbrother, had showed up at her tattoo parlor when Calla was there. Eli had been only fifteen, but he'd been a patched-in member of the Heathens. And the Heathens hadn't been ready to let him walk away. Holly had defended him, shooting one of the Heathens, and she'd been shot herself.

He guessed the violence brought her back to what had happened to her at her old MC. He'd never asked for the full story, but from the bits and pieces he'd gleaned, her old man had been killed in front of her. And she'd been kicked out, with a bounty on her head. Preacher—and Vipers by default—had been protecting her for years. "Let's get to work."

He walked toward the mat but stopped when she asked, "Who's Lila Rose?"

When he turned, she said, "They say you always have them use that code name, to make sure it's safe."

He nodded. "Lila Rose was my mom."

Holly swallowed and then followed him over to the mats.

Chapter 8

The turnoff to Tals's place included a very long and winding private road that eventually would put Maddie's in
front of his house. But it reminded her of the tension she'd
always felt in her gut every time she'd waited outside the
gates of her grandmother's house for him. How they'd gotten that far in under a year's time always amazed her . . .

She'd continued running into him almost daily. Half
the time, she'd learned that Tals simply came to the
school grounds to hang out in their spot without ever
going to class.

She'd ended up eating her lunch there with him,
spending any other free time she had there too. She'd
told her friends that she was going to the library, and
since none of them spent much time there, she didn't
have to worry they'd catch her in a lie.

Then again, she didn't really care if they did. Because the Tals who flirted—and screwed—her friends
wasn't the Tals she knew. That made her happy . . . but
it also upset her, and she'd finally figured out why . . .
or finally admitted it to herself, anyway.

Because why not her? Granted, he wasn't friends with any of the girls he slept with, and she'd watched them try to circle around him only to realize he wasn't after any kind of repeat performance. She couldn't blame him for sleeping with them, because she'd seen the way they threw themselves at him. And every day she tried to gain the courage to ask him about it.

And every day she failed miserably, but didn't care, because she was seeing him daily.

She'd never been with anybody she could simply "be" with. There was a comfort there, an ease that called to her. But still, she didn't share much about her family, and although he talked about Vipers a bit, she didn't know much about that part of his life either. But she knew about him, and that was what mattered.

At the start of their senior year, Tals didn't show up at their spot for a full week. He hadn't ever been gone that long, even during summertime, when they'd had an unspoken agreement to still spend the hot days lying in the shade, each of them doing their own thing but still getting closer.

All she could do was show up daily . . . and go home disappointed and worried. But a week later, he was back. She'd held her breath walking to the shaded spot far enough from the rest of the school grounds to be private, and found him there.

He gave her a nod, like no time had passed, like nothing was wrong.

She noted the bandage on his arm immediately, because he'd stripped his leather jacket off and wore a short-sleeved T-shirt.

He seemed . . . annoyed. Although that wasn't exactly right. Surprised, maybe? Or caught, even when he said, "This isn't your usual time."

Talk about caught . . . "You've, ah . . . been gone a while. And I saw you this morning, so I . . ."

"Cut class?"

"Yes."

"First time?"

"Yes."

"So you're officially a delinquent now?"

"Guess so." She sat, her back against the usual tree. She wanted things back to normal between them. But that was becoming harder. There was tension between them, and she didn't know if it had been growing and she'd simply just noticed it, or if it had suddenly sprung up, but it sat between them like a shot of electricity that couldn't be ignored.

It covered her in waves.

"You had a birthday," he said finally, breaking the silence.

"Yep." She stared at him. "Are you okay?"

"Been better."

"You got hurt."

He looked at the bandage on his arm and hesitated a second too long before telling her, "I cut myself working on my bike."

She accepted the lie with a small nod. "I've never been on a motorcycle."

He seemed grateful for the change in subject, asked carefully, "Do you want to?"

Her heart beat faster when she tried to say, "Sure," as casually as possible.

"I'll pick you up outside your house—outside those gates—at eleven tonight."

He was gone before she got the chance to ask how he knew her house had gates.

Then again, every house in Jessamine had them. It

was its own community, but it didn't have any kind of gate or guard, which was why, right after the new naming, her grandfather had gated in his house. Many of the neighbors followed suit, and now it was customary to hide behind walls.

Which, of course, made it easy for guys like Tals to ride through the wide streets unnoticed. And after she'd chickened out the first night, she'd gathered up her courage and snuck out the very next night.

Tals was early. Waiting for her. She fell in silently next to him as he walked the heavy bike down the block, until they were far enough away from her house. He handed her a helmet in the darkness, which was only slightly illuminated by a lamppost, helped her fasten it securely under her chin. And then he got on the bike and looked back at her.

"Climb on, Maddie."

After a second's hesitation, she did, feeling clumsy. But once she straddled the seat and realized how close she was to him, all of that faded.

"You have to hang on to me, okay?" he told her. "Wrap your arms around my waist—sit close. Don't let go. I lean in to the curves—you just follow my lead."

Her heart pounded when she pressed her chest to his back and she swore she heard a rumble come from him, but maybe it was just the bike vibrating beneath her.

One minute they were still, and the next they were flying down the road with a roar. She was terrified for a moment, but the ultimate freedom made it impossible not to love the ride.

He didn't keep her out long that first night, maybe half an hour. She was disappointed, but they went again several nights later. And again and again, until they were riding for the better part of the night, meeting in their spot on the grass the next day to catch up on their lack of sleep.

And even though they weren't doing anything—because he seemed to want to keep things on the friend level—it was impossible to ignore the rising sexual tension.

That didn't stop them from denying it. At least she was. He was apparently just moving slowly. Circling her so as not to scare her.

He'd always known how to handle her, and honestly, that had probably scared her the most.

Maddie had pulled over on the long private road to his house. As dusk fell around him, Tals waited on the porch, thinking about all the times they'd both waited for each other—him on his bike and Maddie sitting on the stones outside her family's house, then walking the bike with him a safe distance from the house before they got on and rode the night away.

So fucking innocent. He'd seen how good that was with such clarity; at times it was painful. Especially that first night, with his heart nearly pouncing out of his chest. Because she'd chickened out the night before and then apologized. He'd wondered if she'd be there, or if he'd find the police, but this time Maddie was there.

He drove through some of the winding back roads of Skulls and beyond, feeling her clutch him tightly.

When he pulled over, she was flushed . . . and smiling. "That was amazing."

"Yeah, always is." He paused. "Why'd you really not meet me last night?"

"I told you—I got nervous. I don't do things like that—I don't sneak out." Her demeanor changed a little, and she shifted from leg to leg. "You kept busy, though."

Ah fuck. Busted. "Yeah, well, all dressed up and nowhere to go."

She frowned. "You don't even like the Jessamine girls."

He tilted his head. "Did you suddenly move and not tell me?"

"You know what I mean. Why try so hard? Why fake it so much?" she asked, although not unkindly.

He'd suddenly felt completely fucking naked in front of her. Was he that transparent to her, and how did that happen? He turned away from her and walked a few feet until he got to a clearing, where he could look up and see the moon.

She followed.

It'd been getting near spring of their senior year, and seeing Maddie was now a habit, the best part of his day. He was cutting class more and more, but that didn't stop him from hanging out on campus.

"Shit at home," he muttered to her finally. "Gotta fake everything—it's easier that way. What people expect of me, I'll give them."

"I fake things too," she whispered softly, but he already knew that. "I have problems at home too."

He turned to her. "Want to talk about it?"

Because it was easier to talk about her home issues. His were . . . impossible. Things he'd take to his grave without telling a soul outside of Tenn and his Vipers family.

"My dad and my grandmother . . . they're pretty tough on me. I'm supposed to be extra responsible. Not flighty, like my mom, because my mom couldn't handle a husband or a child—and that's why she left."

Tals saw the pain etched in her face. "You never knew her, then."

"I remember bits and pieces, but I was little when she left me with Grams."

"And your dad."

"He's barely home, Tals. It was like once Mom left, he did too, although in a different way. I know Mom wasn't rich . . . or cultured, like my dad. She was a real free spirit." She smiled then. "I have some pictures. I look a lot like her. Maybe that's why Grams and Dad were always lecturing me, so worried I'd turn out like her."

"She doesn't sound so bad," he told her.

"Except for the part that she didn't come back to see me."

"People have reasons, Maddie. There are things you might not understand now . . ." Fuck. He didn't want to do this. He tried to turn away, knew he shouldn't have come back after only a week to see her. Knew his emotions were way too fresh to hide.

Or maybe he'd done this on purpose, so she'd force his hand, which she began to do.

"Please, Tals . . . tell me. I know something's wrong. You were gone and now . . ." She stared up at him, and Christ, where did he even start? The fact that he'd been pretty much born into Vipers? Did he mention that his mom was an escort and starred in porn films and that Tenn had started dipping his toes in those waters, convinced it was a good way to make a living for a guy?

Tals wanted a relationship that wasn't about performing. He did enough of that, in bed and in real life, every time he went out and pretended he was an easygoing guy.

Because he wasn't. Which meant he had to pretend even harder to keep up the facade.

It was always the quiet ones, the ones who seemed the happiest, who carried the most pain. It was how he'd recognized Maddie. And the hours with her were the only times he wasn't pretending.

Of course he wanted to kiss her, roll her in the grass, taste her soft, warm skin with his tongue . . . strip her down . . .

But that would prove to her that he was just as he seemed—out to sleep with all the Jessamine girls. And having an innocent relationship with Maddie made him feel like he was worth something.

"It's easier to pretend to be happy," Tals murmured against her hair. She sniffed and nodded, and then pulled back. "I wish, sometimes, I could be more like Tenn."

"He doesn't hide the fact that he's not the happiest camper," she said wryly.

It was true—there was a smoldering behind his brother's eyes that forced people to give him a wide berth. He wasn't looking to make friends—although his attitude didn't stop him from getting laid.

But Tals got along with everyone. If he got pissed at someone, he told them he was pissed and then it was over. It's not like he was buddies with the Jessamine guys, but they respected him enough to stay out of his way.

"Tals, where were you?" she pressed.

He swallowed hard. "My mom died."

"Oh my God—I'm so sorry." She hugged him this time, holding him tight, and he buried his face against her neck and just let himself be. She stroked the back of his neck, a comforting gesture. It was, of course, electric between them, but they were both ignoring that. Things were getting complicated enough in their friendship . . .

"She was killed," he blurted out. Thought he'd regret it, but strangely, he didn't. Enough so that he continued. "My dad killed her, Maddie. He just got out of prison a day before, and he found us. He was pissed that she took us away from our original Tallahassee chapter. He came into the house, and before Tenn and I knew what was happening . . ."

He got dizzy then, didn't remember much of anything for the next several moments. But she'd gotten him to sit down, and she was propping him up, telling him it was going to be okay.

"You don't know that," he whispered brokenly.

"I don't know that it won't be," she offered, and okay, he could accept that.

"You can walk away, Maddie. It's a fucking nightmare. No one's going to know about it—we're nobodies, so it's not making the papers. It's been buried."

"Your dad?"

"He's gone," Tals said firmly. Because hell, that was the truth. Preacher took care of everything, made it look like his mom had killed herself, and no one knew his dad had shown up in town. And the police were all too happy to wash their hands of things, especially because Tals and Tenn were seventeen and weren't going into the state's care. "Maddie, I'm going to take you home now. And I won't come to our spot, won't bother you for a while. I know this is a lot to take in."

She nodded, didn't protest that it wasn't.

"Look, I know I have no right to ask this, but—"

"I'd never tell anyone, Tals. Promise." She put her hand in his and squeezed, not a handshake as much as a handhold, and she left her palm against his for a while, until he felt steady enough to drive her home.

He'd stayed away a full week and a half. When he'd shown up, she'd been there, looking up at him expectantly.

"I brought us some lunch," she said softly.

He sat down across from her, shared the food she brought . . . and they never discussed what he'd told her again.

*   *   *

Maddie swallowed hard as she thought of Tals's face the day he'd returned after telling her about his mom. He'd looked lost. Worried.

She'd thought about going to his house, finding him, telling him she could still be his friend, but she'd waited him out. And while they never discussed the circumstances of his mom's death, they'd talked about her life, and his.

After that, things definitely heated up. He managed to court her even as he held back, and the fact that it was innocent between them told her that it meant something.

If he hadn't told her about his mom's career, his keeping his hands off her might've bothered her. Okay, it did, but she understood—their relationship was complicated enough without bringing sex into it.

That night she'd ridden on the back of his bike. When he brought her close to home, he left his bike a block away and walked her back. When they got to her gate, he turned to her, asking fiercely, "How much longer are we going to pretend nothing's happening here?"

She wanted to say she had no idea what he meant, deny it, stop the inevitable. But she wasn't that good of a liar. "I don't know. Forever, I think. Because this can't work. You and I both know that."

"Because you live behind a gate?"

"It's so much more than that, Tals. It always was."

"It's pretty damned simple when you're riding on the back of my bike, or having lunch with me, or bringing me movies and books you think I might like," he pointed out.

"You're pushing me away on purpose, because you're scared of how you feel," she told him.

"I didn't want to. But you need someone different from me. You said that yourself."

No, I don't, part of her wanted to cry out. Instead she nodded. "I can't stay here, and you . . ."

"I'm staying," he confirmed. "Family's here. Everything I need is here. For the moment, at least."

He was looking at her the entire time he spoke.

"And the club," she added, because she didn't want to think about what she was throwing away. Because she was seventeen. And not a flake. And not a stupid girl who'd throw everything away because she was falling in love with a boy who could be very, very bad for her.

"My club and my family are one and the same," he told her quietly, and then he left her standing at the gate.

She remained outside until she couldn't hear the roar of his bike any longer.

The next day she didn't go to their spot. Instead she ate lunch with the football team and her friends.

Two weeks later she went to the party after the football game . . . with Earl.

Maddie shook her head, trying to erase that name from her thoughts. She'd been so lost in thought that she'd stopped the car for several moments . . . and then waited a few more to compose herself. These trips down memory lane, coupled with being this close to Tals again, were enough to jar her badly.

To her utter and complete shock, Tals was waiting out on his porch when she pulled up to his house. He was dressed in jeans and his leather jacket and boots, no bandanna. His blond hair was a bit shorter than she remembered, but it looked so good on him. He was the kind of rugged handsome that made women stop and stare.

And she was definitely included in that group.

He walked toward the car and she held her breath, waited for him to walk to her side, tell her he wasn't coming. He wasn't about humiliating her—and she'd been pushing him for sure, but maybe . . .

Before she could continue her thought, he'd opened the door and was sitting next to her. "I'm starving— let's go."

And then he smiled, like he was dialing up the charm. Which wasn't good, because it meant he was taking control of the situation.

"Me too," she managed, pulled away and headed toward a small Italian restaurant that was slightly off the main drag of town. Away from most of the Vipers-related businesses too.

With her luck, she'd find out Vipers owned the restaurant.

Tals was fiddling with the radio, and then he popped in the CD she'd been playing on the drive down. When Stevie Nicks blasted out, she called, "You can change it."

"Nope. She's got good stuff."

She prayed "Stop Draggin' My Heart Around" didn't come on, though. She remembered singing it with Tals, yelling it, no doubt, like they were in concert.

She slid him a glance and got a nod in return. Yeah, he remembered. But the song didn't come on, and the short ride was filled with comfortable silence, occasional singing along. She couldn't help herself.

When she parked across the street from the restaurant, in the small lot, he got out first, then came around and actually opened her door.

"I know you asked me out, but there are some things a man still needs to do," he said, his voice a soft rumble through her.

She stood, almost lost her balance, and he caught her.

They were so close, and the heat she'd always remembered between them was still there. Her nipples hardened, and her body pulled toward him like a divining rod.

He ran a hand over her shoulder. "You look really pretty tonight, Maddie."

She flushed. She wore jeans and a sheer, flowing shirt, hair down. Hippie-chic, she'd call it, much like the way she'd dressed in high school. The clothes were more expensive now, but her style had evolved more than changed.

Could she say the same about herself? "We should go in."

"Right." He stepped aside to let her out and closed her door. They walked across the street as he pointed out a few of the newer stores along the strip.

When they were seated, Tals took a sip of his water, then asked, "How's the tattoo healing?" He leaned back a little, his eyes raking over her side like he could see right through her clothes.

She shifted a little at the heat in his eyes. At least she could tell that he wasn't putting on an act—there was no way to get Tals to fake that look. She'd watched many of her friends hang all over him back in the day, and while he was always able to throw on the easy charm, she'd look in his eyes and know if he was actually feeling it or not.

Honestly, the only time she'd seen the look he was giving her now had been with her. "It's actually good. I thought it would . . . peel or something?"

"Holly's great—just use what she told you and it'll look perfect." He rubbed his arm through his shirt. "She's working on mine too. I go back next week."

"Me too." She took a sip of her wine and wondered how hard it would be to force this from a surface conversation. She wanted her Tals back, the one she'd had for those forty-eight hours. It was one of the worst hours of her life, coupled with the best forty-seven. "It's been great to finally do it. I've been wanting to, but . . ."

"Life got in the way." He leaned back, tilted his head and yes, he'd push them to go there too.

"I got in my own way. It's so screwed up, Tals. I screwed up. I can't believe . . ." She shook her head. Took another sip of wine, then pushed it away. She didn't need alcohol for this, no matter how badly she wanted it. "I thought my ex understood me. My drive. He worked hard. Played hard. I thought he respected me and what I wanted. I believed what I wanted to believe."

"Because he didn't stop you from doing what you wanted."

It was like he saw right through her, to all her fears. And he was right, but it still pissed her off to have him point it out. "So it's my fault?"

He softened. "Ah, babe, no. I'm just saying, if you were really happy, work and play would've been more equal."

"Maybe." But secretly she knew he was right. She'd never rushed home from work. "When people would comment, I'd just say that he supported me completely. I was a fool."

"Worse things than being a fool for love." He shrugged, took a sip of his beer and studied his menu. She did the same, and they ordered shortly after that—him the steak and her the same. It sounded delicious.

"I wish I could cook," she told him. "But you don't want to let me near a kitchen. I can burn water."

He smiled a little, and she realized she couldn't skirt the topic of immediate life post–high school for long, but there was no way she'd talk about the events leading up to her leaving Skulls Creek.

She realized she didn't know where to start. Her strength in life had always been about moving forward, looking back only long enough to respect past mistakes.

But any kind of catching-up conversation would have to include the events leading up to her leaving Skulls Creek.

Tals brought it up first in his no-bullshit way. "You knew I went into the Army."

He didn't seem angry about it, but she still braced herself and started cautiously with, "I did."

"It was me and Cage, and we dragged Tenn along with us."

"I don't know what to say about that. I mean, thank you for your service sounds so . . ."

"It's a nice thing to hear," he said easily. "It was an experience that all MC members should have, if they can. Rounds a guy out."

She swallowed. "You had a hard road growing up. I can't imagine you needed more. I mean, you were the most grounded guy I knew."

"Not sure that's much of a compliment, considering the guys you knew back then."

He tried to keep it light, but she made it serious. "It's definitely a compliment. I knew enough—before and after I left." She wanted to *not* do this here, had to bring it back to . . .

To *what?* They needed to retread if there was any hope of moving forward, and how did she think this could work? Because she couldn't read Tals at the moment—and she vowed to steer the conversation to more casual things. "How is your brother? Tenn, right?" she asked, and he nodded. "Is Tenn part of Vipers?"

"Honorary, but no. He lives in North Carolina, running his own business."

"You guys were always close."

"Still are," he agreed.

"That's nice to have family like that."

"Vipers is my family too." He stretched, like he was trying to ease tight muscles in his neck and shoulders.

"Tough workout?"

"Something like that."

"I've always heard a hot shower and a good night's sleep work wonders."

He laughed softly. "If that works, you deserve a medal. I don't really sleep much."

She smiled, because she remembered that, reminded him, "Same here. I watch old movies or read. I can usually fall asleep just before dawn."

"I remember, Maddie," he said quietly. "What happened when you worked?"

"I used the phrase 'I'll sleep when I'm dead' a lot. It wasn't easy, but as I got higher up in the company, I could work my own schedule. I'd go in late, but I'd stay later than anyone. I put in more hours than anyone." Her tone was clearly defensive, and then she softened, like she realized she didn't have to convince him. "Sorry. A lot of people thought I got special favors. Personally, I think there should be special shifts for night owls."

"Yes, during school especially." He shook his head. "I was late every morning."

She remembered that, because she was always sliding in the door behind him. Now, as they sat here together, championing the merits of three in the morning, she couldn't recall a time she'd had this much fun with a guy. She didn't have to monitor herself or worry she'd insult him.

No, Tals was a big boy who wouldn't turn every innocent thing she said into a sly dig. "Seriously, I'm glad you let me do this. I know I backed you into a corner."

"Yeah, you did." He tilted his head and stared at her. "Why now, Maddie? What the hell's going on?"

"I was trying to show you . . . you did it to me, and I figured, if I was willing to do the same thing . . ."

"Why now?" he repeated.

"I'm going after what I want," she said simply. It was the way she'd gone after her career, with a single-minded focus that had served her well. Once she knew what her heart's desire was, she'd never seen any reason to hold back, and she'd never had any patience for people who did. She didn't understand subtle—and she was pretty sure Tals wasn't looking for a shrinking violet.

"Why now?" he asked, like he really wanted to know the answer.

"It should've been a long time ago." Admitting that took more out of her than she'd thought it would.

"That doesn't answer my question."

Maddie frowned a little at his repeated question, then squared her shoulders like she was preparing for battle. "Why don't you tell me what you think I'm doing back in town? You seem to have an opinion."

And the gloves were off. Good. Not that Tals hadn't been enjoying himself, but there was too much between them to pretend this was all normal. "I think you're back in town, nursing your wounds. Looking for a little action—all the shit you think you missed out on. Midlife crisis hitting you early. So what, I'm your dirty little secret, your roll in the hay so you have a story to share with your high-society friends? Or am I always going

to be your secret?" He sat back. "Not that I mind fucking you. But in case you've got some romantic visions
of where this is going, figured I'd lay it on the line."

He was bullshitting her as hard as he could. He
knew that he could no more simply fuck her than he
could pledge to never steal a car again.

But he'd be damned if he was going to let her have
her way with him so easily, like he was a fucking
woman . . . When the hell had that happened?

When she sent you flowers and shit, that's when. Not
that he minded a woman taking control . . . in certain
situations.

Just thinking of those situations made him hard. Got
him thinking about Maddie on top of him. Riding him.

Yeah, he could get really into that, and then she'd
run off into the sunset. "Forget it."

"Tals . . ."

"Plenty of guys willing to play along with your
games," he assured her roughly, although none of his
friends, because they fucking knew better.

"I don't want anyone but you."

"I can't believe that."

"I refused to. For a long time," she admitted. "I went
out of my way to avoid admitting even feeling the way
I did for you. I thought I'd succeeded. Turns out, you
don't get that many chances at that feeling." She gave
a wry grin. "I thought it happened every time. I was
really wrong."

"Any guy can give you an orgasm, Maddie."

"Not like you, Tals. There's never been anyone like
you."

Jesus, she wasn't kidding.

Or she's a good actor.

Suddenly, he was freaked out at the prospect of either option. "Look, we got close fast. What you went through that night . . ."

As he spoke those words, she changed in an instant. Froze for a second, then threw her napkin on the table. "I'm not talking about that."

"Maddie—"

She leaned in. "No. I'm never talking about that. Got it?" She stood. "I've got the check. You can take the food to go if you'd like."

"So you're dismissing me?"

She wouldn't look at him. Or maybe she couldn't bring herself to, but he wasn't sure it mattered either way.

What did was that he was done following her rules. "This isn't over, Maddie."

She looked at him, her eyes filled with pain. "Maybe you were right, Tals. Maybe it should be."

Chapter 9

As soon as she heard the words come out of her mouth, Maddie regretted them. She'd known they'd have to talk about this—that they would, but in her mind tonight would be them just . . . talking. Flirting. Having fun.

Instead she was back in that moment—the start of the worst and the best forty-eight hours—terrified, humiliated, a seventeen-year-old attempting to fight off a drunk football player and then wishing it to just have not happened.

Having Tals find her, save her, and everything that followed changed her, stripped her denial.

The next best thing was to simply not talk about it. "I'm sorry, Tals. I can't stay. Please." With that one word, she was begging him to understand . . . and to forget everything. Then and now.

She didn't want to see if he'd comply. Bag in hand, she handed her card to the desk, waited, told them it was fine.

She was lying. About that, about everything. About

believing in fresh starts and do-overs. She would always be dragging baggage behind her.

There was no escaping the past . . .

She'd been a senior in high school—seventeen—and she'd been celebrating at the lake with her friends and the football team after their big victory. There were no adults to be seen, but there was lots of beer and pot and loud music.

She'd been dating Earl, the quarterback, for the last couple of months, although they'd been mostly group dates that finished with couples breaking off and making out at the end of the night. He'd never really been pushy, not until that night. It had been exactly the opposite—he'd begun his seduction in a way that made her feel comfortable. Special, even. He wasn't exactly her type, although at that point she hadn't really known what her type was.

Obviously, she'd been ignoring her type for years.

That night he'd somehow cornered her in a more secluded area, and he'd come on strong. She closed her eyes now and swore she could still hear the hardness in his voice, smell the alcohol on his breath as he'd grabbed for her breasts, shoved her back against a tree and held her there.

She'd fought, hard as she could. Cried out, and when he'd covered her mouth with his palm, she'd bitten it.

"Little bitch," he'd snarled, and his language got more abusive. His hand went between her legs and then . . .

And then the pressure had been off her, suddenly. She'd opened her eyes to see Earl on the ground and Tals with his foot on Earl's neck.

"Maddie, are you all right?" Tals had sounded so concerned. He'd looked angry, but that hadn't been directed toward her.

Even so, she'd tried to excuse Earl. "He's not like this usually—he's been drinking."

Tals's expression had hardened, but his voice was gentle when he'd told her, "Don't justify violence against you, Maddie. Not now, not ever. You did nothing wrong. There's never an excuse."

She didn't remember much else about the next couple of hours—she was probably in shock—minor, but she was so cold. She felt out of her body . . . until Tals gathered her up against him.

"You're so warm," she murmured against him.

"Maddie, you're safe."

But she knew that, so she concentrated on burrowing further against his chest, letting the heat from his body unfreeze her.

She thought what had happened would've sobered her up completely, but no, she was definitely still sluggishly inebriated . . . enough so that the horror of what had happened to her—and what had almost happened to her—was numbed over. Was a numbed-over thing she'd deal with tomorrow.

Up until that point Tals had been the toughest boy she'd known, and he was a bad boy without having to bully or abuse women.

That dichotomy stayed with her, and she thought she'd imbibed it. Thought that she'd found those qualities in someone who was in her business, who had similar career goals. "I don't understand," she remembered murmuring. "I told him I didn't want to have sex."

"It's never about sex. It's always about control. Always," he told her. "When someone has to control you that badly, it means they know they have none. They look for someone who doesn't know their own power."

And that had most definitely been her in high school. That night, for the first time in a long time, she'd actually slept for several, unbroken hours—in Tals's arms.

She tried to blame it on stress and the alcohol, but really, she felt safe with him, and so for the first time she could remember, she slept.

When she woke, it was still dark.

"Three a.m." Tals's rough voice answered her unspoken question. "We're in my truck. You're safe. Do you want me to take you home?"

"No." She said it so strenuously she startled herself with how loudly her voice had come out. "Let's go for a ride."

He'd obliged her, brought her down to the river that ran at the edge of his backyard. It was a warm night. Wrapped in a blanket, she'd ventured out with him, scrambled onto the hood of his truck, felt the warmth of the engine under her mostly bare legs.

He'd run a hand over her hair, gently smoothing it from where it had fallen over her cheek, and she wasn't sure how she could go from feeling such revulsion for Earl's touch mere hours before and now feel a shiver of arousal ran through her. "You're so pretty, Maddie."

She'd stopped thinking. Worrying. Instead she wound a hand in his hair and pulled him in for a kiss. And it hadn't stopped at just a kiss, no matter how much he'd tried to back off. She'd begged. She'd wanted him, been wet for him . . . wanted this act to take away what Earl had done.

And it had. Tals had turned what could've been the worst night of her life into the best. Under the moonlight, he'd worshipped her. And it hadn't ended there.

She hadn't wanted to go home, even as the sun started to rise. It had been a cloudy day, she'd remembered, added to the dreamlike feeling. It had been magic.

Tals put on music and sat with her as she sobered up. It was like coming out of a dream. As the sun rose, her sobriety—and reality—returned.

And it hadn't mattered, because she had Tals. He'd been chasing her for years, and he'd finally caught her, for lack of a better word. "I want to hide here forever."

"Yeah, me too." Tals had pulled her close. "Whatever happens, just remember, it's not your fault. You did nothing wrong."

She'd believed him. But he hadn't done anything wrong either, and still, that very next afternoon, when the police came to question her, she'd kept her damned mouth shut . . . and in the process refused to protect Tals.

Now, she started when she noticed he was next to her, outside the restaurant. "Tals, I can't—"

He interrupted her. "Maddie, we're not leaving like this."

"Tals, I can't. This was all a mistake. Coming back here was a mistake. This date was a mistake—just please, let me go."

His eyes widened. "Let you go? Wait a minute—*you* chased *me*. And suddenly you're blaming me for everything that went wrong in your life before this."

"Just everything that went wrong since I met you," she corrected.

He blinked, looking confused, incredulous . . . and like he was ready to explode.

She got there first. "You ruined me, Tals. You chased me and I wouldn't give in. Maybe I knew what you could do to me."

"What I could do to you?"

"Stop repeating everything I say." She pushed him—hard—but he was an immovable force. "You went around sleeping with everyone but me."

"So because I didn't treat you like all the other girls, you were pissed?"

"Yes," she said triumphantly.

He put his hand to his forehead. "I swear I'm having an aneurysm."

"Don't you dare—not before we finish this." She poked at him.

"The Jessamine girls . . . they weren't exactly suffering. I appealed to them on one level, and for one reason only. They weren't interested in taking things further, and neither was I."

"I wanted to be special to you."

He narrowed his eyes, looking at her like she was from another planet. "Jesus Christ, you were. Did you see me going after any other girl the way I did you? Did you see me spending time with them? Picking them up? Giving them rides on my bike?"

"You didn't have to—the rest of them fell at your feet."

"Well, yeah," he conceded. "But I was falling at your feet. You're the one I wanted. You had to feel it."

"I did. Damn you. You ruined me then—you ruined me after we finally did sleep together. I couldn't undo it. It left me comparing everyone else to you."

"You don't think I've been doing the same goddamned thing?" he roared.

She took a step back, stunned. Because no, absolutely not. She'd never considered that.

He took a step toward her. "You weren't just a conquest, Maddie. I wanted you all for me. I wanted to claim you. Make you mine. And when you came for me that first night, you told me that you could love me."

Her mouth opened, breath quickened. For a second she thought—hoped—he'd kiss her.

When he didn't, she began to rifle through her bag for her car key. "It's been a long week for me—"

But when she looked up, she noted that Tals was no longer staring at her, but rather, the key in her hand. His head tilted and froze for a split second, and then he grabbed her wrist—harder than she'd expected. "Give me the key."

She wanted to say no, but the way he held her wrist made her hand open, and revealed the key deposited in her open palm.

Tals stared at it, turning it over. Then he looked between it and the car. Crouched down and looked.

The street was semi-deserted. It was the middle of the week, and they were eating late. She hadn't wanted a crowd around, and she'd gotten what she wished for. "Tals, I just want to go home. Please—"

She moved to take the key from him, but he was faster, almost like a blur, and he was standing next to her, holding on to her biceps—not hard this time, but with enough grip that she wasn't going anywhere. At first she thought he was really pissed that she was going to leave him behind, but no, there was something more. He looked angry, but not at her. And he also looked worried.

"You can't get into that car," was all he'd said. He turned the remote key in his palm, frowning.

"What's wrong?"

But he was dialing his cell phone, asking for Preacher.

Preacher Jones, head of the Vipers MC. Not her biggest fan either, considering what had happened to his charge. She'd had contact with him only once before, when he'd stopped her from seeing Tals. He hadn't been rough with her, but he'd definitely had some bite.

"Yeah, Preach—need your help. Can you bring Cage? I'll explain when you get here. Thanks." He clicked the phone off and then looked up and down the street. "Let's wait inside. It's cold."

"It's really not," she said, but he ushered her in there anyway. Ordered her a glass of wine, which she basically took one sip from and just hung on to so he wouldn't keep hovering. "Tals, can you just—"

"I can't. Just . . . trust me."

Well, she'd trusted him enough to go on this date. Actually, he'd trusted her enough to give her this chance, so she figured she'd wait until Preacher and company got there to find out what was up.

Tals meanwhile spent time on his phone, texting. She was still shaken up enough by his mention of the past that she didn't want to risk him bringing that up again. And, as if he knew that, he reached out at one point and rubbed her back comfortingly.

When Preacher arrived in his big black truck and walked over to them, Tals told her, "Hang out here."

He didn't move far from her, just enough so she couldn't hear what he said to Preacher. Her belly tightened when Preacher looked over at her, looking bigger and badder than he ever had with his bald head and tattoos and black leather jacket that looked soft as butter . . . softer still against the hardness of his countenance. She couldn't believe it when Tals said, "Maddie, Preacher here is going to give you a ride, and I'll meet you with your car in a little bit, okay?"

Okay? No, it certainly wasn't okay, and she had no idea what was happening. But something stopped her from asking the question, mainly because Tals, Preacher and Cage were so quiet. Something was really wrong, and she had to trust that Tals wouldn't do anything to put her in danger.

"Let's go," Preacher told her, his voice rough. He walked next to her, helped her into his truck and then got in. He glanced in the rearview and then took off through town.

Preacher's going to give you a ride . . .

"Are you dropping me off at home? The turnoff to Jessamine is right there," she said helpfully, like he hadn't lived in this town longer than her, but he made her nervous. He ignored her, driving right past the turnoff that went toward Jessamine. "Or not."

"I've had enough of women for the week," he muttered.

"I'm guessing that's not a compliment."

He glanced at her wryly. "Smart-ass. It's always the smart-asses."

Her mind automatically flashed to Tals, and she couldn't disagree with Preacher's sentiment. "Where am I going?"

"To the Vipers clubhouse."

"Why?" God, that was the last place she wanted to go—more time with guys who didn't like her.

"Too many questions."

"First Tals won't let me drive home, and now you won't let me go home. You have to tell me what's going on," she demanded.

"Will you tell me what your husband's into?" he countered.

"We're separated. He's an asshole," she muttered, crossing her arms.

"For a living?"

"For the past year and a half, I've thought so," she mumbled, thought she saw an actual hint of a smile crack Preacher's stoically scary demeanor. "He's the CFO of a major fashion corporation."

"That's all?"

"He sleeps around. He's rich. He's used to being catered to."

There was silence, with strains of "Blue Sky" by the Allman Brothers coming through the speakers. She recalled Tals and Tenn strumming guitars and singing by the lake in the summers, where everyone used to hang out. There wasn't as much of an us-versus-them divide at the lake, which—ironically—physically divided the town in two. It was a peaceful place where many generations of Skulls Creek kids hung out, drank beers and partied. It was where the good girls and the bad boys met (and true, sometimes the good boys met with the bad girls too). Tals would smile as he sang. He always seemed happy.

She'd always pretended to be happy too, so she knew a semi-ruse when she saw one. Although his smile when it came to his brother was completely genuine— she saw that easily in his eyes.

"Look, I don't need to be involved in a fight between Vipers and another club," she started.

"Good. You're not."

"Oh."

Finally, Preacher pulled his truck around the back of the Vipers clubhouse. Although the building looked the same as she remembered—big and sturdy—the surrounding area was now clean and well tended. There was no graffiti on the building or the fences beyond. The parking lot in the back looked new. And there were what she supposed were guards, the only outward sign that this wasn't a normal building. That, and the knife/snake painting that loomed large along the backside of the building.

Preacher's parking space was closest to the door. When she went to get out, she found a heavily tattooed man in a sleeveless T-shirt and a bandanna wrapped around his head waiting there. With a glance over the hood at Preacher, then a small nod, he met her eyes and motioned for her to walk with him to the door.

He was, for lack of better phrasing, covering her. And she hadn't realized she'd been holding her breath until the heavy door of the clubhouse closed behind her.

That is, until she noticed she was surrounded not only by solid walls, but a solid wall of men as well, all in various stages of dress. Some had their leather jackets on, some, only the sleeveless leather vests she'd learned were called cuts. Some only wore T-shirts, looking like they'd been pulled from bed.

She wondered how many of the men actually lived in this building. But it didn't matter, because all of them were intimidating, at least from where she stood.

"I can't do this." The words tumbled out as her arms wrapped protectively—predictably—across her chest and she stepped back. Into another Viper.

Preacher. His hands went to her shoulders to steady her. They were heavy, and oddly a comfort when normally the threat of being held in place would've terrified her.

"Guys, some of you might remember Maddie. She's Tals's."

"I'm Tals's?" she repeated incredulously, glancing back over her shoulder at the man with the shaved head and the fierce eyes. "I'm not anyone's."

There was a soft snigger, but for the most part, it was just her voice of protest echoing in the quiet room.

Preacher's eyes grew darker. He obviously wasn't used to having his authority questioned, especially not by a woman, and he definitely didn't like it, judging by the way he cleared his throat and narrowed his eyes for a moment.

"Like I said, she's Tals's." His eyes never left the group, never flicked to hers.

The guy who'd walked her into the clubhouse caught her eyes and gave an almost imperceptible shake of the head, a "don't contradict him" look.

She listened, because the mood shifted dangerously. She wasn't sure why—Preacher hadn't said anything else, but she didn't have time to dwell before being led down a hall, up some stairs and into a bedroom.

"This is Tals's," the guy explained. "I'm Rally."

She nodded and looked down at the keys in his hand. "Are you locking me in here?"

"Yeah."

"I was kidding," she said miserably.

"Bathroom's that way. Water and soda are in the fridge. You need anything else, hit the red button on the phone. I can bring you food. Tals has movies and all the cable channels."

She didn't have anything on her, not her bag or her cell phone. When the door closed and locked, as promised, she sat on the bed and looked around.

A well-made, comfortably masculine-looking bed. Nice carpet. Walls were clean and painted a light putty color. There were wood blinds, fresh-smelling sheets. A big TV, books, stereo, computer—locked, of course—and a phone with only a red button on it.

She wondered how many women Vipers kept in rooms like this under the guise of protection.

Preacher had already left with Maddie, but when he'd first arrived he'd asked, "You're absolutely sure it's a bomb?" Cage had already been nodding in confirmation of Tals's immediate assessment. There was a motherfucking car bomb hardwired to Maddie's car.

And it hadn't been there before dinner. Because they would never have made it to dinner if there had been.

Now, with Maddie safe—and full of questions—Tals and Cage were left with the responsibility of the bomb. Calling the police was the best thing to do, but somehow they'd blame Vipers. Because they always did.

"Could this be about you?" Cage asked.

"Anything's possible, but hell, there are easier ways to try to kill me."

"None of those have worked, though," Cage offered, completely seriously.

Granted, he was right. Tals had more lives than a cat, and he credited his instincts in helping with that. "If this car blows . . ."

"Looks like a door trigger—or ignition," Cage said, studying the light on the remote. There was no valet service, and no one had touched her key, but when the car was wired, the red infrared button tended to remain lit. Most people wouldn't notice it. Tals and Cage would. "Evac?"

"Again, lots of questions," Tals countered. "If we could defuse it . . ."

Cage sighed. They'd both done time on bomb-squad duty in the Army, but they'd been out a while. And this shit was sophisticated. "You're calling Tenn."

"Yeah, yeah," he muttered, dialing Tenn's number and simultaneously dreading this conversation.

"I'm not calling him," was Tenn's immediate response after Tals explained the situation.

"It's a car bomb in Maddie's car."

There was dead silence and then Tenn growled, "Maddie? As in Maddie Wells?"

Tals looked at Cage, who raised his eyes to the heavens, like he was praying. For something. "There's a bomb and I'm standing right next to it."

"Fuck. Hang on," Tenn said quickly.

And that cut off any further Maddie discussion. For the moment. Tals knew his brother wouldn't refuse, and truthfully, he hated having to force the interaction between Tenn and the fucker who'd broken his heart.

Soon he had two men on the line—Tenn and Ward. He listened to Ward tell him what to look for—and confirm Tals's fear that it was set to blow with the opening of the driver's door.

"I'd blow it."

"'Course you would," Tenn muttered.

Not the time to be in the middle of this. "Public space. Too many questions."

"Can you fake her death?" Ward asked.

"You guys spend way too much time being secretive," Tals muttered. "Not faking it. I need to disarm it to let the fuckers who planted it know they can't get away with this shit."

"Any idea who that is?" Tenn asked.

"Thinking it's something to do with Maddie's ex—Hugh Montgomery," Tals said.

After a few seconds of silence, during which Tals heard him typing, Ward let out a low whistle. "Intel's saying he's currently being investigated. Word on the street is that he's in deep with the Albanian mob—one of the family branches that deals with drug trafficking. Is the wife involved?"

Tals glanced at Cage. "She's almost his ex-wife. She's moved back here to get away from him. I have no idea if she knows any of this, but my guess is absolutely not."

But it made sense to make Maddie the target—these mob guys were smart. Ward put words to it, saying, "Montgomery either wants her dead or he still loves her. And these guys know enough to leverage that."

"Either option sucks," Tenn said. And the silence meant that Ward agreed.

So did Tals.

Cage was silent. Finally, he said, "If you hadn't agreed to go out with her tonight . . ."

He didn't have to finish. If they'd targeted Maddie tonight and Tals hadn't shown . . .

Tals shook his head. "But I was. We'll deal with the other shit later. Can you defuse this?"

"Of course," Ward scoffed. "It's gonna take some time though."

Tals sighed. "It always does."

A little while later, just as Maddie had finally stopped restlessly pacing and actually tried to settle in on Tals's bed, since there was really no place else to sit other than a chair that was covered in clean laundry, she heard a knock on the door.

She got up, listened, then called, "It's not like I can open the door."

The lock opened and a really big guy stood there—she hadn't seen him earlier. He was holding a beer, which he handed to her. She took it promptly.

"You know there's beer in Tals's fridge," he said.

"If you know that, why bring me one?"

"Figured you were probably too pissed to take one."

She smirked, mainly because he was right. Now she was past the point of caring.

"I'm Bear."

"Maddie. But I guess you knew that, being I'm the one locked up. Although it's probably safer for me in here, since most of them can't stand me," she muttered.

"What the hell did you do to them?" Bear asked. When she turned around, he was leaning comfortably against the doorframe, and his question wasn't demanding, but rather genuinely curious. "I mean, I can just go ask Preach and shit, but I figured, you're standing right here."

She rubbed her hands together. "Tals and I . . . in high school . . ."

Bear's eyes widened. "Oh."

"No—it's not what you think. I kind of . . . he got into some trouble with the police because of me. I didn't mean for it to happen, but by the time I tried to stop it, it was too late." It sounded so lame, and Bear was watching her intently.

"I'm thinking," Bear started slowly, "if Vipers really hated you, you wouldn't be here."

"No?"

"We don't let our enemies inside if we don't have to." Bear shrugged. "Then again, Preacher always says to keep your enemies close."

"If you're trying to make me feel better, you're failing miserably," she pointed out. He grinned a little, abashed but unrepentant, which seemed to be a quality of most bad boys. It's what made them irresistible, she supposed. Because she couldn't stay mad at him, especially not over his honesty.

"Try to relax. Not like you can go anywhere anyway."

Chapter 10

Tals returned to the Vipers clubhouse, because he'd never bothered to get another place beyond the familiar bedroom here and his childhood house, which he owned with Tenn.

But Tenn was a state away, in another house with his own business, nursing his loneliness while taking care of other people. The same way he'd tried to take care of their mom.

Tals looked around at the men, knowing all of them had a story that, if not paralleled, was similar to his in its fucked-up-ed-ness. Which was why they'd ended up here—kindred spirits, looking for a family who'd never desert them. It was a similar mind-set to the military, which made sense if you knew that MCs were basically formed by men returning from war, looking for like-minded people. Tals knew that history intimately.

Most MC guys headed to or came to the MCs from the military. At least Vipers guys did. Some of Havoc too—they were a bad bunch of motherfuckers who lived near Tenn in the hills that some said were haunted.

Havoc and Vipers got along.

Vipers and Heathens? Never gonna happen. Not when Heathens pushed drugs like candy and got their own women addicted to keep them in line.

But tonight the Heathens weren't at the heart of this problem. Tals wasn't sure if he should be grateful or not, and decided not. Because there was truth in the expression "the devil you know," and Heathens didn't have the sophistication or the patience to wire car bombs.

It'd taken forty-five minutes of painstaking work, and his shoulders ached from the tension. Cage had stayed with him the whole time, as well as Tenn and Ward on the phone.

"All clear?" Preacher asked.

"Not even sure how to answer that." Tals sank heavily into one of the comfortable leather couches that Holly had insisted Preacher buy for the place.

They'd all bitched and moaned that the clubhouse was just fine as was, that it didn't need a woman's touch. They'd fought especially hard to keep the old couches, which were really fucking terrible. Holly had one delivered and they'd fought to spend time on it. Holly had simply smirked, called them dumbasses and ordered several more.

From there they'd let her do what she wanted, improvements-wise. And Tals had to admit things were better here. She was good at picking simple things that were really luxurious, things none of them had grown up with. Like who knew there were such amazingly soft sheets in existence? Or towels that were all fluff?

Simple comforts that tonight wouldn't take his mind off anything. As if he knew, Cage went to hand him a beer, but Tals shook it off. Fuck, he didn't need his mind clouded now, not any more than it already was.

Rocco went to the kitchen and came back with a soda. "Dude, you look wasted. Sucks to feel like that when you're stone-cold sober."

"Don't I know it." He drank down half, realizing he'd never gotten dinner. Or lunch. What a clusterfuck.

"Maddie's locked in your room," Rally offered, and Tals stared at him. "What? I figured we didn't want her to leave. She seems like the type to."

Tals couldn't argue with that.

By the time Tals opened the door, she'd already worked herself up twice, talked herself down both times and fought—and won—three fights with him in her head.

She was in a deceptively nearly Zen state when he walked inside. There were no signs that he'd been in any kind of fight, and except for the fact that his jaw was clenched tight, no real signs of stress were apparent.

But there was no smile, which meant he wasn't putting on a happy act for her. And she was pretty sure she appreciated it.

It required all her patience not to ask questions, but she was rewarded when he spoke.

"Someone put a bomb in your car," Tals told her calmly.

She blinked. Because that wasn't the kind of reward she'd been hoping for. Her mind reeled as she tried to process it. "What kind of activities are you involved in?"

He let out a short, humorless laugh. "Me? Honey, that was all about you."

"Right. Because the circles I travel in, we always use car bombs. This is ridiculous." She stood, but he closed the door behind him, continuing to block the way to the door with his body.

"I don't know what kind of world you live in," he said slowly, his voice a dangerous rumble. "But someone tried to kill you. They know what kind of car you drove here."

"They made a mistake." She paused. "Maybe they saw me with you."

"You're not anything to me, Maddie, so your theory doesn't make sense."

Those words hit her more harshly than she'd expected. They were truthful, not meant to stab, but they still did. "I need to go home."

"You can't."

"Why not?"

"Someone tried to kill you."

"Call the police."

He shook his head and eyed her like she'd said the most ridiculous thing in the world. "That will make things worse."

She wanted to ask if he was kidding . . . and then she remembered his history with the police. Because of whom he associated with, yes, but also because of her. The guilt tore at her, and she pushed it down. It did nothing to alleviate the helpless feeling. "I can't . . . I don't know what to do, Tals."

"You stay here until we figure this out."

She still didn't want to believe the car bomb was about her. Tals was involved in dangerous things, but throwing blame wasn't going to help matters. And still . . . "After what you're a part of, how can you not think . . . ?"

His expression froze. "Of course you think that. You always have. It's why you avoided me, until you needed my help."

"Tals, please . . ."

"I'm not denying my life doesn't have danger. I've grown up with it. By the time I came here, my dad was already in prison. Mom worked nights, so she wasn't

around a lot. She did the best she could, but, man, she
didn't have it easy. And Tenn and I both worked from
the time we figured out how to make money. I stole
cars and Tenn . . ." He shook his head. "I don't want to
talk about this shit anymore. I fucking lived it while
you were in your ivory tower."

"Tals . . ."

"But that's what you wanted, right? A chance to
make me feel like shit. To remind yourself of why this
was only a fling."

"That's not true. That's not what it was . . . not what
I wanted it to be," she protested.

"Sweetheart, I remember every second of that conversation we had."

"But that was before . . ." she started. *Before everything happened with Earl. Before we slept together.*

*Before I didn't tell the police what really happened and
agreed with Earl's story instead.*

"When you decided to breeze back into town, did
you ever stop to think that I don't want a chick like
you? That you're too much trouble? Not enough sub-
stance under the hood? Because if you haven't suffered,
how do you know what real joy is? How do you know
how to live?"

She stared at him, stunned.

He continued. "My life is dangerous, but I do my
best to protect people close to me. And I always protected you. Let's not forget it was your own Jessamine
crew who posed the biggest threat to you back then. So
why couldn't history be repeating itself?"

His words cut so deep . . . because she didn't know
how to live. She'd come here, to him, to try to learn. "I
wouldn't let that happen."

He didn't push her, didn't try to talk more about the

past. They had enough present to deal with. "Why did you really come here? Are you just fucking with me? I can handle that—just lay it on the line."

"I'm not fucking with you."

He cupped her chin. "Gotta put your trust in me. Sorry there's no other choice right now. But you came into town, shaking your ass at me."

"I did not shake my ass," she said indignantly.

"What do you really want?"

"A fresh start." A kiss. A touch. Recapture lost time.

"Can't look back when you're trying to move forward."

His eyes flashed as she put her hands on his hips. She pressed against him. Seductively. Obviously. Reached up to cup the back of his neck and pull him closer. Tals stopped thinking when she kissed him. Her hands twisted in his hair as she clung to him, and fuck, she could always turn him around like no one else.

This was a mistake. He might not regret it, but she would. Then again, he'd never been mistaken for a saint, so why start now? She wanted it, and so did he. Consenting adults.

Didn't matter that he might be emotionally invested and she most likely wasn't. If history was going to repeat itself, he'd make sure it repeated the good aspects too. And going to bed with Maddie?

Really fucking good.

In seconds his hands spanned her denim-clad ass, pressing her closer. Her response was immediate as she ground against him wantonly, moaning into his mouth.

"Been a while for me," she said shyly. The walls were down, and the Maddie he'd known one-on-one was back. And he had her.

It made him not want to make the mistake of letting

her go again. But he did, at least for the moment. He shook his head. "It's going to be longer than that. I'm not taking advantage of you now."

"Then let me take advantage of you," she told him. She got lost in his eyes, wanted to climb in and drown in the emotions behind them. "Don't leave me alone again."

"I don't make promises I can't keep," he told her, before shutting the door between them.

The entire time he'd been talking to Maddie, Tals's phone was vibrating the fuck out of his pocket. Now he scrolled through the texts—some from Cage, and one really important one from Tenn.

On my way.

Simple. To the point. And a whole lot of anger behind those three little words.

Tals had been avoiding telling him about Maddie. At first he told himself it was because Tenn had a lot to worry about with all his businesses anyway. And Tals was handling things. And nothing was happening with Maddie—just a simple date so they could talk, put the past behind them and move on. Coexist.

The bomb was an unexpected twist. Maddie locked in his bedroom was another. Tals should've known that Tenn was way too calm during the bomb phone call. "He's coming," he told Cage as he came into the kitchen.

Cage was dressed like he was on his way out. "I tried to talk him out of it," he started, but Tals shook his head.

"We both know that wouldn't work, but thanks for the attempt, man."

Cage cupped a hand on Tals's shoulder. "He'll understand."

"No, actually, we both know he won't. But it's not like I didn't know that. It's not going to be pretty." He paused and looked at the man he'd served with, the guy who'd been by his side as much as Tenn had since they'd come to town, the man who was like another brother to him. "I know you're pissed at her too, Cage. You just do a damned good job of hiding it."

Cage gave a small smile. "Don't profess to understand it, but I want you safe and happy. Just let me know how I can help. You worked to free me from hell—I owe you, more than you know."

Rocco's voice came up from behind them. "Sorry—didn't mean to interrupt the brofest, but fuck, you two are getting sappy. You gonna hold hands and braid each other's hair next? Or can we go out and have some fun now?"

"I will fuck you up," Cage promised.

Chapter 11

Maddie waited by herself for as long as she could, but after a couple hours of pacing, she opened the door and padded down the hallway and the stairs until she happened on the main room. It was empty, save for Tals, who was watching a movie in the dark.

He didn't see her right away, and she stood in the darkness, watching him. He still looked so young, so much like that boy who'd swooped in and saved her. And she . . .

"I know exactly what you're thinking about now." Tals's voice cut through her reverie, and she looked up into semi-angry eyes that had no doubt known she was standing there the entire time. "Don't, Maddie, okay? Just don't."

"Tals, I . . ."

"Nothing you say or do can change any of it." His words were harsh but correct. Stirring up the past always caused more trouble than it was worth.

Still . . . "I want to apologize."

"For what?" he ground out. "For being scared?"

Her mouth opened and closed. He took that opportunity to walk out of the room past her, and she remained frozen, angry with herself and with him.

That's when Tenn walked in. And she'd always known he was much less forgiving about this subject than his brother. And if she hadn't known it before, the angry look in his eyes would've clued her in immediately.

He nodded in her direction and went past the table to follow Tals.

"I'm so sorry," she managed, and Tenn stopped dead in his tracks. His back stiffened, but he didn't turn around immediately. Instead, since he was in the doorway, his hands reached out to grab the side of the doorjamb and she heard him just breathe.

"Tenn, forget it." Tals's voice came around the corner, warning his brother.

"You might be able to say that and mean it, brother, but I sure as hell can't." Tenn's drawl wasn't as deep as his brother's, but the anger gave it an edge that made her cross her arms against it.

At Tenn's comment, Tals didn't press, couldn't tell his brother it wasn't his fight. Because especially in those days it had been one for all. What happened to Tals reverberated through Tenn's life, and Tals knew his brother was feeling extra protective of him. Fighting that would do no good. He could simply be grateful and try to mend a fence between the two.

"How's Cage with all of this?" Tenn asked Tals.

"He's . . . ah . . . dealing with it." As Tals's best friend, Cage had been affected by Tals's arrest as badly as Tenn. He was hiding his anger at Maddie well enough, and Tals figured Preacher had something to do with that. Because Preacher was also pissed at Maddie still, although he'd be easier to convince. He understood stupid mistakes of youth.

Tenn waited a beat, staring into Tals's eyes before turning to face Maddie. From the doorway, Tals saw her stiffen, but she didn't move or flinch.

"I'm sorry," she said again calmly, but her voice shook, like she was barely restraining the emotion behind it. "It was a horrible time."

"Right. I'm sure protecting your rich rapist friend was so difficult. Maybe Tals should apologize for putting you through it." Tenn's voice dripped with bitter, vicious sarcasm.

Tenn was typically so easygoing. Gentle to the people he employed. Nurturing. This was a side of him rarely seen.

Out of the corner of his eye, he caught sight of Calla walking by. At the sound of the harshness in Tenn's voice, she stopped cold, looking confused. It was no wonder. Last year, when she'd nearly been killed, Tenn had been the first one to protect her, the one she'd called for help when she'd first got together with Cage. She was so close with Tenn, and Tals could see she was simultaneously stunned and worried about him.

"It wasn't like that," Maddie said, her voice rising in pitch slightly.

"Then tell me what it was like, Maddie. Because from where I'm standing, history's repeating itself. You get in trouble with your rich man and Tals rescues you. I just need to sit back and wait for the police to come, so you can throw Tals under the bus. Again."

"I wouldn't do that," Maddie insisted, and Tals believed her. But Tenn had a right to say what he wanted. And hell, Tals hadn't asked Maddie to defend herself, but she'd needed to.

Still, Tals's gut had twisted all the same as Tenn spoke, because until it had been laid out, he hadn't seen just how uncomfortably similar the situations were.

Granted, in high school she hadn't been playfully chasing him.

Maddie told him firmly, "I know he hasn't forgiven me either, but I'm going to make it up to him. And to you."

Tenn snorted, then walked away from her. He glanced at Calla before clapping Tals on the shoulder. "I'm staying here tonight."

"Tenn, I . . ."

"You don't want me to get involved. I know." His voice softened. "All for one, Tals."

Tals sucked in a harsh breath. Tenn pulled him in for a hug, then walked toward Calla. As they walked toward the rec area, he heard Calla say, "I'm not sure I want to know what that's all about," but he didn't hear Tenn answer.

Maddie was in the doorway Tenn had vacated moments before, wearing Tals's clothes, her cheeks flushed. She looked beautiful and vulnerable.

"It's so different, Tals," she told him. "I couldn't admit how much you scared me back then. Because I knew if I let myself, I could've fallen for you. And then I wouldn't have been able to leave South Carolina. Back then I didn't realize that my freedom had nothing at all to do with my running. My freedom was—is—you. And I wish it hadn't taken me so long to know that. I wish I hadn't brought on so much hurt. I can't take it back, but I can try to make up for it."

"You don't know me well enough to know what I am to you," he managed, his voice sounding like gravel.

"You haven't changed. I know that. I knew it the second you stopped on the road and helped me fix the flat. And then with the car . . . the bomb . . ."

"Just because I helped you . . ."

"You saved me—then and now. And I'm not just talking about physically. You opened my eyes. The first time, it scared me, and I talked myself into believing the opposite of what I knew in my heart. I told myself you were the kind of guy I had to stay away from. I know the kind of boy you were and the kind of man you are. If I could only be so lucky to be a part of your life." She moved forward and cupped his cheek with her palm. "No matter what happens, this would be my loss, or my gain. And I have no problems fighting for that. I want—"

"I want to keep you safe," he cut in. Because that was the truth, and the best he could manage for right now. It would be easy to do what he wanted to do— pick her up, slowly strip off her clothes and kiss every inch of her under the moonlight. He knew that would steam through his windows like finely mapped patterns of hope and pain.

"Go upstairs. And lock the damned door behind you."

She looked startled when his words came out slightly growled. Then she flushed again. "I'll lock it. But I wouldn't mind if you broke it down."

Chapter 12

Preacher had left Tals to deal with his own shit. He'd stomped over to the tattoo shop and stood by the door like an angry bouncer, growling at any guy who got too close to Holly.

Finally, Holly cried uncle by announcing closing time. It was almost two in the morning, and tonight she was limping . . . and unable to hide it.

He ordered Gigi to close up and called Rally over to wait for her. Then he picked Holly up and carried her back to the clubhouse, up the stairs and into her room. It was oddly quiet there, which meant everyone was out. Except for Maddie, he supposed, but he wasn't thinking about that now. Instead he was focused on how good Holly smelled, the way she leaned her head against his shoulder without protest.

The way her blond hair brushed his cheek when he bent down to place her on the bench at the end of her bed. He knelt as she watched, helped her take off her boots, then eased down her jeans, sliding them gently off her calves. It was an act easily misconstrued, and he might've followed through on what that seemed to promise . . . until he got to her right thigh and she winced when he tugged at the jeans.

"Shit," he muttered. "Have to take care of yourself."

"Trying to," she whispered. His hands covered her thigh, massaging it the way the physical therapist had taught him—because one of them needed to take advantage of the PT sessions. After a long massage and stretching, he got up to grab her more medicine. She took it, murmured a soft "Thanks."

He turned away to put the glass down, asked, "Better?" over his shoulder.

"Yes." She stood too fast and almost fell back into her chair. Would have, if Preacher hadn't caught her around the waist and pulled her to him. This time he didn't back away the way he should've. The way she'd expect him to, because no one grabbed at Holly, or crowded her . . . or kissed her.

But that's exactly what he did. He'd been thinking about it, jerking off to it, fucking other women and pretending they were Holly, but now she was pressed against him—the real thing—and fuck, her lips were soft. Perfect. She let him kiss her . . . and then she was kissing him back, her hands twined in his hair, her tongue sliding along his . . . teasing. Tempting. It would be easy—expected, even—to pick her up, bring her to his room and finish this, once and for all. Holly knew the way MCs worked, and theirs was better to women than most. She knew that she owed Preacher, that most methods of collection in the MC world were primitive at best. She would let him in. Not hold grudges. She'd enjoy it—he'd make sure of that—but he wanted more than acceptance and enjoyment. He wanted her. All of her, and maybe that would never happen, but fuck it all, he refused to compromise.

He pulled away, sat her back down. She looked surprised and a little angry. That showed even more in her tone when she said, "I didn't expect you to be a tease, Preacher."

"What did you expect, Holly? For me to treat you the way Mickey did?"

"Don't you dare talk about my husband like that."

"He's gone. I'm just asking if I should do what he did—should I pass you around as I see fit? I know why you'd want that, because that would make it easy for you to dismiss me. And I won't fucking be dismissed." She blinked at his words, but for once she didn't have a smart-ass answer for him. "It's your move, Holly. I'm sure you won't take me up on it, and that's okay. Because I don't want you to if you're not all in this. And I will fucking know the difference."

He walked away, not giving her a chance to get herself together to spout off at him. He wasn't in the mood to hear it, and embarrassing her was definitely the way to get a rejection from her . . . and it was the only way for him to keep his self-respect—to ensure hers.

His mood was beyond foul, and hearing rumblings of a fight with a local gang lying in wait outside Wally's Bar didn't help anything.

He went to the bar, and hearing the bragging of a new probie was the final straw. He threw a chair against the wall, shattering it into a million wooden pieces, along with any last bit of fun they'd all been having.

The music stopped. The crowd stilled. At least they still had that small amount of respect, but it was apparent he needed to pull the reins in, and hard. It was easy to get complacent when the immediate crisis, like the fight between Cage and the Heathens, was over and done with. But that was always the time when trouble struck. And with the impending Maddie disaster . . . he was old enough to know that was going to be a disaster.

"Closing time," he announced decisively, and Calla glanced at him, then moved to raise the lights, the way she normally would during last call. She stood by the switches, and Cage moved next to her, both waiting for Preacher's next move. "Men, get your women home. Meeting in the clubhouse in the next hour. If you're not sober, I don't want to fucking see you. Cage, grab Rally and come outside with me to deal with this gang shit."

With a nod to Cage, he left to go outside. Because it didn't matter how many of these asshole hoods were out there—although a quick count showed six—Vipers had the stronger rep than these upstarts. Now it was time to prove it.

Chapter 13

Tals sat alone in the main room of the clubhouse, in the dark, looking at the flickering TV screen. It was on mute.

So was he.

Tenn might've left with Calla, or he might be just next door at the tattoo shop. Maddie had gone upstairs, and he hadn't heard anything from her for a couple of hours. He couldn't stop his mind from reliving that night, from finding her pinned under Earl, to wanting to break Earl's fucking neck, to making love to Maddie with the promise of a brand-new year. A new start.

He'd resisted the urge to do more than knock Earl out, mainly so he could get Maddie away from him and comfort her. For the next forty-eight hours, he and Maddie holed up together as if the rest of the world didn't exist.

And then Maddie told him that she couldn't stay in Skulls Creek, and he'd told her there was no way he could leave. There'd been more said, of course, but in the end things were pretty certain. He'd taken her home and then he'd gone to find Earl. Because whether or not he and Maddie were going to be together, the bastard needed to be taught a lesson.

Earl thought Tals's anger was based on wanting Maddie for himself. Tals didn't bother arguing, because it would provide a good cover story for Maddie, who'd made him promise to never tell anyone what he'd come across. He'd beaten the shit out of Earl and several members of the football team who'd been with Earl as well. Still angry, he'd found solace at one of the Vipers bars and drunk himself into a stupor.

It was all over, he'd thought. But he'd been proven very wrong, since it'd all gone to hell the next day when the police had shown up to arrest him. He'd called Preacher from the station this time to come get him—to post his bail. It had taken seventy-two hours, and he'd been kept in jail, not taken away. That had to be because of Vipers, but Tals never asked and Preacher never offered.

All Tals knew was that this time the trouble was big, and being associated with Vipers was a strike against him. He'd learned a lot from the experience, especially that patience and stealth were traits he'd needed to acquire.

He'd been seventeen, and he'd refused to speak to the police. A Vipers lawyer informed him that Earl and the other players had come forward to press charges . . . and that Maddie herself had agreed with Earl's statement that Tals had beaten Earl up because he'd wanted her for himself. No mention of Earl's attempted rape or the fact that she'd spent two nights with Tals.

He'd been relieved and angered at that, but the anger was mainly at himself for getting in too deep. Tenn had warned him and Tals had refused to listen. He'd believed in Maddie.

In between getting out on bail and the investigation,

something happened to make them all recant, and Tals assumed that Vipers—Preacher—had something to do with that. Again, Tals never asked, but the main thing was that he'd been innocent and Vipers had known that. Believed him.

When Preacher had finally been allowed to take him home, Tals had been wrung out. He'd let Preacher lead him out with a hand on the back of his neck, guide him into the truck. It was only once they'd pulled out that Preacher murmured, "Tenn's worried sick."

Tals had hung his head. "Fuck, Preach. I didn't . . ."

"What the fuck did you do?" Preacher demanded when Tals just stopped his explanation. "No, forget it. I know what you did."

"No, you don't. You have no fucking idea what I did," Tals had spat, suddenly tired of all the bullshit he'd dealt with over the past forty-eight hours. And even though he'd expected Maddie's betrayal, it still stung like a motherfucker. He'd tried to get out of the truck, even though they were moving at a good speed. Preacher reached out and grabbed him by the collar.

It was easy to forget how strong Preacher really was, since he could be so gentle. Had been to two runaway boys who'd shown up at Vipers' first charter clubhouse and asked for a place to stay.

"Then fucking tell me," Preacher had ground out. "And stop trying to kill us both."

Tals had taken a deep breath and spilled the story. About Maddie. About Earl pressing against her, clawing at her clothes. Hitting her.

How Tals had gotten there just in time.

But even then he'd stopped, keeping Maddie's privacy.

Without thinking, he now grabbed the thing closest to him—a beer bottle—and threw it against the wall, where it gave a satisfying crash of glass and liquid . . . right before some of the guys came pouring into the clubhouse, but quietly subdued, all of them going to their separate quarters.

Meeting in an hour, Cage had texted at some point, Tals noted when he checked his phone now, and whatever the fuck had happened tonight, Preacher was no doubt pissed.

Tals had been brooding and pretending to watch TV, and when Preacher strolled in, Tals swore he saw smoke coming out of the president's ears. He sat and waited for the explosion.

Preacher noticed the broken-glass mess on the wall and floor, but didn't say anything about it. "I called a meeting. Sober assholes only."

"Do I get to know the agenda, or is it a surprise?" Tals asked, comfortable with his level of sarcasm. He'd rather Preacher blow off steam with him before the meeting. He and Cage were two of the few who'd seen Preacher's temper full force . . . and it wasn't something he wanted to see unleashed on their own, unless completely warranted.

Preacher's eyes flashed. "Don't fuck with me, Tals. You brought this shit here. All I do is clean up your fucking messes, and that's not what Vipers is for."

"Funny, but I thought that was the point. Family helping family, right?"

And that was Tenn's voice, booming across the room. Fuck.

Preacher's head snapped in that direction. Tals stood as his brother strode across the room. Preacher approached from the left, Tenn from the right, leaving Tals squarely in the middle. As fucking usual. He'd done it for Cage and Preacher at various other times, and he was sick of it. "Fight your own damned selves," he told them now, and stepped away.

"Fuck that. You don't get to bring trouble and then walk away," Preacher told him.

"Then I'll take my fucking trouble and go," Tals told him, stepping up and walking over the coffee table rather than trying to walk through Preacher and Tenn and the pathways they blocked.

"That's not your decision to make," Preacher reminded him.

"Maybe it should be."

"Not your choice to make, especially not now." Preacher didn't have to threaten—it was simple MC fact, and that's what Tals had signed up for all those years ago.

This was why Tenn refused. It was the one time they'd parted ways in a life decision. Until that moment Tals had never regretted it.

But he couldn't turn to Tenn now. At this point Tenn would be the first to tell him that he needed Vipers' protection now. Because whatever Maddie was involved in, Tals was now smack in the middle. And confused as hell.

"I know you think she's using me." He turned his attention to Tenn now.

"All I know is that you rescued her, got her sober and she screwed you over," Tenn said.

"That's not all that happened, goddammit," Tals bit out, then wished he hadn't. Because now they were all staring at him.

"You . . ." Preacher paused.

"You slept with her?" Cage finished.

"Why didn't we know that?" Tenn demanded.

"I didn't know I needed to send a memo on my love

life." Tals was trapped, and he waited for one of them to yell at him or call him an idiot.

But Tenn muttered, "It all makes sense."

"Really? Care to explain it to me?" Tals asked, his tone heavily laced with sarcasm.

"It was sex, *Tals*. Maybe it felt like more, but—"

"But what, *Tenn*?" There was a challenge in his voice that Tenn took head-on.

"I don't know what the fuck to think." Tenn's eyes blazed. "Except that you usually don't get caught up like this."

"I always help," he challenged.

Tenn's voice softened. "You do, yes. But you don't usually help people who fucked you over so thoroughly."

Fuck, Tenn was right. But Tals was right too. "She didn't mean to . . . Fuck, she was seventeen. Scared. You have to remember what that's like."

"I do," Tenn said through gritted teeth.

"Then think about how much worse it would've been for a girl. We were used to violence. She wasn't. She doesn't deserve it. Dammit, no one does." He was done with this conversation, and he was done with staying away from his feelings for Maddie and from Maddie herself.

He got to the end of the hall. Second floor. He tried the door, found it locked, the way he'd asked. He had a key somewhere, and he could easily pick the lock too. But he'd made her a promise, and he didn't break those without a damned good reason.

"Maddie, I'm coming in." His voice rumbled, and he heard the lust rumble through his own voice. "Move away from the door."

He kicked it open. Thankfully, it still closed behind him, because the plans he had definitely required privacy.

Chapter 14

Maddie's body flooded with need as the door slapped the jamb uselessly behind it. Tals didn't seem to notice or care—his focus was solely on her, even as he slowed his stride and began to strip. First he shrugged his cut off and placed it on a chair.

He was nowhere near as careful with the rest of his clothes. His T-shirt flew across the room as she watched his chest, mesmerized by how broad, tattooed, utterly capable it was. She wanted to trace her fingers into the dips of the six-pack of his abs. His arms were muscled—dusted with light hair, strong, ready to hold her down, pin her . . .

A cross between a cry and a gasp escaped her throat as he unbuttoned and unzipped his jeans, and it was obvious he wasn't wearing anything underneath. His thick cock immediately took center stage, and he gave her a lazy smile as she sank into the other chair.

In return he put a booted foot on the seat next to her and waited.

She was so close to his open zipper her fingers shook.

She reached up to touch his abs, but he caught her wrists.

"Boots," he said, and the inherent command in his tone, the order, made her wetter than she'd been. Her fingers went to the laces of the heavy steel-toed motorcycle boots. and she clumsily unlaced the first. When he eased it off, he let it drop with a *thud* before she did the second one.

He hooked his fingers into his belt loops then and tugged his jeans down his hips maddeningly slowly.

Her breath caught as he stood naked in front of her, and all she wanted to do was his bidding. Right now she'd do anything he asked, and oh, how she wanted him to ask.

She leaned forward again, her fingertips trailing along his abs, and a slight shiver from Tals was her reward. She got a groan when her finger trailed a drop of precome from his cock before bringing her tongue down to taste him.

His hand slid along the back of her neck as she took him into her mouth, licking and teasing, growing bolder as his body began to vibrate. Her fingernails dug into a firm ass cheek, keeping him close. His hand twisted in her hair, a reminder that, no matter how out of control he appeared to get, he was still in control—of himself and of her.

It made her even more aroused to know that she was helpless, her mouth around him while she was fully clothed, pleasing him without him touching her . . . at least not where she wanted—needed—him to.

And yet she was getting so much pleasure from this. Her nipples pulled taut, brushed almost painfully against the cotton of her T-shirt. She wanted to wrap her legs around one of his thighs and just grind against him.

When she glanced up, the heated look he gave her seared through her body, telling her that he wanted her as badly as she wanted him.

She wanted more, willed him to come. His expression pulled taut, and then he growled and tugged her away from him and to her feet.

Before she knew what was happening, she was in the bed, her sweats dragged down. By the time she got her bearings, Tals was grinning wickedly, his face between her legs. And then he dipped his head down and began to lick her.

The room spun as he licked and laved her. His hands slid up her wrists, then found her nipples. It was the perfect storm. She arched up simultaneously into his palms and his mouth, and he seemed to encourage her quickening orgasm. It slammed her. Her muscles locked as her body thrashed against the mattress, although firmly held in place by him.

She heard the crinkle of a condom wrapper, and when he slid inside of her, she instinctively wrapped around him, pulling him deeper, locking him in. Melding him to her.

"I'm back, Tals," she murmured. "I'm here with you."

He wanted to believe her, and it was his choice to accept her words or remain skeptical. At that moment he accepted them, sank into her warmth and let her lull him into a post-orgasmic haze and out the other end as she revved him right back up.

"You're insatiable."

"Yes," he agreed seriously.

"Incorrigible."

"And it turned you the fuck on."

It was her turn to say, "Yes."

He smiled, then got serious. "Are you all right?"

She gave him a warm, lazy smile. "How could I not be?" Then she paused. "Right. My life outside that door is falling to shit."

Thankfully, she laughed a little, and he shook his head. "It'll work out, Maddie. It always does."

"Tenn seems pretty immovable."

"Honestly, I'm more worried about your ex."

"Yeah." She gnawed on her bottom lip. "He can be unpredictable. A little out of control sometimes, but—"

"Did he hit you?" Tals demanded.

"God no. He never laid a hand on me." She paused. "But his hands were all over other women."

"When did you find that out?"

"A while ago," she admitted, locking her gaze to his. "I knew we were falling out of love. Maybe he was never really in love with me. But I was focused on work. So focused, I made it my everything because I don't have anything else."

Her whole explanation was a challenge—and her chin jutted, eyes defiant.

If she'd been a man, no one would give a second thought to her work ethic. But she wasn't a man. Emotions got the best of her, and really, Tals always admired women and their emotions and how easily they could express themselves.

But Maddie was more like him—circumspect. A loner, despite all the girls and guys who crowded around her most days in high school. She was always surrounded, and she'd never appeared to like it.

She admitted as much to him the night he'd rescued her from Earl, the star quarterback who was currently on his fourth wife, thanks to a combination of family money and alcohol. Following in his family's tradition of all fucked-up.

"Do you want me to call any of your friends? Let them know where you are?"

She frowned, like he was speaking a different language. "These people aren't my friends. I knew it then, but . . . geography. High school seems to be all about geography."

She was referring to the two distinct sides of Skulls Creek, but she was right. "Life is all about geography."

"You're right. And I can't help but think . . . what we had, it was so innocent and perfect."

"I was never innocent, Maddie. Trust me. If you could've read my mind . . ."

"Don't think I couldn't." She smiled. "But it was innocent. I don't care what you say. It was romantic. You were romantic."

"Past tense?"

She shook her head. "You've still got it. You set the bar high. You were always a gentleman to me, when the other guys who were supposed to be gentlemen weren't."

"Earl had been on me for a while. He found out we were hanging out," Tals admitted. "I told him to fuck off, that we were just friends, that if you wanted to date him, you would."

God, it was making so much sense now, Earl's anger at her that night. His taunts of, "You're already giving it away to trash, so why not to me?" rang in her ears. She hadn't thought anyone knew, but she supposed that was naive. It's not like she spoke with her friends much beyond the superficial, who's dating who, what are you wearing to prom . . . and now she knew they were gossiping behind her back about a time in her life that was probably the most special.

She'd been in a vacuum. Her own little world, leaving Tals to deal with the fallout. "I had no idea . . ."

"I know. I didn't want you to deal with it." His face was grim. "You weren't the first girl Earl pulled this on. It's just that most of them didn't make him wait and wait before going out on a date."

She squeezed her eyes shut as she swore she could still hear the sound of Tals's fist hitting Earl's cheek, the snap of Earl's cheekbone, the swift curse of Tals as he ever so gently got her out of Earl's grasp and into his truck. "The morning I went home, you went to Earl's."

"Damn straight." The anger in his voice was still apparent. "I didn't tell anyone. Didn't ask for help. Didn't think to wait before I beat the shit out of him."

"You blame yourself for what happened? Tals, that's on me."

"No, it's not. You have no idea, but it's not."

And then she stared at him, pressed her lips together like she was deciding whether or not to say something. Finally, she did. "If you hadn't stopped Earl, we both know what would've happened. I shouldn't have put myself in that situation. I'd heard rumors, but . . ."

Tals broke in. "It wasn't just you, Maddie. There were others, and they weren't so lucky."

She shuddered, like she was just realizing that there were so many predators in the world. They were all so vulnerable. "So you took care of it."

Tals gazed at her with clear eyes and, she guessed, a clear conscience. He had a code, and he lived and died by it. He had his line in the sand, had drawn it early and refused to step over it. And he'd hooked himself up with a group of men who held to the same standards. "I've lived a lot, Maddie. MC, military, not counting the early years. And I've seen too many things not to take a stand, no matter the cost. And trust me, there's always a cost."

"And you bear that burden because of me."

"It's not that part of it that bothers me," he told her.

"I should've said something sooner. I wanted to go to the police after you brought me home. But I told my father and Grams, and they both said—"

"That Earl was from an old Southern family. That no one would believe you. That you shouldn't have been alone with him, that I was trash and who would believe me," he told her, and she couldn't deny that all of those things had come out of her father's mouth. "I can't believe you told them."

"I wanted them to know how I felt about you. Grams loved Earl, and I wanted her to know what a bastard he was. And even if they told me not to say anything, I was still old enough. I could've spoken up to the police the very first time they came to me and asked me about your supposed obsession with me—they talked to me alone," she admitted.

His gaze was steady, his eyes taking on that haunted look again. "I don't know what you want me to say. I think you want me to excuse you and tell you it was okay to run. And I've done that. You did it before the Earl incident and after, and I know you were scared as fuck. But you had a phone—my phone number. And if you'd stuck with me . . ." He cleared his throat. "Forget it. I'm probably expecting too much from a seventeen-year-old."

"But I expected the same thing, and I got it," she admitted, then practically whispered, "You knew he wasn't a good guy."

"I have radar for that shit."

"I wish I did. Wish I could spot the good."

"You do."

They'd had almost the exact same conversation that night after Earl. At the time, she hadn't realized he was talking about him.

"Why did you come back here?" he asked.

I had nowhere else to go.

But the truth was, no matter how hard she tried to forget Tals, the more he invaded her mind.

When you love someone, you lose control. Love makes you powerless.

Chapter 15

In the end the meeting hadn't fully rectified the issues Preacher had with some of the younger Vipers members. But the very next night, he got a call that he knew would drive the point home to his MC.

"Bear, get everyone here ASAP."

Bear nodded, then frowned and asked, "Everyone?" before letting his eyes drift upward. He didn't have to mention Tals by name—everyone knew he and Maddie had been holed up together since last night, and that they were doing more than talking.

"Leave him. Everyone else," Preacher reiterated.

"Big trouble?"

"Just a wannabe one-percenter club who likes to ride through cities and towns, making trouble."

Bear smiled, because Bear loved a good fight, and then he began assembling the others.

Of course this new MC knew Vipers was in town, but they assumed that Vipers was part of the MC brotherhood that would allow another MC to fuck up their town—as long as they weren't fucking up a Vipers-owned business.

They assumed fucking wrong. Even though Kelly's Pub wasn't Vipers-owned, it was part of Skulls Creek, and what was good for Skulls was good for Vipers and vice versa. And this fly-by-night MC? They were going down.

Less than forty minutes later, Bear had efficiently rounded everyone up—and those working the bar and the tattoo parlor were on speakerphones and Skype. Preacher informed them what was going on, how they were going up against this MC that needed a good beatdown.

"Let's put what we discussed at the meeting last night to the test. Like I said, you're all drinking and fucking around, and that's motherfucking great when everything in town is going fine."

But some of the younger members still didn't get it. One of them protested, "Vipers is fine—no one fucks with us now that we took care of Heathens."

Preacher's controlled wrath focused on him. "Vipers might be fine, but Skulls isn't. And we owe Skulls."

"Even though they hate us," the kid muttered.

"Yeah, even though they hate us. We don't shit where we eat, and we don't let anyone else do it either. Even though Skulls might not appreciate us, we live here—that means we have a responsibility to control what others can't."

"And law enforcement can't—that's for damned sure," Rally added firmly, and that was a truth. Law enforcement in Skulls up against forty violent bikers? A fucking disaster.

"Let's roll," Preacher told them. "Bear and Tim, you'll stay here with the bar. I've got two guys at the tattoo shop and Tals is at the clubhouse."

Those were safeguards in case of retaliation, plus

that left Vipers behind to post bail, because arrest was always a possibility.

Next he called Holly directly. He didn't doubt for a second she'd been listening in to the meeting with the Vipers guys who bodyguarded the shop. It was the first time he'd spoken to her directly since he'd kissed her. She hadn't made a move to come into his room, and even though it killed him, he'd stayed in his room last night.

He hadn't slept alone in a year. Holly barely noticed he slid into bed with her—or so he told himself—but damned, he'd gotten used to the comforts of her scent, her soft breathing . . .

"What's the problem?" she asked calmly, sounding almost bored.

His hackles were already up. He growled, "Go to the clubhouse and stay there."

She remained unimpressed. Slightly exasperated even. "I've got clients. A business to run."

"Cancel your appointments. The shop can stay open." There was a pause, enough of one to know that Holly wasn't going to follow his orders. "I swear to fuck, I'll have the guys carry you out of there."

"Let them try."

And she hung up on him.

Hung. Up.

He almost threw the phone across the room, let it shatter with the anger Holly seemed to bring out in him more and more lately.

He got why she'd fight to stay in the shop, even with the threat of violence—last time she'd been forced into that situation, she'd handled it, saved Calla and Cage's brother and herself.

And then she'd nearly had a breakdown. Her PTSD

had gotten worse for a bit, but he had to grudgingly admit that it had receded and she seemed stronger than ever.

Maybe that worries you?

And maybe he should stop Dr. Phil-ing himself and go beat the shit out of some assholes.

Before Maddie knew it, nearly forty-eight hours had passed. Tals kept reassuring her that things were okay, that some Vipers guys had been watching Grams's house and it was all quiet there. But they knew no more than they had last night.

When Tals went to talk to Preacher, Maddie had no problem staying behind and showering. She wrapped herself in a towel after inspecting her healing tattoo and went to rifle through Tals's drawers, since all her clothes were at Grams's. She certainly wasn't troubling Tals or any of the other guys to make a trip inside.

No, there was a fragile peace happening now, especially between her and Tals. She needed to make sure they got past forty-eight hours this way.

The door opened and Holly strutted in without knock or explanation, wordlessly dropped some clothes on the bed, smirked at Maddie and walked out.

"Wait," Maddie called out, but clipped British tones simply said, "I'm late for work. Make sure you're putting lotion on that fresh ink."

With that, the door shut. "See you at the shop," she murmured to the closed door, but hey, she was more than grateful for the pile of black leggings and plain V-neck tees. Casual. Chic. Comfy. She pulled on another outfit, tried on the gauzy top that floated around her. She felt like Stevie Nicks. In fact, when Tals walked in, she was humming "Gypsy" and fighting the urge to twirl in front of the mirror.

"All dressed up and no place to go," he mused.

"Literally."

"I'll make us some dinner. It'll be quiet tonight. Lot of guys go to the bar. Holly's at work next door. There are still guys guarding the building—and others are near your grandmother's house," he added.

"I can help."

He looked doubtful. "You can't cook, remember?"

"Well, I don't know if that's technically true. I've never tried to cook."

"Honey, you're not starting now. Not when I'm starving." He turned and walked away, but she followed him to the kitchen, asking, "So what am I supposed to do?"

"Stand there and look pretty?" he suggested, and when she turned around, scanning the open surface, he asked, "What are you doing?"

"Looking for something heavy enough to throw at you."

"Check the cabinets," Tals advised. "And let me know when to duck."

Instead she sat there while he made them breakfast for dinner. Tals was flipping pancakes expertly—with chocolate chips threaded through them.

"God, these smell delicious," she moaned, leaning in toward the pan.

"Hey, let the cook work in peace," he admonished. "Grab the plates."

"Jeez, you're bossy." She hip-checked him lightly, and the teasing smile he gave her made her heart flip. Those damned butterflies again. He'd always been the only one to give her butterflies.

How could she have let that go?

He's here now, she reminded herself. That was the only thing that mattered for the moment. That was always the only thing that should've mattered. And so she reached up and kissed him, and it went from hot to scalding in about five seconds, and it had nothing to do with the stove. No, in fact, she heard the click of the gas shutting off, and then he was carrying her—although she helped by wrapping around him like she'd never let go—and then they were back in his bedroom.

Naked. Under him. *God, yes.*

He moved between her legs before she could protest. This wasn't something she'd had done to her often—and she hadn't realized what she'd been missing. Not until Tals's hot mouth found her most intimate places and owned her. Completely.

In between the next round of orgasms, Maddie's stomach growled and he laughed softly. "After this, gotta make you new pancakes."

"Can we eat them in bed?"

"I'm not sure we'll ever get to eat them that way," he mused.

"That's not the worst thing."

"Definitely not," he agreed.

"Gotta make it past forty-eight hours," she murmured, more to herself, but the look on Tals's face told her she'd said it out loud—and that she probably shouldn't have. "I didn't mean—"

"I know what you meant, Maddie. It's okay. I wouldn't mind breaking that record either."

And then, in the middle of that romantic moment, her stomach growled. Loudly.

He grinned. "Hold that thought." He tugged his jeans on and left the room, only to return fifteen minutes later with plated pancakes on a tray. He put it on the bed next to her, then picked up the syrup and whipped cream he'd also brought and stared at them like he was making the most important decision in the world.

"What's up?" she asked.

"Not sure which one I want to use." He sat next to her and motioned for her to come closer. "Gonna need a taste test."

She stared at him as he tugged the T-shirt she wore—his—off her shoulder. Then he grabbed the whipped cream and drew a line of it across her shoulder . . . and promptly licked it off.

And looked way too pleased with himself. "Good?" she asked.

"You tell me." He kissed her, and she tasted Tals mixed with the sweet cream.

"That's nice."

"Now the syrup." He poured it lightly, licking before it could drip down her shoulder. And then he kissed her again.

Before she could say anything, he was yanking the T-shirt up, covering one of her nipples with the syrup and sucking it off, the delicious friction of his tongue against her nipple causing her to shiver. "We're never getting to those pancakes, are we?"

"Not anytime soon," he agreed, already covering her nipple again with whipped cream and licking it off, teasing her nipple. She twined her hand through his hair and hissed his name.

He stopped, then casually tugged her shirt down. "I'm going to use both," he said decisively.

"Now that I'm sticky." She mock pouted.

He sighed, shook his head. "I guess I'll have to take care of that." With that, he picked her up, forcing her to wrap herself around him. He didn't let her down until he reached the bathroom, and even then he kept her close, her body between him and the wall while he turned the water on.

While they waited for the steam of the shower to float around them, she wrapped a leg around his waist and pulled him down for a kiss. She wasn't thinking about anything but Tals and orgasms, and that felt so good. She couldn't remember the last time she was this relaxed, and she planned on stretching it out as long as possible before real life dropped in on them again.

When the bathroom was sufficiently steamy, he made quick work of the sticky T-shirt and his jeans, and he carried her into the shower. It was a large glass enclosure and Tals fiddled with the handles so water was spouting from all directions. Under the main rain shower, he turned her around, and she grabbed the towel bar, leaning forward slightly. His cock brushed against her ass cheeks, his fingers brushed her belly, then moved between her legs to tease her clit. He bit her shoulder lightly, then licked, then nipped again, and just when she felt his hardness between her legs, it disappeared, only to be replaced by his tongue.

He'd gotten on his knees, burying his face between her legs while she stood, helpless, grabbing the towel bar while he took her. She was aware she was crying out, moaning—rocking her hips as much as she could, but he held her pretty well in place, tugging at her hips, forcing her to lean forward farther.

He exposed her in a way she'd never been, and he made it feel so right, so natural. It would never be like this with anyone else, and she'd known that well before she'd ever made love to him for the first time.

That time had been so tame compared to this, and it had still been amazing. But this . . . they were older. Wiser.

She was still in love with him. She'd never stopped.

With that thought in mind, she came with a hard jolt, and she probably would've slid to the tile floor if he hadn't been holding her. But he was, even as he got off his knees, pressed his chest to her back and entered her.

She went up on her toes as he filled her, his mouth wet against the side of her neck. He sucked hard, and it would leave a mark.

She wanted it to.

From there it was a blur of orgasms, soapy-smelling suds as he gently washed her . . . and then proceeded to get her dirty all over again.

Tals couldn't get enough of her. They could stay in this shower, this room for days and months, and he could remain inside of her like he never wanted to let her go.

Because he didn't. Had no idea what would happen when they left the shower and the room, no clue especially what she'd do when she was out of the clubhouse. Because that would mean she was safe. Free to go—back to her family, her ex, her old life. Free to run.

Right now he didn't care. Couldn't. He'd take his fill, the way he should've all those years ago. He should've gone with her to her house, taken her out of there.

At the very least, he could've visited her when she left Skulls. Fought for what he wanted.

Except you were in the military to avoid getting into more trouble, he reminded himself, and then he shut down the thinking part of his brain in favor of simply feeling . . . her smooth skin against his, the beat of her heart against his chest when he brought her to the bed, toweled them off and lay next to her. He ran his hands through her long, damp hair, untangling it, watching it dry wild, making her look sexy as hell. Like a real MC chick.

His MC old lady.

He wouldn't make the same mistakes. He'd protect her—and himself.

The knocks interrupted them . . . right after Maddie had come. And she hadn't been quiet. "Oh my God," she whispered against his shoulder. "Did they hear?"

"No, I'm sure they didn't," Tals reassured her, even though she felt him fighting to hold in a laugh. "What's up? I'm busy."

The door cracked. "Dude, I realize that. But Detective Flores is here," Bear said in a mock whisper. "She's saying you've kidnapped Maddie."

At that Maddie turned to look at Bear, who continued. "Obviously, she doesn't know what those moans mean."

Maddie's cheeks flushed hot, but Bear was grinning conspiratorially at her. He even winked, as if to say, *You go, girl.*

Sex was nothing to be ashamed of here.

Sex was nothing to be ashamed of at all.

"Tell her Maddie will be right out," Tals said, and Bear nodded and shut the door.

With that she straightened up, grabbed Tals's discarded T-shirt, which went to her thighs—and slid off her shoulder—and prepared to go talk to Detective Flores. "Is this bad?"

"It's never good when the police show, Maddie," Tals said as he tugged his jeans on and grabbed a flannel shirt that he buttoned a few times over his bare chest.

It was painfully obvious what they'd been doing, which, as Bear said, eliminated the whole kidnapping charge. "How do the police know I'm here? Do you think they went to Grams's house and saw your guys or something?"

Tals sighed. "No. I don't think that's what happened."

"Then what? You didn't tell them about the bomb in my car, right?" She looked into his serious eyes. "You really think this car bomb is about me, don't you?"

"I think it's all connected to your soon-to-be ex. You might not want to hear what I'm going to say, but I think he's a selfish prick. Whoever's threatening you has to promise blowback on Hugh, or else he wouldn't give a shit enough to try to make sure you were safe."

She snorted softly at his assessment. "That's why you wanted me here and not home, because it would be even more dangerous for her to be close to me." She paused. "Which means I'm dropping the danger right here on Vipers' doorstep."

"Trust me—we can more than deal with it. And we made sure your ex knows it."

"When did all this happen?" she asked, but he shook his head. "Okay, probably better I don't know. But that's how Detective Flores knew where to find me. Through Hugh?"

"He's probably the one who sent her here, yeah," Tals agreed. "We definitely got his attention. Let's get out there before she gets more suspicious."

She followed him out the door and down the hall, but she went into the kitchen first, where Detective Flores sat right at the table where Maddie had sat watching Tals cook pancakes only an hour ago.

"This is Maddie," Rocco said. He was standing by the fridge, wearing just a towel around his waist, his hair wet.

The detective shot him a look before turning her attention to Maddie. "You're Maddie Wells?" She was a pretty woman, even with the severe suit and the even more severe way she slicked her hair back into a bun.

Maddie smiled a little. "Yes, and I'm here willingly, of my own volition. Sound mind and body and everything."

"Miss Wells, I'd like you to come with me so we can talk alone. Preferably down to the station so I can be sure you're not under any undue influences."

Tals snorted. "Like me?"

"I don't understand—what makes you think I've been kidnapped? Did someone call you? Is Grams okay?" Maddie wasn't the greatest liar, but she was excellent at playing the game. It was a skill she'd learned quickly in the business world, not giving away too much and throwing out red herrings. Acting innocent.

"As far as I know, your grandmother is fine. She's not the one who contacted us," Flores said. "It was your husband."

"I don't have a husband," Maddie shot back.

"Tell that to the courts, because you're still legally married," Flores told her calmly.

"Why is he calling the police about me?" she pressed. "That doesn't make sense. We've separated. I came back to my hometown. And I've known Tals longer than I've known Hugh Montgomery."

Flores's eyebrows rose at that, but all she said was, "I think it's better we have this conversation down at the station."

Maddie began to shake her head instinctively, and then Rocco's voice broke in, asking, "Is she under arrest?"

Maddie peered out to see Rocco leaning against the opposite wall, staring at Flores so intently, Maddie swore the detective blushed a little. But she got her composure back quickly, which Maddie gave her credit for, since Rocco wore only a towel and was basically dripping wet from a very recent shower.

And Rocco was something to see. Tall, dark and handsome, he didn't have as many tattoos as the other guys had, but there were enough to show off the hard planes of his body. And his intense gaze was focused only on Flores.

Interesting.

"Of course she's not," Flores said. "But cooperating would end this matter more quickly than putting up roadblocks."

Rocco turned to Tals, and when Tals nodded, he turned back to Flores. "We need to talk. Without her first. Then you can have some time with her, with me in the room, in this clubhouse."

"I'm not speaking with you until you're properly attired, counsel or no counsel," Flores muttered.

Rocco smiled, and Maddie was sure it gave Flores goose bumps. Unless the detective was a robot. "There's nothing proper about me, Detective. But you already knew that."

Flores turned and walked down the hall. "Kitchen. You've got two minutes."

Maddie definitely couldn't be the only one who'd noticed that you could cut the tension between Rocco and Flores with a knife . . . It was such a raw, physical energy passing between them that she'd actually felt a little like a voyeur.

"How can she order us around in our own clubhouse?" Bear asked.

"She can't," Rocco said easily, obviously in no rush. "You all right, Maddie?"

"I think so. Wait. You're a lawyer?" she asked, and Rocco nodded. "Are you going to tell her about the car bomb?" she asked him.

Tals put an arm around her as Rocco nodded. "I'm sure your ex isn't telling her anything at all about that," Rocco added.

"Supposed the detective doesn't believe you?"

"She will. Eventually." With that Rocco pushed off the wall and went back to his room, no doubt to dress.

She realized it was time for her to do the same. Tals thanked Bear and closed the door so they could both do just that.

Chapter 16

It had been months since Rocco had been this close to Detective Lola Flores, and it hadn't been official police business back then at all. Not when he was murmuring "Lola" in her ear and she was dragging her nails down his back while she came.

She'd been drunk, but not as drunk as she'd like to pretend—that much he knew. She'd been reeling with guilt after Calla almost died. She'd been doubting herself . . . and she fell into Rocco's arms. Literally.

Although he definitely hadn't taken advantage of her.

Since then the closest he'd come to seeing her after Calla's rescue from the hands of a fucking madman, who'd also been a lawman, was having her speed by in her police-issued Chrysler Cutlass, refusing to turn her head to glance at him when he knew damned well she'd spotted him.

Not that he'd been expecting anything to come from their tryst. Hell, how could it? He'd been shocked enough when it happened, but not too shocked to enjoy the hell out of it. Or to wish it would happen again. And again . . .

He'd put on a shirt and jeans, sauntered back into the main room to find her stalking around in full angry-detective mode.

When she saw him, she quickly closed the distance between them, stabbing a finger in his direction. "If you're trying to undermine me—"

"I'm doing nothing of the sort," he said casually. "Trust me—sleeping with you isn't something I'd trumpet around here. I'm pretty sure it's grounds for expulsion from the club."

She smirked a little at that. "I'm sure it is."

"You'll be my dirty little secret."

"There's nothing dirty about me."

He knew she meant that completely different from the way it sounded, but he couldn't resist telling her, "Lola, you dirty talk better than any woman I've ever known."

"I'm sure you know many women, Rocco. But we're not doing this. We're definitely not doing this here," she told him furiously. "It's *Detective* to you."

But it hadn't been when she'd been rolling her hips under him, crying out his name. He didn't point that out, not out loud, anyway, but they both knew he was thinking about it. Hell, so was she, if she was honest with herself. "Don't get yourself twisted, babe."

"I'm not your babe," she said calmly. "If you think you can blackmail me with this . . ."

"I know that's the way the police think," he answered flatly. "I don't use sex as a weapon. So what happened that night—"

"It was a mistake," she interrupted quickly. Decisively.

He didn't take the time to examine why that cut him—and way more than he'd expected it to. "I tend to see it as a learning experience. And I learned a lot."

She glared at him; then her expression settled back into its serious-cop face as Maddie came back into the room. Rocco bit back a smile, because although Maddie had put pants on, she still wore Tals's Vipers T-shirt, and she'd tied it to show the edges of a healing tattoo. With her wild-looking hair and sex flush, she definitely looked like a Vipers chick.

At that moment, Preacher's voice boomed across the room, demanding, "What the fuck's going on in my house?"

"Didn't want to bother you, Preach. It's handled," Rocco said easily as Maddie tensed visibly, which, of course, Flores took note of. "This was a misunderstanding. I'm sure the detective is beginning to realize that. Once she talks to Maddie, she'll confirm it."

Preacher stared steadily at Flores even as he addressed Rocco. "You stay in here during that conversation. Tape it if you have to."

"Guilty people think like that," Flores told him with a smile.

"People who don't get caught think like that," Preacher corrected her, with zero trace of a smile.

"Reports referencing a brawl at Kelly's came in tonight," Flores said casually as she stared first at Preacher's bruised face and then glanced down at his equally banged-up knuckles.

Preacher shrugged. "Did you talk to Jessie?"

"I heard he had nothing to say, but his bar's intact. No one's talking." She smiled tightly. "Know anything about that, Preacher?"

"Nope," he answered easily. "But if I get wind of anything, law enforcement is on my speed dial."

How the guy could say that with a straight face was beyond Rocco, who had to duck his head to hide his grin.

"Riiiight," an equally unconvinced Flores drawled. "I'll be on pins and needles waiting for that call. In the meantime, don't make the mistake of thinking you're untouchable."

"I don't make mistakes that would cost my club members or my town, Detective. Skulls is my home and Vipers is my family," Preacher told her steadily. "Got it?"

She stared at him.

"I'm going to assume that's a yes. I'm also going to assume you know that at any point, I can tell you to get the fuck off my property and try to catch some real criminals, and not to come back if you don't have a warrant." And then he crossed his arms. "Clear?"

"Crystal," she said through gritted teeth.

When Maddie had come back in to continue her talk with Detective Flores, Rocco was dressed, but the tension in the room was thicker than it had been when he'd been nearly naked. Which was . . . odd. Maybe Preacher wasn't noticing it—maybe it was something only another woman could pick up on.

She had bigger things to worry about than Detective Flores's sex life. And after Preacher marched away, still grumbling about this being his house, she settled in to answer some questions, glad Rocco was there with her.

"Hugh Montgomery claims he was alerted to your whereabouts and was told that there was a bomb attached to your car last night," Detective Flores began.

Rocco nodded, and Maddie said, "I know the second part of what you said is true."

"Do you have enemies, Mrs. Montgomery?"

"Not that I know of. And it's still Wells. I kept my last name."

"Of course you did." Flores's smile was tight. "You're hanging out with some very dangerous men."

"Right now it appears that my husband might be the dangerous one."

"Can you elaborate?"

Maddie sighed. "We're going through a divorce."

"So you believe he's trying to have you killed?"

"She didn't say that," Rocco shot back. "Give her a break."

"Sorry. That's not part of my job." Flores kept all her attention focused on Maddie.

"I honestly have no idea what's going on with Hugh. I don't think he's trying to hurt me, but . . ."

"Did you consider the bomb might've been for the Vipers MC? You do know that this is a gang, don't you?"

"I grew up here, so I know what Vipers is," Maddie told her, feeling the anger rise up. Rocco gave her a small head shake of the keep-it-together variety, and she took a deep breath before continuing. "It doesn't make sense for enemies of Vipers to randomly go after me. I'm nobody to this club. I came into town a couple of days ago."

"But you're dating Tals."

"We've been on one date. Before this I hadn't seen him since high school."

"But obviously there's more to it than that, since Tals spoke with your husband."

"Ex," she said, distracted by what Flores had just said.

"Tals is the club's enforcer. If someone messes with the club, it's his job to stop them," Flores continued. "You emphasized that you grew up here. I'd expect you'd know more about who you're dealing with. Maybe you are here under false pretenses—in which case, I'd be happy to help you by taking you down to the station and hearing what you have to say."

Maddie looked Flores in the eye. "I know everything I need to know. I'm right where I want to be."

In reality she was confused as hell, but she could clear it up after she finished with Flores.

Flores wasn't ready for that to happen. "Do you really believe your husband is involved in something illegal?" she pushed. "You were married to him, and this is the first time you're mentioning anything about his illegal activities."

"Who would she mention it to, Detective?" Rocco asked.

Was Flores purposely using the word "husband" to goad her? Maddie assumed the answer was yes, and remained calm, letting Rocco add, "Since the bomb found in Maddie's car was rather sophisticated, I've got to assume it's not a rogue MC that's come calling."

"MCs do tend to be more heavy-handed and simplistic, yes," Flores agreed, and Rocco's face hardened. Then Flores said to her, "You had a reaction when Preacher Jones spoke."

"Did I?"

"Yes. It was fear." Flores stared her down.

She wasn't wrong, but she'd taken it wrong. "Preacher, Tals and I have a history." She attempted to use her words carefully. "They're still deciding if they can trust me. I don't have the same issue with them or I wouldn't be here."

"Where would you be, exactly?"

"With my grandmother."

"Who's being guarded by Vipers members, I'm assuming without her knowledge," Flores pointed out. "You can see how odd it looks from my end."

"I really can't," Maddie countered, praying Flores didn't plan on breaking the news to her grandmother anytime soon. "Not when I can only surmise that whatever—or whoever—Hugh Montgomery is involved with is threatening my life. I don't have those kinds of enemies."

"What, exactly, do you think Mr. Montgomery's associates are involved in?"

"I have no idea."

"Really? Wives always say that."

"Maybe some of us mean it. Maybe that's why I'm soon to be an ex-wife." Maddie couldn't keep the bitterness out of her voice. Flores wrote something down in her notepad. Slowly.

Damn her.

"What now?" Maddie asked.

"Now I go back to the station and give my report to Mr. Montgomery," Flores answered.

"What are you going to tell him?"

"If you're that interested, you'd accompany me."

"And put myself in danger? I don't think so." Maddie stood and glanced at Rocco. "We're done?"

"I'll see the detective out," Rocco told her.

Flores snorted. "Trust me, I know the way."

"What kind of game's Montgomery playing?" Tals murmured.

"One he's trying to win," Rocco said distractedly.

They were in the kitchen. The one good thing was that there'd been no sign of Tenn through all of this, and Tals figured he was staying at Cage and Calla's place. He'd already warned Rocco not to call him, but Tenn would be back tomorrow and he'd get an earful for sure. Tals had waited for Maddie to fall asleep, more from exhaustion than anything, because despite Tals telling her not to worry, she was worried as hell.

So was he. "He's trying to kill her."

"Or scare her so she'll come back," Rocco offered.

"Or his associates are trying to kill her to get to him. Preacher thinks that's the most likely scenario."

"So do I." Maddie's voice was sleepy but firm. Both men glanced up at her, and she shrugged.

"Come here, baby." Tals pulled out the chair next to him, and Maddie curled her legs under her and half leaned on him, taking a sip of his coffee. "Is there any business associate of Hugh's who made you nervous?"

"He was the bigwig," she explained. "He was the head of my organization."

"We're thinking it's someone outside of that," Rocco started. "Sometimes businessmen look for funding outside of the normal venues. Especially with the economy tanking the way it did."

She winced. "Like . . . mafias?"

Rocco nodded. Tals rubbed her shoulder. "It's going to be all right, Maddie."

"Look, the thing is . . . I didn't really socialize with Hugh outside of work. He cheated, but the marriage fell apart because of me. I put my work first. Everyone noticed it. Everyone but me, not until the last minute. And obviously, I put that barrier up on purpose. So I honestly couldn't tell you what color socks he wore, never mind the company he kept." The words came out in a rush, and she took another sip of coffee.

"Ah, Maddie." Tals shook his head. "It takes two to keep things afloat."

"Do you think Hugh would tell me?" she asked suddenly.

"Tell you what?" Rocco's tone held a suspicion Tals himself felt.

"Forget it," Tals told her flatly. "You're not talking to him—he'd want to see you alone, and no fucking way am I letting that happen."

"It's the best chance I have of finding out who's trying to hurt me. You both know that," she insisted.

Tals shook his head. "It might be. Still doesn't mean I'm going to let you."

"Let me?" Maddie asked.

Rocco threw his hands in the air. "Here we go again."

"I could just call him," Maddie started.

"You know he wants to see you in person," Tals interjected.

"Could he come here?"

Tals and Rocco both stared at her like she'd lost her mind. And probably she had, a little bit. A side effect of amazing sex, she realized, but hey.

And neither man was saying no.

"He won't do it," Tals muttered.

"Suppose he does, though?" she persisted.

"Supposed he plants a bomb?" Rocco asked. "Granted, it's not like our clubhouse is exactly a secret location."

Tals sat back and ran his hands through his already rumpled hair. "Even if he tells us what's going on, what then? What does it change? We're still protecting Maddie. Is he going to want our protection too?"

Maddie jerked her head in his direction. "You think that's what this is about?"

"Partially," Tals said easily. "He also wants you back."

"Why? Because he can't have me?"

Tals shrugged and she sighed. Rocco took that moment to slide out, leaving them alone. When they were, she took that moment to explain, "I called Grams earlier," she told him now. She'd been checking in nightly, lying and saying she'd decided to stay in town in a hotel for a while to get herself together. But then Maddie's presence was requested at home.

"Everything all right?"

"Yes . . . and no. I've got to get back home."

"Not happening," Tals said, like he was shutting down the conversation completely.

"Tals, I don't have a choice unless I want a lot more questions. My dad's coming in tonight. Obviously, she's concerned with how I'm quote, 'living my life these days.' And I'm sure she's told Dad everything, including the fact that I've resigned. He wants to have dinner with me tomorrow night. I put him off twenty-four hours, but that's the best I can do."

"The great thing about being an adult is that you don't have to do what other people want you to do." He glanced up to where Preacher had appeared, his broad shoulders framing the doorway. "Most of the time."

Preacher snorted. Tals smiled, then said, "I'll go get your stuff for you if you're not ready to deal with them."

"I'd love to let you do that. But I think I need to go talk to them. Explain a little." She reached out for Tals's hand. "Tell them I'm going to stay with you. Unless . . ."

"You're definitely staying with me."

She wasn't sure whether it was because there was still a possible threat of danger or because he really wanted her here. She smiled at Tals, then looked over at Preacher, who nodded, raised his bottle of beer like he was making a toast before he left.

Tals started again, telling her, "I know you're going through a lot of shit—"

"I know. But I'm through that. I'm here. Going after what I want."

"You wanted the city. And Hugh. You wanted everything you have."

"Had," she corrected. "I quit my job. Opened my eyes to my marriage."

"And came home to live with your grandmother."

"And ended up here with you." She frowned. "It's not the ideal way for this to have happened, but this, with you, that was the last time I felt right, that I didn't have to pretend. I could let myself be vulnerable without being scared—and I haven't done that since . . . well, not until right now."

She was being more honest than she'd been at dinner. Maybe because her life was at risk. Maybe it was the orgasms, because Tals knew he was good.

But hell, he didn't know what to do with this. "Is this your way of asking me for another date?"

He expected her to frown, get pissed at the joke he'd made in the middle of her serious confession.

Instead, she nodded. "Maybe you should drive, though."

And he was sure that if he hadn't fallen in love with her in high school, he would've anyway, and right about now. Because anyone who could have this much upheaval going on, anyone who could be this strong while still showing emotions . . . hell, that was a sign of someone who could fucking partner with him for life.

Suddenly he was choking again. It's not like he'd had great marriage role models around him growing up. None of the men here had had that. None of the women, either, although Cage and Calla were giving him hope. There were some stable family men, but the relationships were still a constant struggle.

Tenn assured him that would happen in an MC as well as outside of one. That it was normal. But to Tals, anything that required that much work wasn't the real thing.

Chapter 17

"Heard you had quite the club meetings the past two nights," Holly said languidly. She'd stayed in bed all day, taken an Epsom salt bath he'd forced her into to soothe her leg and finally agreed to take the painkillers the doctor had prescribed. Half of one, at least.

Now she lounged against the pillows. Preacher had already informed her that he'd called in help for the tattoo shop that evening, that she had the night off. She'd been too high to argue at the time, but he was pretty sure that, once the painkillers wore off, she wouldn't be this pliable.

She was still pissed about what he'd said to her last night. She hid it well, because that's what an MC woman did—waited for the right time. And Holly definitely knew how to handle him. She'd let him stew in his own guilt, which was exactly what happened.

It didn't take a genius to see what he'd been doing— he'd been losing control of his feelings for Holly, and he was trying to rein in the club to combat that. Ridiculous. Stupid as fuck.

But he wouldn't take advantage of her, not the way

her husband had, the way her old MC had or the way she expected him to.

But that was easier said than done. Last night he'd gone in to check on her, and he'd found a guy's phone number—the same one who'd been hanging on her in the shop, because Preacher had made sure to get the guy's name. It must've fallen out of her jeans, and it was on a piece of paper folded up into a tiny square, like it was being saved. Otherwise, why not toss it?

Maybe she forgot it was there . . .

Why would she accept it in the first place? Fuck. He didn't bother confronting her about it now, instead, telling her, "Club business is none of your concern."

"It is when you take out your anger at me on the club."

"Trust me, these guys do enough wrong that I don't need to misplace any blame." It was true enough—the club could always use a good ass kicking, especially the younger members. Preacher had no problem laying down the law when need be.

"Good to know." She tapped her own cheek, then pointed to the bruise on his. "Who were you really fighting last night?"

For the first time since coming into her room, he took note of the travel brochures on her bed. His heart lurched. "Making plans?"

"I'm thinking of going on holiday." She had a haughty way about her, and it came across even more strongly when she was trying to hide any kind of emotion.

"Running?"

She gazed at him coolly. "Both our lives would be easier."

He knew exactly what she was trying to do. Since he'd claimed her, in order to keep her safe from the No'Ones' retaliation, as well as any other Vipers member, she wasn't supposed to make a move without Preacher. The men he was closest to knew the claiming was in name only, but rules were rules.

In her eyes, by not asserting his rights to sleep with her, she was rejected. Especially because he slept with other women, which was also his right.

She never complained. Mainly because she was claimed but she wasn't an old lady, and there was a real difference.

She wore short jeans shorts. The scar on her leg healed well, and it did nothing to detract from her long-legged beauty.

You should let her go . . . set her free.

From this life.

From *him*.

When she'd come to Vipers . . . Damn, if he shut his eyes, he could see her so clearly, and it still made him want to go out and kill the No'Ones' president with his bare hands.

She still had nightmares. She needed the antianxiety meds less and less, and strangely, the violence she'd meted out and received twice in the last months while defending both Calla and Eli had made her stronger.

If she wasn't, she'd never be considering this holiday bullshit. They both knew that if she went to London, she wasn't coming back.

"It's the same as it was when I was with the No'Ones," she challenged. "The place isn't mine."

"The money you make is," he reminded her.

"Right. So I won't be left with nothing," she said sarcastically. "Don't worry, Preacher. I've always known history would repeat itself."

"What's really going on?" he demanded. "Stop bullshitting and talk to me."

"Right, as you're always such an open book," she

replied. Then she sighed and admitted, "My parents have been writing."

"Really?"

She glanced up at him, her voice slightly mocking. "Yes, really. Some people don't hold grudges against their only children."

Holly's worst crime had been running off with a man her parents had deemed not good enough for her.

"So you're going for a visit, then?"

"I was thinking of something a bit more . . . permanent." She met his gaze defiantly.

"And here I thought you were having fun." He couldn't help the bitterness in his voice.

Her response was just as bitter. "You raise people, Preacher. I've no need to be raised. I'm all grown-up, in case you hadn't noticed."

God, that fucking accent could still do it to him, all these years later. Granted, it was the combo of the accent and Holly's beauty plus the attitude that made him alternately go insane and want to kiss her all at once.

She knew it too. Used it all against him. And no matter how many times he told himself it was for her own good, he also knew telling her the same exact thing wouldn't change her mind.

But this development . . . this was new. And the trip she was talking about wasn't just a holiday. "So what, you'd move back there with them? Start over?"

She shrugged. "That's what they'd like. Of course, I realize I'd need your permission." The tone was anything but subservient, with just enough pretend bowing down to make his temper rise.

"That's right."

"But I'm sure you can find some new strays to take in and occupy your time."

What she was saying was nothing new, but something pushed his buttons more than usual tonight. She'd taken it a step too far, and although he'd certainly curbed his temper, there was still no real low setting on his boil. And as he moved toward her, she backed up. And for the first time she showed a flash of fear in her eyes, especially as her back hit the wall.

He was on her in seconds, pinning her, anger flooding his body. But there was nothing sexual about this, nothing punishing . . .

Nothing beyond the fact that he was done putting up with Holly, once and for all. "Those strays I've taken in? They'd lay down their goddamned lives for me, every single one of them. I've made only one mistake in twenty-two years, and I'm looking at her. So you're free, Holly, if that's really what you want. Consider your bank account yours. But I suggest you buy a ticket and be on the next flight out, because once the No'Ones find out you're not with me anymore, I can't make any promises as to what they'll do."

The No'Ones wouldn't follow her to London. For chrissakes, they could barely find their way across state lines half the time. The ball was in her court.

She'd never realized it always had been.

Chapter 18

"Missed me?" Rocco asked. Lola Flores straightened her shoulders and stared him down from the back door of Vipers clubhouse. "Maybe we should let you use the front entrance—that is the one most guests use."

"Trust me, I'm no guest."

"Would you like to come in? Harass some of our members? Search the place?" Rocco offered.

"At this moment, I'm simply a messenger."

Oh, this was gonna be good. "Then by all means, deliver."

"Hugh Montgomery is missing."

He leaned against the doorjamb, giving his best bored impression. "How's that Maddie's problem?"

Flores smiled, almost too sweetly. "Witnesses place her as the last one to see him."

That was, of course, impossible, which made it a complete lie. "I'd like to take a crack at some of your witnesses."

"I'm sure you would. Is Maddie here?"

Rocco kept his expression neutral. He'd had enough practice.

"She is. And she hasn't left the clubhouse since she came in here two nights ago. And we have plenty of witnesses to that. She's neither seen nor spoken to Hugh Montgomery, so I think we're done here."

Lola took a step closer. "Don't you think someone should mention to Maddie that you acting as her lawyer is a conflict of interest?"

She was wearing perfume. Did she always when she was on duty and he'd never noticed? Or had she put it on just for him?

On purpose? Was she trying to screw with his head, or was something else going on with her, unconsciously? "You're one to talk about conflicts of interest, Detective."

"I'm a professional."

"So am I."

She gave him a small smirk. "Really? Where's your practice?"

"I keep current enough." He sat back. "Detective, you don't have to worry about me using what we did against you. That's not the way I operate."

She snorted, and he leaned in toward her. "You have a certain idea of the kind of man I am. Or at least you did when my head was between your legs and you were begging for more."

The flush on her cheeks told him she had fond memories, while the narrowing of her eyes said he'd hit the mark with his crudeness. It was what she wanted to believe of him, and it galled him to prove her right, but he understood why she needed to believe it. She was more determined than ever to expose the Vipers, to prove she could never like them. She was also punishing Rocco because she'd slept with him. Female logic.

"I'll be back, Rocco," she warned.

"I never doubt that."

*   *   *

Tals barely got any warning from Rocco before she was back, less than an hour later.

"She planned this," Rocco muttered as Tals stared out the window at the cop cars she'd brought with her, like there was going to be some kind of MC-police war on the premises.

"Maybe she and Hugh are in this together." Fuck, he wished Maddie didn't have to see this. But hey, they'd made it past forty-eight hours.

Barely. But still, it counted.

"You ready for me to open the door?" Rocco asked.

"Let's get it over with."

"I already set up bail plans," Rocco assured him, because they both knew she wouldn't be back with this many officers if she wasn't planning an arrest.

At the last minute, Tals grabbed Rocco's arm. "No way we're not getting dragged in with some fucked-up evidence, but you don't think she'll arrest Maddie, do you?"

"Collusion is circumstantial at best. If Flores does it for a scare tactic, we get the grandmother involved. Maddie's family has enough weight to step on some necks," Rocco assured him. "But honestly? She's gunning for us. Maybe you more than me—I'll just be collateral damage."

There was an edge to Rocco's voice in a situation he was usually cool as a cucumber in. And he was staring out the window at Flores.

Ah, hell no. What the fuck was wrong with all of them? Maybe it was in the water. He made a mental note to have it tested as Rocco opened the door and stood back to allow Flores to enter.

To arrest them, she'd have to ask them to step outside, and they always made her ask and follow procedure down to the letter, as per Rocco's teachings.

"Back so soon, Detective Flores?" Rocco called to her.

"Why don't you step outside so we can talk?" she asked.

"No, please, come on in. We insist." Rocco held the door open for her. She pushed past him, walked in and stopped in front of Tals.

"I'm here to place you under arrest," she told Tals, point-blank. "And Rocco and Rally too."

At the mention of his name, Rally walked into the room, standing there silently, staring Flores down.

"What are the charges?" Rocco asked while Tals stood there, hoping Maddie didn't come down in the middle of this.

"Extortion. Threats. Kidnapping and battery. Such a nice checklist. Because someone tried to kill Hugh Montgomery tonight," she told them.

"That's funny—because an hour ago, you told me Hugh was missing and that Maddie was the last one to see him. Remember, you had all those witnesses," Rocco reminded her.

Flores tapped a finger against her chin, like she was trying to remember. "Oh, right—that. Faulty information. We all know how unreliable witnesses can be."

"So what witness do you have now?" Tals couldn't help but ask.

"Well, your woman never mentioned that you called Hugh and had a nice clarifying chat with him. A threat and then a kidnapping."

Rocco rolled his eyes. "Hoping you'll do better than that."

"Of course, Counselor—we definitely have something better. Evidence." She held up a Baggie that had been stuffed in her blazer pocket and flashed it quickly. "Hugh called the police after his attackers left him behind. Someone came by and stopped them from going further, or I have no doubt he'd be dead. Police found this Vipers patch on the scene."

"That's your evidence?" Rocco asked in amazement. "Bullshit."

"Do you really think we're fucking stupid enough to leave a calling card like that?" Tals asked.

"Yes, I definitely think anyone in a gang is fucking stupid," Flores told him pleasantly. She was enjoying this way too much.

"Shut the fuck up, Tals," Rocco murmured.

Tals did what was recommended. This would never stick—and he could practically guarantee the patch was fake. But none of that was the point—who the hell was behind all of this, and were they trying to hurt Tals, Maddie or both?

"I've got more than just the patch," Flores assured them. "Including the fact that Hugh Montgomery heard you calling each other by name. Coupled with the fact that you, Tals and Rally were caught on videotape walking into Hugh's hotel and getting out of the elevator on his floor . . ." She trailed off and shrugged. "I think that's more than sufficient for now. Gentlemen, you know what to do next."

Unfortunately, Tals did. He pushed outside, hands in the air and knelt on the ground. Immediately, an officer came up behind him, yanking his arms down and behind his back before cuffing them. The officer kept a hand pressed to his shoulder.

He glanced to the left and saw Rally, kneeling and cuffed. From behind him, Tals heard Flores say, "You too, Rocco."

"What are the charges?" Rocco asked.

"Vipers patch. You've been defending Maddie, so I have to assume you're in collusion."

Rocco shook his head, and Tals swore he could hear the guy mentally counting to ten before turning around to offer his wrists for the cuffs.

"We'll be out by morning," Rocco told Tals, even though it was more for Flores's benefit than anything.

"I wouldn't count on it," Flores countered.

It was happening again—Tals getting arrested because of her. And this time Maddie wasn't allowed to say a word. If she hadn't gotten out of the shower in time to hear the ruckus happening below, she'd have missed it. And Preacher would've probably told her Tals was out on club business.

Instead she got to watch Tals being put in the back of a police car along with Rocco.

And Preacher was literally holding her back, his hands on her shoulders.

"You can't do this to me," she told Preacher, refusing to tear her eyes from Tals. Tals, who wouldn't even turn his head, no matter how hard she stared. "You can't put me in this position again."

"The way I see it, you owe all of us. The way you pay us back is by doing what we say," Preacher told her. "Besides, you put yourself in this position, Maddie. You dragged this to our clubhouse steps. It's out of your hands and on our backs now."

Even though he spoke the truth, she still hated him at this moment. "You have to take me to the station. Let me talk to Hugh. I'll get him to drop the charges."

Preacher shook his head. "Won't matter. Even if he does, the state will try the case."

God, this was horrible. And to top it all off, she was still in danger, along with the Vipers. Because whoever had framed the MC still wanted her dead.

Chapter 19

Holly was still here. As far as Preacher could tell, she hadn't made any airline reservations, but then again, with everything going on, Holly would never abandon the MC now. She was nothing if not loyal to the life-style.

Or maybe she's just staying for you.

But he refused to believe that, to acknowledge it. They were both way too fucked-up—about love and everything in between—to make this work.

Tonight, though, she marched in and didn't wait to be acknowledged—or seem to give a shit that he was on the phone—before saying, "There are men staying in the next town you need to look at."

Preacher wanted to tell her to sit down, to stop inter-rupting, but dammit all, he couldn't. "Talk."

"I've seen them. More important, I've seen their tat-toos. I know what they mean." She had an iPad with her, and she passed it to Preacher. He studied the pic-ture as she outlined the three men and the tattoos she'd been able to see, growing more concerned by the minute.

They were definitely Albanian, most likely mafia.

He'd heard rumblings that they were breaking into the stolen-luxury-car market, trying to horn in on East Coast territory. He figured it was more about running drugs inside the cars, a kill-two-birds-with-one-stone type of crime. But if they were really after Hugh, and Maddie by default, Vipers would be caught in the middle.

"Did they recognize you?' Preacher demanded of Holly.

"No."

"Holly, you don't exactly blend," Preacher told her.

"They didn't see me. I was sitting down, anyway. I had a hat on. My hair was up. I was in sweats. Trust me—they didn't glance in my direction once. And they weren't exactly in hiding or trying to cover up."

"You're lying," Preacher said bluntly. "And I'm going to find out the truth one way or another."

Her bravado faltered for a brief second, and then the mask slipped back into place. "I've given you necessary information, and now you're trying to punish me?"

"If I make you so fucking miserable, why are you still here?" he challenged. "I'm telling you right now, if you're staying, things are going to goddamn change around here."

She crossed her arms. "Really?"

"Don't push, Holly. You're putting yourself in danger, and by extension, Vipers. Maybe that's what you do, though—"

"Fuck you, Preacher."

"I'd stop there."

"Going to put me in line?"

He paused a long moment before he told her, "It's time someone did."

She looked like she wanted to say something, thought better of it and simply walked away. That was more frustrating than anything (and of course she knew it) because now he was all pissed off, revved up, with no outlet.

"Preach?"

He looked up to see Tenn standing in the doorway. Preach said, "Bail's being posted for Tals and Rocco now."

"I know. I was going to ask when the last time you got laid was."

The only other person who'd dare ask him that so bluntly was Tals. And Tenn was not only completely unapologetic, but he was also completely serious.

"Tenn, I don't have time for your shit."

Tenn pulled out a chair, turned it around and sat so his chest leaned against the back. "I mean, look. I'm not one to take my own advice on a regular basis, but hell, man, you're driving everyone fucking nuts."

"And they called you to tell me where to put my dick?"

"No one has to tell me. I can see it. And what the fuck is up with you and Holly?"

"There's no *me and Holly*, Tenn."

Tenn leaned back a little, holding on to the chair's back like he was stretching. "Why're you pushing her out the door?"

"She wants to go."

"Then why hasn't she?"

"That's what I'm trying to figure out."

Tenn nodded, then suggested, "Check her bank account. Usually when someone can't leave, either they really don't want to, or they're too broke."

"It's good you remind me of why I keep you around."

Chapter 20

Maddie was practically climbing the walls. She couldn't go anywhere, since there was obviously active danger, which meant she was stuck inside the clubhouse, waiting for Tals, Rocco and Rally to be arraigned and praying that bail would be set.

The clubhouse was a big place, but she couldn't settle in at all. Plus, the tension was incredible, because all the guys were intent on figuring out who was trying to frame Vipers. Preacher had sent out groups of Vipers to try to get to the bottom of the mess, but then he'd called that off.

He wasn't going to tell her why, and she knew better than to ask. But ten hours after Tals was taken away, she was exhausted from stress, unable to sleep and she had no one to talk to.

Was it like this for all the women with Vipers men, or just her? Her circumstances were definitely different from most who dated Vipers . . . or at least, that's how it seemed.

She was lingering in the kitchen, staring at the fridge like it might produce something to quell her anxiety, when she heard loud voices coming from the other room. A definite argument—and she recognized Tenn's voice immediately.

She closed the fridge and steeled herself. She hadn't seen him since the other night, when they'd been arguing. She'd known he hadn't gone back home yet, though. Tals told her he'd been staying with Calla and Cage at their apartment a few blocks away.

"Tenn, she didn't do this," Preacher was repeating.

"Tals is in jail because he's accused of assaulting her husband—how is she not involved?" Tenn yelled over his shoulder as he walked into the kitchen.

Preacher was right behind him. "This is Flores, trying to take us down any way she can."

"If there's smoke, there's fire." Tenn was staring right at her. "Am I right, Maddie?"

"My ex called the police after someone tried to kidnap him," she started.

"And there's video of Tals, Rocco and Rally headed to your ex's hotel room. Plus a phone call. And at the scene of the kidnapping, there just happened to be a Vipers patch," he finished.

"Nothing concrete," Preacher added.

Tenn glanced at him impatiently, saying, "You forget how much pull I've got—I know exactly how concrete the evidence is," before turning his full attention back to Maddie. "Your ex knew where you were staying, who you were staying with, since he accused Tals of kidnapping you. Did you even try to talk to your ex, to tell him to leave Tals out of your goddamned drama? Now you've got Rocco and Rally involved too."

"Tals didn't want me to—"

"Of course not. My brother's great at protecting everyone but himself. But you knew that, didn't you? Is that why you're walking all over him, leading him by the goddamned nose?"

"Tenn—"

"This is the third goddamned time he's been arrested for something to do with you."

"I didn't ask him to," she whispered.

"Right. And he was supposed to just let Earl hurt you?" Tenn pressed his lips together, then said, "You should do Tals a favor and leave him alone. Leave Vipers, go back to your rich family and let them protect you. If you really do give a shit about him, like you claim to, you wouldn't break up his family."

She wanted to tell him that she wasn't trying to break up his family, but that's exactly what was happening—she was pitting brother against brother. And so she remained silent, because she was never going to win this.

Tenn wasn't exactly angry, but rather, honest. And he wasn't done. "Maddie, look, I get that this all might seem really great—Tals rescues you. He takes care of you. He's dangerous. But I think what's happening between you is different for you than it is for him."

"You think I'm here for a fling."

He nodded. "And Tals is a lot like our mom. She was a romantic. She was convinced that there's 'the one'—a soul mate. The right one."

Maybe their mothers had been friends. "Who was the right one for your mom?"

Tenn smiled tensely. "Unfortunately, it was my dad."

Maddie just nodded, because what could she say to that? All she added was, "So Tals is still looking, then."

Her voice sounded neutral, but she felt all hollowed out inside. She wanted to end this conversation, go back inside, crawl under the covers with ice cream and stay there in hiding.

Tenn looked at her strangely. "No. He hasn't really been looking for a long time. Not since high school."

He sounded disapproving . . . and she was confused. "He found someone in high school?"

He shook his head. "For someone so aware . . ."

"Wait. You're talking about . . . ?" She couldn't get the last word out, so she simply pointed to herself.

"Clueless," Tenn muttered. "You're it for him, Maddie, okay? The two of you, you're like ghosts haunting each other. And I know ghosts too damned well to know it's not going to end well. It's going to fucking kill him when you leave. Again. And I know you will, so do me a favor and go ahead and do it already."

And then Calla came in and gave Maddie a sympathetic look while putting a hand on Tenn's forearm, urging him to "calm down" and "come with her."

Thankfully, Tenn listened. Preacher started to say something to her, but sighed instead and followed Tenn.

She fought tears. Sat on the table and buried her face in her hands, looked up when she heard Bear ask, "You all right, Maddie?" He added, "Of course you're not."

She raised her head, wiped her eyes. "I guess you heard. I'm sure the whole clubhouse heard."

"Everyone's worried. When Tals bails out—"

"I think I should do what Tenn says and leave."

Bear shook his head. "Tals will not be happy about that."

"Well, I'm not happy at the thought of breaking up his relationship with Tenn. And Cage and Preacher. All of this is my problem, not theirs."

"He can handle it."

"I know he can, but . . ." She shook her head. "He shouldn't have to. He's had to pretend too often."

"He's not pretending with you."

"I know that. It's just that he's not what most people think."

Bear went to the fridge, took out two beers, opened one and handed it to her. "He's easygoing. Fun. But—"

"He's not happy—not the way he appears," she told him. "It's not an act, exactly. He's trying to convince himself . . . It's like wish fulfillment."

Bear stared at her, his surprise obvious. "How'd you know that?"

"Because I'm exactly the same way." She gave a one-shouldered shrug. "I know that's not who he is. I know he's a good guy. I've just started scratching the surface. I didn't want to in high school. I never wanted to get that close."

"Scared he wouldn't be what you wanted?"

"Just the opposite," she said ruefully. "How did you get involved with the MC?"

"Through Tals." Bear took a long drink of his beer. She thought he wouldn't elaborate, then, "I was about ten. He was just out of high school. Almost. Then . . ."

Bear stopped. Shrugged. And she realized that, along with everything else, she was also responsible for separating Bear from Tals for a while, since he'd gone into the military after the Earl incident.

"Maddie, listen, he was going into the military no matter what. Preach got involved, and when Tals finished his tour and was doing the National Guard stuff, he started to pull me in more. Got me into repo work."

Bear was perfect for that job based on size alone. He had an intense expression too—when he didn't let through the inherent kindness she saw in his eyes.

And obviously, it was Calla's turn to try to help Maddie feel not so alone. Or responsible, because she came in next, apologizing. "I'm sorry—I tried to talk Tenn out of coming here. He's upset."

"He has a right to be."

"Maybe. But he shouldn't take it out on you." Calla

sat next to her. "I think he's angrier at himself that he can't protect Tals all the time. From everything."

"He's a good brother. I'm an only child." She shrugged.

"Me too, for all intents and purposes. My stepbrother was a bad guy."

"How long have you been involved with Vipers?" Maddie couldn't help but ask.

"I met Cage—well, technically, I met Tenn first. I was working for their Army CO and there was some trouble," she explained. "I was in trouble. And I fell in love with Cage from a phone call." She laughed. "I'm sure some people would say that was crazy, that it couldn't happen. But all I can say is, if it doesn't happen to you, how can you be so sure?"

Maddie nodded. She understood, because she was pretty sure she'd fallen for Tals the first time she'd seen him in the halls of the high school. "This lifestyle . . ."

"You grew up around here, right? I mean, you see what these guys do. I used to tend bar in Upstate New York, so I had a good idea what MCs were like. It's not always easy, but Preacher's smart. And since he raised Cage and Tals and Tenn . . ." Calla trailed off. "Anyway, Tals will land on his feet. These guys always do."

Maddie agreed, but this time she was going to take herself out of the equation in order to facilitate that.

When it was too late to take back, when Maddie knew the security guards her dad hired for her were close to the Vipers clubhouse, she found Preacher and broke the news to him. She dressed in the outfit she'd worn on her date with Tals—seemed like a lifetime ago.

"One of the guys will drive my car home," she said. "I just need the key."

Tals had parked it in the back lot for safekeeping.

Preacher didn't answer her at first; then finally he

said, "We can't stop you, Maddie. But you're putting yourself in a hell of a lot of danger."

"My dad's got security coming to get me. He talked to Hugh. He said Hugh needs to talk to me." She stared into his dark eyes. "It's better this way, for everyone."

Preacher looked like he was going to say something, but ultimately he simply told her, "If this is what you want, I'll let you know when your security detail's here."

And he did, ten minutes later. He gave her the key to her car and walked her outside, delivering her into the waiting SUV, pointing out her car to the big man who got out. She watched Preacher give him the side eye, would've laughed if she wasn't so miserable.

"Do you want me to give Tals a message?" Preacher asked right before she closed the car door.

She bit her bottom lip, then said, "Just tell him I'm really sorry."

Preacher nodded, let her close the door, and the SUV left Vipers territory and headed back toward Jessamine. The driver was quiet, but kept looking back at her in the rearview mirror.

Finally she asked, "How bad is it back at the house?"

He sighed. "You shouldn't be involved with Vipers. That's all I'm saying."

"I'm sure you're not the only one with that opinion," she muttered.

Chapter 21

Half an hour later, her father was repeating, "I don't understand, Maddie," over and over. Like she'd disappointed and confused him so much, he'd become a broken record of disbelief.

Her grandmother's silent, icy treatment was actually preferable at this point.

Although neither of them seemed to remember she was a grown woman, way too old to be lectured like this. But she'd put herself in this position. She wasn't stupid enough to think she could handle what was happening without protection.

As her father finally broke out and used his words, things got worse. It didn't matter what she countered with. He couldn't seem to get past the fact that she'd, according to him, thrown her entire career away, jeopardized her future and now she was acting just like her mother.

From everything she'd heard about Margaret Wells, she had to agree.

"And after all of that—after leaving Hugh, quitting what you worked so hard for—you come back here and hook up with Tals Garrity? The same motorcycle-gang juvenile delinquent who nearly killed Earl?" her father demanded. "Maddie, do you have any idea how hard I fought to keep what happened under wraps for your sake? Earl's parents were not happy. They could've ruined you—"

"Ruined *me*?" she repeated incredulously.

"I really thought you understood what you needed to do, Maddie. I wanted you independent. I wasn't thrilled when you got married, but at least you were smart about it. Divorce is one thing, but what you're involved in—"

"What I'm involved in? Dad, I don't think you understand."

"I understand that Vipers Motorcycle Club is responsible for almost killing Hugh and that Tals is under arrest. I'm thankful you came to your senses and came home. Hugh has been waiting to speak to you."

"Hugh's here?" She glanced around, and her grandmother nodded.

Her grandmother sniffed. "He's very worried about you. In fact, he was the one who informed us of where you were. I thought you were at a hotel, which I didn't understand."

"I'm sorry I lied. I wasn't ready to talk about Tals yet."

"There's nothing to talk about, Maddie. There is no you and Tals," her father said sternly. "I've spoken with Hugh about you returning to work."

"I'm not working for Hugh any longer."

Her father studied her. "Fine. I can pull a few strings and get you seen."

"I'm capable of getting my own job. And I'm not talking about this now, Dad. You don't get to come in and dictate my life. I've been doing fine on my own."

"If fine is almost getting yourself killed," Hugh broke in. She whirled around to see him standing in the doorway of the sitting room.

"We'll leave you two alone," her father said, extending a hand to her grandmother to help her up and walk her out of the room.

Hugh looked as exhausted as she felt. Had it really been less than two weeks since she'd left him at the party? "I can't believe you're here," she hissed.

"I can't believe your boyfriend tried to kill me."

"He's not my boyfriend. He's someone I knew in high school," she lied casually.

Hugh was pacing the room. "I almost got killed tonight."

"Join the club."

"What are you talking about?"

"Didn't Detective Flores tell you about the bomb? I told her, the same night you tried to have me brought to you by the police." She crossed her arms in front of her body as he pulled up short. "It's pretty obvious you're trying to frame Vipers because I'm with them."

"You're *with them*?" he asked sarcastically. "What exactly does that mean?"

"It means they're protecting me from whoever tried to murder me last week," she shot back, and Hugh started. "Or at least they were. What aren't you hearing? There was a bomb in my car. If Tals hadn't noticed something funny with the remote . . ."

Shit. She'd never really let herself think about that, because Tals had been there. Her knees trembled a little as the realization of just how close she'd come to being killed flashed through her mind.

It obviously hit Hugh too, because he started, "The detective didn't . . ." before sinking into the closest chair. "She told me you were staying with Vipers, that you refused to leave and she couldn't be one hundred percent sure you wanted to be there. But she said there wasn't much she could do to get you out."

"Vipers isn't trying to kill you, Hugh. But they are trying to figure out who you pissed off. So maybe you could share that information with me?"

"Jesus, Maddie, what's wrong with you? I'm the CFO of a major corporation. You're the one sleeping with criminals, and I'm the one who's doing something wrong?"

Hugh was lying to her. He was capable of sleeping around and lying about it, but this was a whole other level. Had she ever really known him? "Someone's trying to kill us, Hugh," she reiterated. "Don't try to bullshit me—I know you're involved."

"And you don't think it has anything to do with the company you're keeping?" he demanded.

"Let's not even talk about 'company.' Obviously, you neglected to tell my father any of that. So he thinks I just walked away from you and quit my job on a whim?" Of course he'd believe that—he'd always lectured her that she was too much like her mother, which really, was a horrible thing to say to a child.

"No one I slept with ever tried to kill me."

"Give it time," she told him through clenched teeth.

He pointed at her. "The man you're fucking is trying to have me killed, and you're caught up in whatever illegal shit he's into, Maddie. Wake up and deal with that. He's on video coming to my hotel room."

Maddie knew that the only way to get Tals off the hook—and Rocco and Rally too—was to convince Hugh to recant his story. Especially since it wasn't the truth. But this was . . . "If you really and truly believe that, why not tell him you'll take him up on his offer to protect you?" she asked, as the pieces began to click together in her mind. "Don't you think it's possible that Tals was coming to get you, but he was too late?"

Hugh's mouth opened, then closed. His jaw clenched.

"Think about what you really heard and why. Do you think men who kidnapped you would use their names? Be scared away that easily? Tals was going to protect you even after the trouble you've gotten me in-to—or maybe because of it. You still need that protection, Hugh, so don't be stupid. Make a call to the police and maybe Vipers will still consider that protection."

There was a long pause as Hugh considered this. And then he took out his cell phone, dialed and said, "I need to speak with Detective Flores please."

Because he knows he needs protection. The thought chilled her.

She turned and walked away from him, went upstairs and locked herself in her room. She hoped to God he wasn't staying here in the house, but she had to assume he was.

Chapter 22

Twenty-four hours after Tals, Rocco and Rally had been escorted into jail, they were released. They'd figured they were out on bail, but as it turned out, there was a sudden lack of evidence to hold them.

Or at least, that was the company line they were fed—Tals knew they'd get the full story soon. Although Rocco was always in charge of the club's legal matters, they retained a woman named Callie for matters like conflicts of interests . . . and for when Rocco was arrested himself. Tals assumed she and Preacher had worked some magic, and he was damned grateful for it.

None of them had slept much, even though they were in a quiet cell, just the three of them. Any longer, and Tals had no doubt they would've been transferred to the state-run facility.

"What the fuck happened?" Rocco demanded when he saw Preacher.

"Witness recanted. Said it was a misunderstanding. Said he never heard your names. Flores knew the patch was bullshit anyway . . . and the surveillance video? Hugh said he invited you guys to come see him,"

Preacher said. "Hugh even admitted he was jealous of Tals and that's why the whole thing started."

"Fuckin' A," Rocco muttered.

"Must've killed Flores to let us go," Tals muttered, his voice rough as he rode in the backseat of Preacher's truck, Tenn and Rally next to him, Rocco up front with Preacher.

"Just about," Preacher replied.

"How's Maddie?" Tals asked, and he swore there was a noticeable tension that passed through the car before Preach assured him she was fine.

But Tals wasn't going to believe that until he saw it with his own eyes. And so when he first noted that her car was missing from the lot, he tensed. When he went inside and headed to his room, from behind him Tenn said, "Don't bother—she's gone."

She's gone.

That echoed through Tals's mind, turned him cold, but he didn't turn around when he asked, as calmly as he fucking could, "What do you mean, gone?"

"She went home," Tenn said unapologetically. "To her grandmother's house. They have security for her."

Tals drew in a breath. "Whose idea was that?"

"Maddie's."

"Just out of the blue, she decided to go hang out at home?" Tals asked, his resolve not to punch his brother beginning to wane.

And when Tenn finally admitted, "I think I know why," Tals turned to him slowly, his hands fisting.

He took a couple of steps toward Tenn, whose jaw was clenched, and asked, "What the fuck did you do?"

"She thought she was breaking up your family."

Tals frowned. "She told you that?"

"In so many words, yes."

"And you did nothing to dissuade her of that?"

Tenn shook his head. "Look at the trouble—"

And that's when Tals lost it, shoving Tenn back. As his brother stumbled a little, Tals told him, "You're the one breaking up our family—it's you, Tenn. You don't get to pick who I love."

Tenn stood up straight, dangerously still for a moment before he lunged for Tals. Even though Tals was ready for him, it still motherfucking hurt, because Tenn hit him like a brick wall. They slammed to the ground, rolling, punching, Tenn trying to get his hands around Tals's neck.

They didn't fight often, but when they did, it was messy and dirty and so goddamned bad that Tals could taste the anger for days afterward. It was like fighting with himself, with his own conscience.

With that in mind, Tals slammed Tenn in the ribs and rolled out from under him, simultaneously coughing from the hold Tenn'd had on his throat while trying to draw in air.

"Who you love got you arrested three times now. Are you just waiting for one to stick?" Tenn challenged, even as he panted, holding his side. "Fucker. You're listening to your dick. You're living out some teenage fantasy."

"That's rich, coming from you. How's your love life, Tenn? Still running Ward off?" Tenn looked like he'd been slapped, but Tals pressed on. "Yeah, I know you tell everyone he left you. Maybe you even believe it yourself, because that's what you need to do to convince yourself it's not your fault. But you pushed him away. You can lie about that to everyone but me."

Tenn stared at him. "Go fuck yourself."

"You've done a good enough job of fucking me over already."

Chapter 23

The first thing Maddie did when she went upstairs to her old room was grab her favorite blanket and her slouchy beanie cap and head out onto the deck. From that vantage point, she could just make out the security detail out by the gates.

It had started to snow a little. The grounds always looked so pretty this time of year, and she was reluctant to go inside, despite how cold she was. It didn't matter—she felt cold and numb on the inside anyway, so at least now her outsides matched.

A huge part of her hoped Tals would come to her, demand she go back with him, but that's not what she'd hoped to accomplish by leaving Vipers. No, she'd needed to talk to Hugh, which she'd done, but she had to not get in the way of Tals and Tenn, or Tals and Vipers.

Still, she wondered what Tenn would tell him . . . or how betrayed Tals would feel when he got out and she wasn't there.

If he got out. Her heart lurched at that. Even though Hugh had told the police he didn't think Tals tried to kill him, it was possible they wouldn't back down. According to Hugh's last text to her, Flores was threatening him with jail time for perjury, then telling him that they could protect him from Vipers.

Hugh also said that he wouldn't let Flores change his mind, but to please put in a word for him to Vipers. Yes, he was scared. And yes, she would do what he asked, once Tals and Rocco and Rally were released.

And once Tals was out and this was over? Where did she go next? She couldn't stay in the same town with Tals and not have her heart break over and over.

Her head ached along with her heart. She pressed her fingers to her temples as if that could alleviate anything, felt the hot tears warm her cold cheeks.

"Maddie." It was Tenn's voice. Several stories up on guarded, alarmed property. She stood slowly, looking around. "Behind you."

She whirled around and saw him sitting in a chair, like he'd shown up for a casual drink. "You almost gave me a heart attack. What the hell are you doing? And how did you get up here—"

"Because you're supposed to have security in place?" he said. "Don't worry—it'd be hard to find security that works against me. Or Tals."

"Or the men who are trying to kill me?"

"They seem to be not as subtle. The guys you have are all right for the moment, but I think you really need to let Tals protect you."

She swore she had whiplash. And he obviously knew that because he added, "Tals is out of jail. Charges dropped. Patch was fake, but Flores knew that already. And yeah, we had a huge fight and I told him what happened. How I felt. But in the end . . . you're what he wants."

She shook her head. "I will not come between you

guys. No way. I know what you're doing, but you don't have to feel guilty."

He stood, told her fiercely, "I don't, Maddie, okay? I don't do shit out of guilt. But if you're willing to sacrifice yourself for our family, then maybe you really are our family."

She felt a flutter of hope, at the fact that Tals was out and off the hook . . . and about Tenn possibly not holding her accountable for all the bad things happening around her. But they weren't out of danger yet. "Look, I appreciate what you're saying, but I'm still at fault."

"You didn't know what Hugh was doing. Not any more than you knew what Earl would try," Tenn admitted. "I'm a protective older brother." She frowned and he added, "I'm older by four minutes, but that's still older, dammit."

"He won't stay angry at you—he has to know why you did it." And why was she comforting Tenn after the awful way he'd been to her?

Maybe because he loves his brother more than life.

Tenn looked up at the sky for a long moment, then back at her. "I shouldn't have put him in that position. I forced his hand."

"You were protecting him."

"And also not seeing that if he can forgive you, maybe I can too."

"I put him in danger."

"He puts himself in danger every damned day he's in this MC," Tenn reminded her. "Have we really reversed positions here, that I have to talk you into going back to him? Because that's insane. Fucking insane." He rubbed a hand over his head—he wore a skullcap— and looked puzzled.

"It's just . . . maybe you really can't go home again.

Or maybe you can, but you shouldn't." She'd ruined things back then. She was ruining things now—people, families, Vipers. Maybe, like her father, like Grams, she was meant to be alone. It was probably better that way.

"You know what? Don't use me as an excuse," Tenn told her.

She narrowed her eyes. "First you drive me away and now it's my fault for letting myself get driven away?"

"Yes. Gotta be tougher if you're gonna hang with Vipers." He glanced down at her hand, which had fisted unconsciously . . . and grinned. "Atta girl."

Preacher convinced him, along with Rocco and Cage, not to do anything stupid.

"You just got released, Tals—you go over to Maddie's like a bat out of hell, when you don't know what headspace she's in, you'll get arrested again," Preacher warned. "Cool off. Make a plan."

So Tals's plan had been to grab a bottle of whiskey, sit on the roof in the cold air—alone—and try to figure out how things had gotten so fucked in such a short span of time.

Bear joined him a little while later, with a blanket to wrap around him and some hot coffee. Tals immediately rejected the latter, threatened to throw it off the roof, and grabbed the former.

He took another swig, and then another, enjoying the numbness.

"If it makes it any better, she was as miserable as you are right now," Bear offered.

"Right. So miserable she can't wait to get the fuck away from me."

"I think she was trying to get away from Tenn. Your

brother can be a real asshole when he's sticking up for you."

"Tell me about it," Tals muttered. "Tenn says I'm asking for trouble. Cage is on the fence, but that's because he's all gooey-eyed romantic right now." Tals took a swig from the bottle, then passed it to Bear, pretended to ignore the fact that Bear never took a sip.

Like a chaperone. But hell, it was a move Tals himself had pulled, and right now he just wanted to get fucked-up drunk.

He was well on his way.

"And what does Tals think?" Bear asked patiently.

"Don't get all child psychology on me," Tals warned. "You being the child and all."

"Right."

"You're just going to keep drinking instead of trying to get in touch with her?"

"I'm not allowed to."

"Since when do you follow directions?" Bear asked. And Bear would definitely know, since he and Tals had known each other since Bear was ten and Tals, seventeen.

Bear and Tals rarely spoke about where Bear came from . . . what he'd been doing before this, before Tals had recruited Bear and urged Preacher to take him on as a probie when he turned seventeen. Ultimately, Tals put Bear on his team of enforcers.

Now he was twenty-three, a big brick wall of a guy, blond and good-looking. Football-player type. Because he had been at one point, but it wasn't an injury that had pulled him off the field. Not physically, anyway.

Tals never doubted him, which meant he'd not allowed Bear to doubt himself. And now Bear was comforting him as best he could. "If you want to go see her, go see her. I don't doubt that she wants to see you."

And that was the problem—Tals didn't doubt that either. It wasn't her wanting him that was the issue . . . It was her commitment. It was fucking with him, with Vipers . . . with everything. He glanced at Bear, told him, "I keep fighting for her . . . and she keeps running. Skirting out. Deserting me. Betraying me." Tals couldn't keep the anguish out of his voice. His fists were tight, his throat burned, and Bear just watched him. Listening, no judgment, which would be more than Tenn could do. "I don't think I can keep doing this. I was doing fine and then she came back and fucked it all up."

Even as he said that, he knew it wasn't true. "I'll be fine," he told Bear.

"I know that." Bear clapped him on the shoulder. "Doesn't mean you shouldn't lean on everyone."

"Yeah. Thanks, man."

Bear nodded. "Yell if you need me."

Bear knew when to leave Tals alone, not to push. Tenn knew it too, but that never stopped him from pushing.

A few minutes later, he heard, "I didn't mean to hear that," from Holly, calling from the other side of the roof. She stepped around now. "I came out for a smoke."

She grinned like an errant child—Preacher didn't like when Holly smoked, and everyone but Preacher knew that she would often come out here and sneak smokes. Particularly when she was stressed, which was a lot lately.

She hid a lot from Preacher. Preacher hid a lot from her. Maybe all relationships were fucked-up.

"That's all right. Nothing you don't know. Nothing everyone doesn't know at this point."

She nodded. Walked over, crouched down and held out her cigarette. He accepted it, took a long drag and exhaled. While he did that, she cleared her throat and said, "She feels helpless, Tals, and when a woman feels helpless, she'll do anything to gain back any sense of power. Even if it's the stupidest possible thing she can do."

Holly took back the cigarette and straightened then, and it was obvious, based on her tight expression, how much it pained her to admit it, never mind say it out loud. She took a last drag, tossed it and said, "We're training the day after tomorrow, right?"

"Right," he echoed. As she walked away, he murmured, "Thanks."

"Welcome." And after a pause, "We like to be bossed around too. Never admit it, though."

He smiled into the darkness for the first time in twenty-four hours, even as he muttered, "Women."

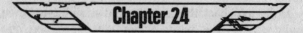

Chapter 24

What made Tals finally leave the roof was seeing a man in a dark car pull across the street from Vipers. He was alone, and he was carrying, but he looked more worried than anything, kept looking over his shoulder as he walked toward the clubhouse.

Tals was down the stairs to confront him in under sixty seconds, but the guys guarding the door had gotten to him first. Rally was holding him in a choke hold as he brought the guy toward Tals. "This is Hugh Montgomery. Says he's here to talk to Preach."

Tals nodded, way more calmly than he felt. Assessed the struggling man for a quick second, then said, "Rally, let him go and you can tell Preach he's here. I've got this."

"No problem, Tals. I took his piece already," Rally assured him, then went inside.

"You alone?" Tals asked.

"I want to speak to Preacher," Hugh demanded, then narrowed his eyes. "I recognize your voice."

"Good," Tals growled. They were the same height. Tals was lean while Hugh was soft. And even though

Hugh was pretending to be all tough guy, Tals could see the sweat beading on his forehead, the way his eyes jerked around. Like he was nervous as hell.

Could be because he was surrounded by MC members.

Could be because he knew someone was targeting him . . . and by extension, Maddie.

Hugh tried again. "I'm not dealing with anyone but the head of your organization."

Tals rubbed his chin. "Not sure why you think you get to make demands. Seeing as how I'm the guy you framed for trying to kill you, maybe I should actually make the punishment fit the crime." He didn't move when he said it, but Hugh paled and seemed to shrink a little. Then he put up his hands.

"I had nothing to do with that. The police found the patch. I didn't see who grabbed me."

"Pretty convenient story—you're forgetting you gave the police names. Plus, you sent the police here to fetch Maddie before that. Seems like you had a plan in place. And you're going to tell me what it was."

Preacher walked in then, nodded at Tals to continue. Tals told Hugh, "This is Preacher. For right now, you and I are going to talk. Got it?"

Hugh nodded. Then he looked at Preacher and nodded again before explaining. "Look, I called the police and told them I was wrong about the names. That I couldn't be sure. I said that I never got a call from anyone at Vipers, but that I made the call because I was trying to get Maddie back."

"And they believed you?" Tals demanded.

"I know how to convince people," Hugh told him, and there wasn't anything like bragging in his tone.

"And you did this from the goodness of your heart?"

Hugh glared at him. "I did it because Maddie asked

me to. And because I owe you. You offered to protect me. I threw you under the bus. But to be fair, whoever took me planted enough to make me think of Vipers—I didn't kidnap myself."

Tals nodded, his heart racing. Now the dropping of the charges made sense. So did Maddie's leaving. "I'm going to tell you straight out that we didn't have anything to do with your kidnapping. Any idea why there'd be a bomb wired to your ex's car?"

"She's my wife," Hugh said through gritted teeth.

"She's in danger because of you. So I'd start talking."

"Or what?"

Tals smiled and it unnerved the hell out of the executive. Hugh shifted. Stuck his hands in his pockets while Tals pretended to have patience.

And then he was tired of pretending, so he grabbed the man by the back of his collar and shoved him down so his cheek kissed the hood of the pool table.

Tals spoke casually. "Going to ask one more time. What the fuck are you involved in?"

Rocco chose that moment to enter. "Is there a party going on and you forgot to invite me?"

"We're entertaining Hugh Montgomery," Preacher explained. "Tals might strangle him before he has a chance to talk, but I'm not going to stop him."

"I came here for you to protect me," Hugh managed. "I want to take you up on your offer."

Preacher raised his brows, Rocco snorted and Tals laughed, saying, "That's a good one—we make you an offer and you frame us."

Preacher leaned down. "For someone who's asking for help, you're not giving us any incentive."

"I made it right with Flores. And I have money," Hugh promised.

"I don't need your money," Preacher told him. "I'm

interested in keeping Maddie safe. So start talking and I'll make my decision then."

"Can you tell him to let me up?" Hugh asked.

Preacher looked at Tals and smiled. "This one? You can't tell him anything."

Rocco let himself into Lola's unmarked car while she was inside the café getting coffee. No one noticed, because it was pouring rain, a freaking Noah's ark kind of deluge, and everyone was tripping over themselves trying to keep covered while running for it.

He was soaked too. Wiped the hair off his face, glad he'd let Cass, their local bondsman, know he might be getting another call. In a few minutes, Lola came out of the coffee shop, bag in hand, and got in.

Even though she appeared to be looking down at the ground as she walked fast, Rocco had no doubt that she'd spotted him. Maybe even before she'd left the shop.

To her credit, she was calm. She pushed her hood down and opened her coffee. "I guess you really did miss me, Rocco. Or at least, the handcuffs. Don't worry. I'm sure you'll be spending time with us—on the state's dime—very soon."

"If I'd known you were so focused on handcuffs, Lola—"

"Cut the shit and get out of my car. You know I can arrest you just for this," she warned.

"You could, but you won't, Detective. I'll keep it short—you're focusing on the wrong people."

"You say my title like it's a curse."

He shrugged, not denying it. "You've had issues with Vipers since you got here."

"Is this going somewhere, Counselor?" she prompted, pretending to be bored.

"Hugh's tied in with the Albanians. Has been for years." He pulled a small tape out of his pocket and put it on the console between them. "He told us everything."

"He'd tell you anything to escape your wrath. Where is he now?"

"He's safe."

"Safe?" She laughed. "I don't have to frame you with false information or false evidence. There's enough there for me to make arrests legitimately. I know that. It's a matter of time before one of you screws up big enough to dismantle the whole crew."

"You and what army? The DEA and the ATF and other agencies have been trying to shut MCs down forever. If you'll notice, their focus is on one-percenters, which Vipers isn't."

She laughed, shook her head. Stared at the roof of her car. "There it is. The argument my sister used on me all the time. Like the fact that you're not classified as killers or drug runners or gun runners, the fact that you don't identify as such makes it all better."

"I'm not defending the Heathens. Never will. But—"

"But nothing," she spat fiercely. "You killed her as surely as if you'd been in the room. This whole MC mentality, the culture, the lifestyle . . . you pull innocent women in."

"Like Calla?"

She froze. Raised her chin defiantly. "Pound for pound, let's compare law enforcement and MC men, and we'll see who has the higher percentage for abuse."

But she was nervous. If he hadn't slept with her, he wouldn't have known, but because he'd been intimate with her, he had the keys to the kingdom.

It was nothing he wanted to use against her. But if she was going to fight dirty, he had no choice but to do the same. "Your sister wasn't killed by a Viper. It was a Heathen—and that's an entirely different animal. If you don't get that after what happened with Calla and Cage's stepbrother . . ." He trailed off, shaking his head.

Her face hardened. "If you think I'm discussing my personal life with you—"

"But you'll get naked with me?"

"That was a mistake."

"Like your sister made? And you think getting rid of Vipers will erase it?"

She clutched the wheel hard. Her knuckles whitened, and tension filled the car. For a moment he did worry she'd arrest him, no matter how much she knew it wouldn't stick.

That didn't stop him from pushing it. "At the end of the day, arresting the wrong people will fuck you up."

She hadn't moved from her position, and he turned and opened the door to leave. Before he could, she spoke. "Tell me, Rocco, if I looked into your background, what would I find?"

He stilled. Closed his eyes against the rain pouring into the car, slamming him with what felt like sharp pins. "Are you going to tell me, Detective?"

"Based on what you just told me, you don't need any reminders."

He didn't wait to hear if she said anything else—he was out of the car, closing the door, walking through the rain until it soaked him to the skin.

And then he walked some goddamn more.

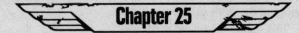

Chapter 25

Tenn exited her deck as silently as he'd come, leaving Maddie with the ball in her court. If she'd wanted, he would've taken her back to Vipers—to Tals—but there was still a lot to think about.

Maybe too much thinking has always been your problem.

Irritably, she told herself to shut up. Out loud. She could see her breath laden with frost more clearly now as the temperature dropped. She stared out over the railing toward the driveway. The view wasn't the best, but it had been harder to see in summertime, with the trees in full bloom.

But the night Tals had stolen her car, the cherry-red Mustang had been parked so she could see it. Probably the result of her being careless when she'd parked, or maybe a recent rain tamping down the branches, but either way . . .

It was one of those perfect end-of-the-summer nights, a little bit cooler and infused with the scent of yellow Jessamine that bloomed abundantly around what was arguably the largest, grandest house in all of the Jessamine community.

Maddie leaned over the railing of the porch that connected to her third-floor suite of rooms, listening to the sounds of mockingbirds as they searched for their perfect mate. This ritual had been going on for weeks, alternately frustrating and fascinating her. They were searching loudly in the trees this season, and even if she tried to sleep before they started their night calls, the cacophony was loud enough to wake her.

But tonight she hadn't been asleep. She'd taken a cup of tea with honey onto the porch, and she moved away from the railing to sit in the padded chaise. She pulled the blanket she'd brought with her over her legs, as she wore only shorts and a tank top.

Grams's house was so secluded that she didn't have to worry about anyone seeing her. Even if they did, she was hardly wearing anything scandalous.

But tonight she wished she'd been scandalous. If she'd flirted a little more, or even smiled in Tals's direction . . .

What? You'd invite him up here for tea?

"Get real, Maddie," she murmured under her breath.

She noted a figure on the property, and she stilled, not wanting to call attention to herself in case it was a thief. Or worse.

She blinked as she struggled to focus in the darkness, but when the figure got under the soft lights of the driveway, she saw exactly who it was.

Tals.

Had he come here for her? When she'd left the lake, he'd been deep in conversation with Sissy, and Sissy was practically in his lap, listening to whatever stories he was telling her and giggling.

But no, he was circling her car now, the one she'd gotten as a present on the day of her sixteenth birthday. To her it signified guilt as surely as if the word had been placed on the vanity license plates instead of her name.

It was embarrassing to her, but her friends in Jessamine loved it. She'd let many of her girlfriends and several members of the football team her group regularly hung around with take the sporty car for a drive.

She'd refused to put it into the garage, as she was still having trouble navigating backing out. Now Tals was stealing her car. It gave her a thrill, even as she got angry.

If her grandmother and father hadn't been away, she probably wouldn't have called the police. But they were. And she knew the police would grab him and she could simply decline to press charges. But she'd show him that he couldn't just come in and take what he wanted . . . not after he'd ignored her.

Even though he'd been chasing her for years before that.

She ignored that and dialed the local police.

"I knew you didn't sleep, but damn, this is how you knew I stole your car." Tals's voice came quietly over the railings behind where she sat, putting her mind squarely back in the present. Somehow, she didn't jump or get scared.

She swore she'd sensed him on the grounds in a way she hadn't sensed Tenn. Calmly, she stood and turned to see Tals standing on the deck behind her, almost right where Tenn had been. "It's not like I was waiting for you to show. You were quiet . . . and if I hadn't been on the roof, looking at the stars, I wouldn't have noticed you."

He shrugged. "You wouldn't let me drive it."

She raised her chin. "You stopped asking."

He said, "Ah," and nothing else, like it was the secret to a puzzle he'd long been trying to break. And maybe it was.

"Tenn was here."

He gave a small smile. "I figured. He runs hot when he's in protective mode. Then he cools off and thinks shit through. He's more protective than I am, which is damned hard to do."

"He told me that the charges were dropped." She paused. "Hugh is here. He says he has no idea what's going on with the bombing and the kidnapping—the real culprits behind both."

Tals's face darkened. He glanced toward the closed glass door and then moved closer to her. "Flores and the DA weren't happy about releasing us, but after Hugh recanted . . ." He paused and she gave a brief nod, her concession to already knowing that. "Flores tried to say that we planted the fake patch on purpose, but hell, Flores knows better. We don't fuck with our symbols. Ever."

"How would she know that?" she asked.

"Her sister dated a guy from another MC. Didn't turn out that well, which is why Flores is hell-bent on lumping all MCs together and making sure we all go down. But the counterfeit patch trick is an old one—in this case, we'd have no reason to attempt to kill Hugh. And if we went to kill him, we'd have succeeded."

A chill ran through her at how easily he said that—and meant it too. "You went to the hotel to bring Hugh into Viper protection."

"Yes. Because we found out some new developments. We had a hint of it before the arrests, but now we know for sure."

"Like what?"

He sighed. Glanced back at the door, then motioned for her to sit down. It wasn't until she did that she realized her legs were trembling.

He sat next to her, close but facing the door to her room. He hesitated a second before telling her, "Hugh's involved with some really bad guys. Has been for years. I don't expect him to admit it to you, but you have a right to know that this isn't just going to end."

"How bad?"

"He's been doing a lot of creative accounting. Nothing that would seem suspicious to the shareholders, but he's basically laundering money."

"How's that possible? And why? He's got money."

"Sometimes enough isn't enough. Sometimes guys get pulled in unwittingly, and once you're in, you can't get out. From what I know, he's caught up with a group who's got ties to the Albanian mob."

"I can't . . . This doesn't . . ." She stopped. Caught her breath. "I never knew anything about this. How's that possible?"

"He didn't want you to know. It's not like he'd have them over for dinner."

It's not like she had dinner with Hugh all that much over the course of their marriage either. "We didn't share bank accounts. It was his apartment. He paid those bills and I paid mine. Things were separate. Everything was separate. How did you find all this out?"

Tals looked grim. "We didn't have to dig too much. Cage, Tenn and I have some connections—it might've raised some flags, but hell, they're pretty much waving in the air like beacons right now anyway."

She shook her head, trying to clear it. "I ran part of a major corporation. I had a team of people under me. I placed millions of dollars' worth of orders, flew all around the world. I knew the business inside and out . . . but I had no idea what was happening with the man I lived with. But wait . . . I didn't know. So why are they after me?"

"He was trying to get out from under them. They're pulling him in deeper, which is what happens with this shit. Once you do a job for them, they own you. And it's exactly what I figured—they threatened to hurt you if Hugh didn't continue."

Her heart dropped, and as bad as that was, she could just tell there was more. "Don't try to protect me, please."

"Fuck." He pounded his fisted hands on his thighs, then told her, "They told Hugh they'd kill you and then frame him for the murder."

"And then they showed him they know how to frame someone . . . because they kidnapped him," she whispered.

"When you ran here, to me, they saw a convenient way to get rid of both of you, and they could easily force us to shoulder the blame. And that shit makes Preach really unhappy."

"I'll bet."

"He's trying to make contact, to convince them that they need to leave you the fuck alone."

"And Hugh?"

Tals laughed somberly. "He already came back to us for protection. He told us what you had him do . . . and I understood why you left."

"He needs protection . . . from me," she promised, and she noted he was biting back a grin.

It was nice to see him smiling. "That's the Maddie I know. At this point, Hugh claims he'll call them off you. That you won't report any of it. And you won't. I know you want to be honest, but there are better ways of dealing with it than going to the Feds. This kind of shit needs to implode on itself."

She knew she wasn't in any position to take on this battle, or drag Vipers into it. "Do you really think that it's true? That Hugh can call those guys off that easily?"

She wanted an immediate yes, but, like Tenn, he'd give her honest. "I want to believe it," he started carefully. "I don't think the Albanians want a war with us. They've dealt with some MCs on the East Coast before and it didn't end well."

"But?" she prompted.

"If Hugh could pay them off so easily, why didn't he do it earlier?"

She sighed. "I was thinking the same thing. Dammit. How does a guy like that end up involved in such bad stuff?"

Tals laughed harshly. "Hard to believe that good guys can do bad shit, right?"

She sighed. "You'd think I'd remember that."

And here they were. Again. She knew they'd get there, but she'd been enjoying their peace treaty.

"For the future, I'm going to make sure you know it," he promised.

"I know you, Tals. I really do."

"I know you too. There was something about you. I could see it clearly from the first time I walked into the school freshman year, and I didn't get how no one else could. You weren't like the other kids from your group. I used to watch you, earphones on, smiling. You'd get lost in the music. You were okay being alone. You never looked completely comfortable in the crowds down by the lake."

He knew her—he'd always known her. "I should've stayed. I should've tried with you."

Tals shook his head. "When it's right, it's not trying."

"You're right," she relented. "Back then it was less about that and more about me. At first I wanted to get out of here, be independent like my dad wanted me to be. And then, after what happened, Grams wanted me out of here. It was an escape. But it's different now. I didn't come back here with any expectations, but . . . I'll admit, I was hoping you were here."

"And what happens when you need to escape again, Maddie? Because you're running. Rare to see a woman doing it, but I recognize the signs."

"Because you've run?"

"You see the men in my family? Extended and otherwise, they specialize in that shit."

"And you?"

"I'm not stupid enough to throw away the real thing."

His honesty cut right through her, but it was refreshing. He'd do exactly what he said he would. He'd be there for her. And she hadn't done the same.

As if reading her mind, he caught her chin in his palm. "Hey, I understand why you left."

"I threw it away."

"No, you walked away. Big difference."

Could she ever convince him of what she knew in her heart—that she belonged with him? Before she could attempt it, he told her, "This isn't about a simple conquest. Although make no mistake, I've already fucking claimed you. In my mind, you're mine. I know you feel the same. I can't fool myself that badly, but I know now why you ran this time—you came to find Hugh. You think you brought bad shit on the MC. But the thing you need to learn is that you don't get to make those kinds of decisions."

Her mouth dried. She couldn't have said anything if she tried, but he didn't really need her participation for this, beyond listening.

He began to walk toward her as he spoke, his voice low. Husky. Dangerous. "Gonna tell you something— I'm done handling you. You need to make your decision right now. If you're with me, you are fucking with me."

"Handling me?" she repeated.

He ignored her. "This decision isn't just about us, baby. That's what you're not getting."

She was getting something—hot and bothered by the way he was actively stalking toward her. She should feel pressured. Threatened. At the very least, annoyed by the way he was speaking to her.

Instead? She was ready to take her clothes off even more than when he'd broken down his own door to get to her.

As much as she wanted that, she wanted his demands to go on a little bit longer. "Then maybe you should explain it to me."

A slow, lazy smile slid across his mouth. He was on her, pressing her to the railing at this point with just his presence . . . and oh, how she was impatient for his hands. "I'll break it down for you, Maddie. If you're mine, then you are mine. You don't get to pull this in-and-out shit. There's no running away because you think it's good for me—no running home because your family demands it. You are with me. You run shit by me instead of running from me. Because you're mine, it means you're part of Vipers. And if you have Vipers' best interests at heart, Vipers will have your back. I don't expect you to put yourself in physical danger for us, but part of that is listening. Staying put when you're told."

"When I'm told—"

"So we can keep you safe." He paused. "See, you can stay here. Hang out with your father, grandmother, ex, whoever. And that's your decision. Or you can come back to me. So you can call me if you're ready. When you're ready. Because your running shit? Ends today."

She stared up into his eyes. He looked fierce and handsome. She wanted to go with him immediately, but he put a stop to that before she could even say it out loud.

"If it were up to me, I'd put you over my shoulder and take you out of here right now. Walk you out in front of your family, tell them that I'll keep you safer than you've ever been in your life. But there's more to it than that. This shit with your ex? That will pass. But you came here . . . and I still don't know if you're ready to actually stay here, or if this is a passing thing to get you back on your feet. I won't hold you back, Maddie, just like I won't let anyone hold me back. I've made my decision—I'm where I want to be, and I'm old enough to know that you're who I want to be with. Ball's in your court for this. I'm not letting you make any decision with me standing here—it's got to be on your own terms. Because once you step back across Vipers' threshold, you are mine."

He kissed her then, hard, fast, with a ferocity that she swore she could come from. He ripped his mouth away, muttering, "So fucking sweet. Addicting."

And then he was . . . leaving. Really leaving her alone, with her decision to make. It took everything she had not to run after him.

Even though she did. But by the time she looked over the side of the porch, he was already gone.

Chapter 26

A few clicks through Holly's bank account, thanks to Rocco, and several phone calls later, Preacher had exactly what he was looking for.

And then he went looking for her. She was still at the clubhouse, although she was getting dressed to go to work.

"Going in late?" he asked from the doorway. He hadn't bothered knocking this time—and he always knocked.

She knew something was up, because her shoulders tensed a little before she said, "It's good to be the boss. And my first client's not until midnight."

"You don't take walk-ins anymore?" he pressed.

She turned, hands on her hips. "What's this all about, Preacher? I don't have all night."

"You'll have what I say you'll have," he warned. "And I didn't say you could have a hired gun looking out for you."

She threw her hands up in the air. "Fine. I should've run it by you. From now on, I'll keep notes on everything, including my toilet schedule."

"Holly—"

"You guys have enough going on. His only job for me is to keep an eye out for suspicious newcomers."

Preacher was grateful as hell for the information she'd gleaned about Hugh, but that didn't erase the anger. "What the fuck do you think you're doing? We provide protection for you—that's why we let you stay."

"I know, Preacher. You're very clear on that every single time you mention how indebted I am to you. How lucky I am to be here. I know how precarious my tenure is." Her arms crossed.

"You can't make decisions like that without consulting with us."

"It doesn't affect you—it actually helps you," she pointed out. "I don't ask you for money to pay him."

And then it all clicked—that's where most of her money was going. She wasn't being irresponsible—just paranoid. Justifiably so. "What about your holiday?"

"You know as well as I do I wouldn't leave you short-handed in a crisis," she said coolly. "But I am going, Preacher."

"You don't have the money to go. Because you're paying some asshole."

"He's not an asshole."

"Did you ever stop to think that by observing you, he's observing us? That that could hurt Vipers in the long run? Even in the short run? Suppose he decided to sell information—or suppose he went to Flores?"

Judging by her expression, she hadn't thought about that. "Consider him gone."

"Damage is done."

"Well, like you said, you've got good information, so let's consider it a fair trade and call it a day." She brushed past him and left then . . . and he let her.

For the moment.

And then he followed her, down the stairs and through the clubhouse, catching up with her in the main room. She was almost to the hallway that led to the alleyway, and she quietly passed by everyone who was there.

He was nowhere near as quiet. "Stop, Holly. And get back upstairs, because we are far from fucking done," he told her through gritted teeth, noting by the way her eyes widened that she knew she'd gone too far, pushed him just a millimeter over the edge of his normally careful control.

She'd done this to him more often than he could count, pissed him off beyond belief, but he'd always taken those energies out on other people.

Tonight he was going to take it out on the right person.

"You wanted to play with fire, Holly?" he asked, backing her against the wall as the rest of the men— and a few women—watched. There was a deadly silence in the room, the energy so highly charged that he swore an orgy could break out in the room at any moment and no one would be surprised. Holly swallowed hard, her look at once defiant and vulnerable.

She knew better than to talk back, to smart-ass him in front of anyone. She'd already done enough.

He could order her upstairs, watch her march proudly, attempt to hide the small limp she still had, but he didn't have the damned patience for that. Instead, he picked her up, forced her over his shoulder and without another word, carried her upstairs. To his damned room.

When he put her down, she looked around in surprise. Jumped when he slammed the door shut and stared at him when he locked it behind them. And then she tried to regain some of the power by pulling her shirt over her head, sliding out of her pants and walking toward the bed, shaking that perfect ass of hers.

"You're trying to tease?"

She pulled out her ponytail before turning to look at him over her shoulder, her blond hair tumbling over one shoulder, eyes green and wide and anything but innocent. "I'm yours, Preacher. You don't take advantage of—"

He didn't let her finish. Instead he was on her in seconds, turning her, putting her on the bed and pinning her there with his weight.

She looked frightened. At the same time, he knew she didn't want him to stop. She knew what to say if that's what she wanted.

Her nipples were hard. She unconsciously rubbed her pelvis against his as he studied her.

"Everything will change if we do this," she implored him, and he honestly couldn't tell if she thought that was a good thing or not.

He honestly couldn't give a fuck. "I know," he told her, his last words before lowering his mouth to hers.

The kiss was punishing, meant to show her that she was no longer in charge. Because she'd definitely been under that impression. Time to shatter that illusion for good.

And shatter was exactly what happened when her mouth opened, forced at first, and then her tongue met his tentatively. He pushed her arms up over her head, held them there with one hand circling her wrists. She pushed back against him, with her arms and her pelvis, and that just ended up forcing her to grind against him. She gasped with surprise in his mouth—it had been a hell of a long time for her. He knew that.

But going slow wasn't an option.

He continued to hold her arms pressed down against the mattress. She continued to buck her body up against his, trying to take charge. As always.

"Gonna come a time I won't mind you taking charge, Hols. But until you learn to submit . . ."

"I just want to get laid, Preacher. I submit to you in other ways," she retorted haughtily.

"Like what?" She stared up at him, unable to answer. Because it was a total damned lie. "That's what I thought." He shook his head. "You know, sometimes I know shit. And the things I'm going to do to you? You're going to be begging for more."

"That sure of yourself?"

"Reason to be," Preacher promised, bent down and sucked a spot right behind her earlobe . . . and she shuddered underneath him.

"I want you, Preacher," she murmured. "I don't know if I can do this though."

"Trust me," he growled.

"Because you deserve it?"

"Because you have no other choice." He kissed her then, to shut her up, to calm her enough to deal with being held down. His voice was husky when he asked, "You giving me permission, Hols?"

She studied him. And then, for just a moment, her arms went slack against his touch. For now she'd given up the fight. But he knew she'd fight everything he did.

He counted on it.

"Good. Baby. Just hang on and enjoy the ride."

She whimpered—it was low, but he caught it, smiled against her tit as he suckled her nipple through the soft cotton of her T-shirt.

This time her moan was audible. At least before she bit it back. Holly had a hard time letting go, and he wanted that to stop—at least when she was with him.

"Preacher . . ."

He stared down at her soft green eyes, her lush mouth . . . her flushed cheeks, the wetness between her legs . . . All of it screamed she was so ready for this. She looked up at him as he touched her, her expression beautifully taut.

He took his hand off her wrists. "Don't move," he warned her. She bit her bottom lip but complied.

He reached up to the neck of her T-shirt and she stilled. He ripped it down the front with little effort, opened to expose her beautiful body. He'd seen her naked many times—she was always trying to tempt him, and she had no idea how close she'd come . . . how often he jerked off to her image burned into his brain.

There was no going back now. This could bury them both.

He took his own T-shirt off and wrapped it around her wrists—not tight, but definitely secured well enough that she couldn't take the bindings off herself. She tugged, trying, but he flipped her onto her belly before she could get too panicked. Soothed her with kisses down her neck, a kneading massage on her shoulders and neck, a finger inside of her, making her rock back and forth, seeking more of him.

Her scent filled the room, made him dizzy with need. She'd love to know that and he'd never give her the satisfaction. Instead he urged her onto her elbows and then roped the ends of the bindings around the headboard. He pulled her onto her knees, then pulled her hips back until she was hard-pressed to do anything but concentrate on balancing.

He'd never let her fall.

He spread her legs, leaned down to lick her, and she jolted so hard he thought she came. Hell, maybe she did, but he held her more tightly, buried his face between her legs until he felt her contracting around his tongue. He sucked her clit hard, felt her body quake, her muscles contract until she finally released with a scream of his name, a curse and an orgasm that seemed to go on forever.

He wasn't letting her off the hook, even when she begged. He licked her through her climax and straight into another one, until she was barely coherent. Her body was strung taut like a bow even as it was oddly relaxed at the same time.

When she was sagging, unable to hold herself up any longer, he helped prop her as he entered her from behind. She was so prepared for him, so ready and still so goddamned tight.

It'd been a long time for her—he took his time filling her, even as she tried to push back against him. But every time she did so, he stopped, until she cursed at him.

"Stay still until I tell you to move," he warned. "Or you don't get this."

"Fucker," she hissed, but she ultimately complied. And when he was seated deeply inside of her, he took her, hard and fast, holding her to him until they were both completely wrung out.

Only then did he let himself come, near silently, his face buried against her back.

Hours later Holly crawled into his lap, and he let her bite his neck, his head, sink her teeth into his ear like she was somehow claiming him. Then she murmured, "Fuck me, daddy. Now."

He pushed up into her, hard enough to make her gasp. Two more strokes and she was coming, clawing at him.

"We're not done," he told her. "You're not done."

"Why, Preach? Why do you want to break me?" she murmured as his cheek pressed hers.

Because you already broke me, dammit. Figured we could put ourselves back together . . . together.

That's what he wanted to say. But he didn't. Instead he made her come until she stopped asking questions.

Chapter 27

By the time Maddie went inside, it was after eleven at night. She took a long bath and couldn't get her body to stop strumming over Tals's words, his kiss.

She'd made her decision the moment she'd pointed her car in the direction of Skulls Creek. And so she packed up, grabbed a bag she could carry easily and headed down the stairs.

She knew her father would still be awake, but she was surprised to see Grams. She might've been dozing on the couch at one point, but she was awake, drinking tea and reading.

"Maddie, you couldn't sleep either?" Grams asked.

Her father looked up from his laptop. "Why do you have your bag with you?"

She shifted her weight but kept the bag on her shoulder like a combination talisman slash security blanket. "I'm leaving."

"But it's not safe. We have security," Grams said, dropping her book onto the couch and pulling her glasses lower on her nose.

"I'm going to stay with Tals again."

Her father stared at her like she was a complete stranger. In so many ways, she was . . . and he was one to her as well. Her grandmother shook her head. "Tals is why you're in this mess in the first place. Hugh said—"

"Hugh lied," she said dully.

"Where is he, John?" Grams asked her son. "Call him in here."

"He's not here, Grams. He went to Vipers, to ask them for protection." She let that settle in for a second before adding, "He's done some bad things. The people trying to hurt him—and me by extension—are because of him, not Tals or Vipers."

There was silence. She took advantage of it. "I'll come back for the rest of my things when it's safer. I don't want to put you at risk, although that's not why I'm leaving. I'll make sure Hugh doesn't come back either. Please, keep the security detail, although once I'm gone, I think you should both be fine."

"Maddie—" her grandmother pleaded.

"Grams, I'll be right in town. I'm staying. I don't know what I'm going to do, but I'll figure it out. But I'm happy with Tals. I know you find that hard to believe, but it's the truth. And you'll see me—I promise that."

"I don't understand your choices," her father started.

"Did Hugh tell you he cheated on me?" she demanded. "Multiple times? In fact, through the entire time we were married."

"And you left a job because you were angry he cheated?" her father asked.

"You're missing the point."

"No, Maddie, I get the point. What I don't understand is how you could throw away your career for a man like that. For any man. For anyone." He looked so driven at that moment that he reminded her of how she used to feel about her work. And honestly, it didn't feel good to revisit that. "What are you planning to do around here? Open a leather shop?"

"Maybe," she said defiantly, suddenly feeling twelve. "I have lots of options. I came here to start over. I didn't quit just because Hugh cheated."

"You won't be satisfied, not here and not with Tals," her father predicted. "You have to think ahead."

"Maybe my problem was always thinking too far ahead. I refused to let my guard down for Tals once before. I'm not making the same mistake twice. I'm not missing out again." As she spoke, she realized how strongly she meant every word.

"I agree with your father—you're making a terrible mistake. Tals is a nice guy, but he's still a member of a hard-core motorcycle club. A criminal."

"He's not a criminal. And you even dated an MC guy."

"Dated. Not married." Grams sniffed. "It's fine to sow your wild oats, but when your father brought Margaret home, I tried to talk him out of it. And I would've, if it hadn't been for one thing."

"Mom, enough," her father warned.

But Grams looked pointedly at Maddie, and suddenly Maddie got it. "She was pregnant when you married," she said to her dad.

It was Grams who answered. "She was. And you're a wonderful addition, Maddie. But your mother wasn't cut out for this life."

"What does that mean?" she demanded. "You keep telling me she was flighty. My whole life I had to be responsible so I wouldn't end up like her. What did she do that was so wrong? She loved you—right, Dad?"

Her father nodded. He looked pained. "Sometimes love isn't enough."

"For you, or for Grams?" She turned to her grandmother. "Did she leave . . . or did you drive her out?"

"She was better off. She never fit in. It never really worked."

"I don't even know what that means. I don't even know you two. And right now I'm not sure I want to know you." She started to walk to the door. "Don't even think of calling the police like Hugh did. If you do that, I'll never speak to either of you again," she warned. "Although I'm not really sure you'd care."

"Maddie, please, of course we'd care," her grandmother reasoned.

"Let her go," her father said. "Security will get you to your car safely and will escort you over."

There was nothing more to say. She walked outside, prepared, and saw security.

And Tals.

Tals was *there*. Waiting. His truck parked, facing the gates.

With a line of Vipers MC members on bikes lined up just outside the gates.

He'd never left. And now he was walking toward her, slipping the bag off her shoulder. She hugged him as hard as she could. "You never really let go," she whispered against his cheek.

"Definitely not. Neither did you. Because the second you came back to Skulls and inserted yourself in my life, you became Vipers."

"So that whole thing about letting me make my own decision?"

He gave a playful smirk, but his voice was steel. "The second I kissed you, it was made."

She didn't have to ask which kiss he was talking about, because it was the first kiss . . . and each one after that. It was all meant to be. She'd just taken the long road around. "I love you, Tals. You brought me color. Took my life off mute."

He shook his head. "You did that when you stood up and realized how you'd been living. Took a chance. Came back to me, because a part of you knew I fell in love with you the day I laid eyes on you." He touched her cheek. "We both had a long road."

She hadn't realized she could have both independence and love. In her world—her family—the two were mutually exclusive. Her mom had, inadvertently, left Maddie to pay the price.

Maddie had promised herself, along with Dad and Grams, that she wouldn't be that foolish. She somehow always believed that that's what her mom would want for her too.

Then again, maybe her mom would want her to fall in love, over and over again, no matter how badly it hurt.

But being left with nothing . . .

There had to be a happy medium. And she had a strong feeling Tals was her happy medium. "No going back."

"Right, baby. No going back." With that, he pulled away from her house and toward the Vipers clubhouse.

Tals turned up the radio and drove fast to Vipers, holding on to Maddie's hand the entire time. When he pulled into the lot and the guys pulled in behind them, and the gates to the lot were closed—and man, they never closed those gates—he turned to her, asking, "Want to talk about it?"

She gave him a soft smile. "I'm where I want to be. With who I want to be with. What's to talk about?"

He snorted. "Take your pick. Your family, for one. Your head's still back at that house."

She sighed. "It was pretty bad. I expected it to be, but I didn't expect what I learned about my mom. I mean, I told you that she left and never got in touch, never came back. All this time I thought she just didn't. But she couldn't."

"What happened?"

She looked up at Tals. "Grams kept her away. I don't know exactly how, but she all but admitted it."

"Can you look for her?"

She stared at him steadily. "I already did, Tals. Last year I hired a private detective. And he found her."

"And?"

"She died about a year after she left me. The PI talked to her best friend at the time." She bit back a sob. "The woman swore she died of a broken heart."

He hugged her fiercely. "Then it's up to you not to. You owe her that. You owe it to her to let yourself just be you."

She pulled back and wiped her eyes. "I know. I'm more angry that they're so disappointed in me, like because I want happiness, everything I did before that is thrown away. I had a lot of success. I already lived a whole other life, you know?"

"Did you want success because you wanted it, or because you wanted your dad's approval?" At his question, she glared at him and he held up his hands. "Just a question. I didn't have to fight for my dad's approval. I just stole a car and I was in."

"God, that's . . . horrible?"

"Father-son bonding," he replied with a lightness she knew he couldn't totally feel.

She sighed. "I think you're right, about trying to please my dad. I never realized that my success was a way to get his attention. I thought it was just a part of me."

"Probably is. But there are lots of different measures of success." He ran a hand over her breast. "Like, to me? This is success."

She giggled, and to Tals it was the best sound in the world. "If you're going to do that, best get me inside first."

"Right. Let's go."

He got out and was around to her side to open her door, grab her bag and help her slide out. She looked up at the clubhouse, with the painting of the dagger and snake—the one Tals had tattooed on his back, along with the wings, and she asked, "Did you ever want to leave?"

"I did leave, remember?"

She frowned, then, "Right, the Army."

"See the world. Blow shit up." He took her hand and led her past Rally and inside the main room. "I had choices. Could've stayed in. Could've moved to one of the agencies. Imagine me, working for ATF." He snorted. "In the end, this is my family. It's where I belonged."

And then he looked toward the doorway that led to the hall. She turned and saw Hugh standing there.

"I was going to tell you, Maddie," Tals started. "He's not staying, but we're trying to take care of things. I figured you might want to talk to him."

"I want to kill him," she said, and watched Hugh's eyes widen.

"Join the club," Tals muttered. "I'll be right outside this door if you need me. Rally's got that door. In case you were going to try to leave." He pointed at Hugh as he spoke, and Hugh looked nervous. And angry.

She was all anger. "Tals, please stay. And, Hugh, you lied to me. For years. I can almost understand that, but once I was almost killed, you still kept it up. I could've been killed because you didn't warn me."

"Look, they came to me," Hugh started, and her heart sank. "I didn't go looking for this opportunity."

"It's the Albanian mafia, Hugh—how you can think of it as *an opportunity* is beyond me."

Hugh scowled. "They're blackmailing me, okay? I got involved with a woman who turned out to have connections to them. At first it was one of those too-good-to-be-true things. But it was easy—an easy job and easy money, and I didn't have to do much."

She couldn't even feel sorry for him—she really couldn't. "That's what you get for putting your dick where it doesn't belong."

Behind her she heard Tals's soft whistle. She was pretty sure it was approving, but she didn't turn to check. No, because she wanted more information, and dammit, she was going to get it.

"It wasn't like that, Maddie. It was a business deal. And let's be honest. You never cared where my dick was—especially once we got married."

His words hurt, mainly because they hit their mark. "We never should've gotten married."

He crossed his arms. "Probably not. We were a better couple on paper. I think, deep down, we both knew that."

She sighed at the honesty—and the truth of his words. "We were good friends," she agreed. "Comfortable."

"Marriage is more than that. Should be, anyway," Hugh agreed. "Look, I've made mistakes . . ."

"We both have."

"But yours aren't putting you in danger." He gave her a grim look. "Is this really where you want to be?"

She glanced around the clubhouse. "A couple of

days ago I couldn't have said yes. But now . . . I belong with Tals. Wherever that might be."

"And your grandmother?"

"She's not happy. She thinks I should've outgrown bad boys in high school. But I was too busy looking to the future."

"Guess it's never too late to look back." Although he looked unsure as he said it, which she assumed was because he was thinking that his future was in jeopardy. "I'm going to make sure that you're kept safe."

She crossed her arms. "How are you going to do that, exactly?"

Hugh glanced at Tals. "I made a few calls. The smartest thing I can do is testify against them."

"And get killed," she said flatly.

"Not if I go into Witness Protection. It's the best bet. The only bet at this point. Although Vipers is trying to broker a deal, to make sure you're untouched," Hugh told her. "I just wanted to say good-bye before I went."

"Are you really going into Witness Protection?" she asked hollowly.

"I really don't know. I don't know anything anymore," Hugh said honestly. And then Preacher came in and escorted him away. She was left staring after him.

"Preach took a meeting with some of the guys who're after you and Hugh. They claim they don't want any trouble from us. They just want Hugh."

"But you won't give them Hugh."

Tals sighed. "Trust me, I thought about it. But he's not my fish to fry. If he does testify, maybe he can reverse some of the trouble he caused."

When he said that, Maddie sank to her knees in front of him, tugged at his belt. And smiled.

He touched her hair, asking, "What're you doing?"

"Trying to make up for some of the trouble I caused."

"Ah, babe, I'll never turn this down, but you don't have to make anything up to me."

"I know. But I want to. Let me, Tals."

He nodded. "Go ahead and try."

A challenge, a dare, a tease . . .

She was up for the challenge. She tugged his jeans down—boxer briefs too—and she dug her fingers into his hips as she swiped the broad head of his cock with her tongue. A low groan escaped him—his hips stuttered a little. She put her mouth around him, swirled her tongue as she sucked. Ran a finger underneath his balls and heard the longest, lowest growled groan—she almost came from that groan.

And he was watching her—that was the biggest turn-on of all. His eyes were glued to hers as she pleasured him. Held him literally in her hands, drove him wild, the way he'd done with her. She wanted to bring him to the edge—and then she pulled back, teasing him, loving the way he cursed under his breath as he tried to regain any sense of control.

She kissed down the rigid length of him, pressing her tongue on a particularly sensitive part near the head of his cock.

"That's it," he murmured, and before she knew it, he was picking her up—God, she loved how he just threw her around like she weighed nothing at all—and carried her over to the room with the pool table.

Tals kicked the door closed behind him. This was typically the place for exhibitionism—usually the young girls who knew what they were getting into and had no problem showing off their bodies while they were being pleasured.

It got as much action from people having no interest in playing pool because it was a good height. And hell, it got cleaned nightly.

Still, he grabbed a clean towel blanket from the closet and laid it down before placing her on top. Moved between her legs even as he tugged her jeans and underwear down. He moved aside only to take them off, and then he was back, his jeans unzipped, condom on, her sex warm and wet against his cock.

She shivered against him, her body taut and ready.

"Used to fantasize about bringing you here," he told her as he gazed at her. Her lips were red and a little swollen from sucking him. Her hair was messed. She looked . . . wanton. Sexy as fuck. Better than any fantasy he'd ever had of her. "Wanted to show you off in my clubhouse. Wanted to mark you here. Used to daydream about you on this table, under me. Just like this."

Because as much as what happened here on this table ended up as public-club fodder, it was also the place where women went from mamas to old ladies, where the respect of being alone with your woman happened.

To anyone outside the MC, it probably sounded like the most unromantic shit ever, but to an MC guy? They got it.

Maddie's eyes were a little wide. "Would you have done this here, in front of everyone?"

He grinned. "Why? Would that have turned you on?"

She blushed. "Not actually doing it, Tals . . . but thinking about it . . ." She squirmed, and fuck, he had to have her. Now.

"Trust me, this is better than any fantasy I've ever had about you." He hitched her legs up so her calves were on his shoulders, and it was so dirty and hot:

Maddie, with her arms thrown over her head, shirt pulled up to reveal her firm breasts with rose-colored nipples.

"You haven't changed, Maddie. If anything, you've gotten more beautiful." He pulled her hips toward him, which made her full of him, deliciously so with him inside of her.

She held to him fast, with his elbows locking hers in place. "You have too, Tals. Always . . . beautiful to me."

Chapter 28

The next morning, Maddie woke tired but happy. She knew Tenn was still in town, splitting his time between the clubhouse and Cage and Calla's, and she knew she wanted to grab him alone for a few minutes. Although he'd seemed happy to see her, and he'd gone to her house to talk her into coming back, she still felt like she needed to clear some things up with him.

He was in the rec room playing a game of pool—or practicing—when she walked in. He glanced up and she said, "I need to thank you."

Tenn straightened. "We're good."

"I know you think that. And I want to believe it. I came back to Tals—I'm not running again. But I needed to explain." Tenn nodded, took a seat at the edge of the pool table, and so she jumped into her speech. "I wanted to be in charge of my own life. I wanted to make my own way. Make my own money. And I did. I don't care what my ex says—my record speaks for itself. I got to my position on my own. We worked side by side. I thought I was in love. I think now that I was all about power and the excitement of being in the top position I'd always wanted to be in. I was at the top of my game. I had everything I wanted. And I thought maybe he came into my life now because I was ready. I'd conquered. It seemed like a sign and . . . I was wrong."

A big admission. She blew out a breath and stared up at Tenn, so opposite in demeanor from his brother. "You probably don't understand how important being in control is for me."

He snorted. "No, that I get."

"I thought I was in control, but while I trusted and worked, he cheated. And the worst part? I was angry. Humiliated. Betrayed, but I didn't care. Because by that point, I knew we weren't right for each other. I just didn't know how to get out of it." She glanced up at Tenn. "I know how pathetic that was."

"Maddie, none of that is pathetic—it's human. But when you were in high school, you let Tals get into trouble. You let him take the blame."

"I know. I was so scared . . . and Tals . . ."

Tals broke in then. "I knew she didn't want anyone to know what happened. I told her not to say anything."

"She didn't have to listen," Tenn pointed out.

"I told Earl that I was pissed at him because Maddie wouldn't give me the time of day, that that's the real reason I grabbed her from him. I lied to keep my promise to Maddie."

In the wake of Tals's confession, they both just stared at him for several long moments. Maddie was up out of her seat before Tenn could react. "Are you . . . ? What did you . . . ? How could you do that? How dare you make that decision for me?"

Tals blinked, stone-faced. "Had to."

"No, you didn't have to. I went to the police and told

my side of the story after the fact. They didn't believe me—and no wonder—and I have to live with that."

Tals shook his head. "I told you that I didn't want you involved."

"But I was. I am. Just because you say it doesn't make it true."

"I did what I needed to."

"You did what you needed to." She was getting more furious by the second. Tenn was cursing at no one in particular. Cage walked in with a frown. Tals just said, "I did what was necessary to protect you. You have no idea what they could've done to you. So yeah, I took your choice away. I dealt with things. I absolve you of guilt."

"I don't want to be taken care of, Tals. I don't need to be. What don't you understand about that? I grew up watching it. I won't ever let it happen to me again."

"But you did let it," Tals told her calmly.

"I tried to do the right thing. It might've taken me a little while, but I told the police exactly what happened. Now I know that you sabotaged it."

"Sabotaged?"

"You want me dependent on you. You're no different . . ."

"Don't." His tone was enough to warn her from continuing. "You wouldn't know different if it bit you in the ass. And I guess all this time I was fooling myself. Guess I don't know different either."

He walked out, leaving her with Tenn. She swallowed back tears, mumbled, "Why is this so hard?"

"Love always is, babe," Tenn drawled.

"He brought me back here—"

"To keep you safe."

"He's making decisions for me."

Tenn narrowed his eyes at her. "To keep you safe."

"Because that's what Tals does," Cage explained. "He protects. He doesn't want you to know. He wanted to make the bad disappear for you. For everyone."

"But he can't always do that."

"Not going to stop him from trying," Cage pointed out. He clapped Tenn on the shoulder. Tenn, who'd been strangely silent during Tals's confession, caught her gaze now.

"What do we do now?" Maddie asked.

"Hell if I know," Tenn muttered.

"Just love him. S'all he's ever wanted," Cage told them both calmly. "Don't shut him out."

"Now you're the one who's running," Maddie pointed out.

"I'm not running—I'm getting my space." Tals had gone to the roof, assumed someone would point her in his direction.

She walked over, sat down next to him on the double lounge chair. "Do you come up here a lot?"

"Top of the world, babe."

She nodded. Wrapped her arms around her calves as she pulled them to her chest and rested her chin on her knees. "I don't want to fight with you anymore."

"So don't."

"It's that easy?"

"It should be," he muttered, and then he turned to her and kissed her, catching her off guard. But after a second, she opened her mouth to him easily, moaning into his kiss, uncurling her body and wrapping herself around him as he lay back. "See?"

"I can't decide which one of us you're calling easy."

He laughed. "Me. Definitely me." Then he sobered. "I get why you're pissed. I just didn't see a better way to keep you out of it. Part of it was the truth, that I was into you. And then I went further, told him I'd been trying to get into your pants for years and it was a no go, and there was no way I was going to let him have you first."

Maddie took his hand in hers and he sighed, continued. "I wasn't going to let Jessamine—or your grandmother or father—know about what almost happened to you, Maddie. You told me you didn't want anyone to know at all, that you weren't going to the police, that you'd avoid Earl. That you were lucky and you would just put it behind you."

And then she'd told him, that next morning, that they couldn't be together. But it hadn't changed his plan at all. There was no other way to get rid of the anger than to take it out on Earl, and several other members of the football team who'd just happened to be there.

"I didn't want you to do anything—I never meant for you to get in trouble. He deserved to be in trouble."

"I'm okay, Maddie. I've gotta take some responsibility too. I could've fucking killed him. I almost did," he told her.

"And I went along with the story you told Earl . . . I thought it was Earl's version. And all the while you were setting it up. Setting me up . . ."

"Did you think Earl would tell the truth?" Tals asked her. "I knew you couldn't."

"I tried," she admitted. "It wasn't until the next day. I didn't sleep for days afterward. I was a mess. And I realized that, even though you might never forgive me, I had to do the right thing. So I went to the police, without my family knowing. At least I thought they didn't know. Turns out the chief of police called Grams and told her what I was trying to do. She put it together, told me I was going to throw my life away, and it would be way worse than what happened to my dad because I was a woman. That I had fewer choices. She told me I'd ruined things, that I couldn't stay in Jessamine. I told her I'd never planned to. It was a huge fight. The next day, I left for the spring program at college and I didn't come back home for a year."

He nodded, because he'd known where she'd gone. He could've gone to see her too, but things had ended with a brutal finality that, even though he'd orchestrated it, devastated him.

The Army—and Tenn and Cage—had helped to put him back together. It'd been a long road, and he'd always assumed he'd just never settle down, be content stealing cars, screwing around and having Vipers as his all-knowing family.

He'd never counted on the fact that Maddie had taken a piece of his heart with her when she'd left.

"You know, leaving Skulls wasn't just about leaving you behind—it was like escaping my own conscience. Because you knew me better than I knew myself. Back then—and probably even now. You saw right through me, and I liked it, but then I hated it. Because it interfered with my plan. It was too good. And when something seems too good to be true . . ." She stopped.

"What?"

She shook her head. "It's just . . . that's exactly what Grams always said about my mom. She used to tell my dad, 'This relationship is too easy and too good to be true.' And then Grams drove her away and told him, 'See? I was right.'"

"Ah, Maddie."

"It's okay. Better that I know." She bent down and kissed the side of his neck. "I'm sorry about getting so angry about what you told Earl. I just . . . I wish you'd told me sooner."

"I didn't because I knew you'd react like that."

She rolled her eyes. "Tals—"

"What? I knew it wasn't right. You're not wrong to be mad . . . but I'm not wrong to do what I did."

"Even back then you were trying to be in charge of me."

He raised his brows. "Trying?" His hands went under her shirt, a thumb brushed her nipple and she gasped softly. "Unless you want me to stop?"

"No. Never, Tals."

The sound of bikes interrupted them—she leaned up to look over the roof, and Tals said, "It's Bear and Preacher," because he knew the subtle differences between each of the Vipers' bikes.

She turned back to him. "How did you know that?"

"I've been around a long time."

"And you never let anyone in?"

"You mean any women?" he asked, and she nodded. "Not until you. Unless it's serious, we try to stay insular. It's safer for all of us. I deal with the probies or guys from other charters who need to be set straight on shit like that—letting too many outsiders into our private business, among other things. And I have to reach out to other MCs. I'm the first line. If Preacher has to get involved, there's no turning back."

"So you're like a peacemaker?"

Tals snorted. "You put a nice spin on it, but no. Kind of the opposite. But I also do some racing and some repo work for our shop to keep busy. I also own a shit ton of real estate, thanks to Preacher."

She smiled a little. "Me too. I learned to invest, thanks to my dad." She paused. "Will you . . . show me what you do?"

"You can't come with me on enforcing jobs. It'll make you a target."

"What about repo?"

He rolled his eyes. "Maybe an easy job."

"That's fine. And the racing." Her eyes glowed.

He was going to tell her he absolutely wasn't going to drag her into anything illegal, but he didn't bother. Because *women*.

And then he smiled.

"So was this your goal, Tals? To be a Viper?"

He didn't say anything for a long time. Finally, he told her, "I wanted to survive. To make it out of the mess my family had made—Tenn and I both wanted that. And then I wanted to help Preacher keep my family safe." He studied her. "I wanted to be happy. So I've tried to do things that made me happy. Do no harm, except to those who cause harm. Life's too short, Maddie."

"Yes, it is. Too short to not be doing what you love. And I thought I was doing that, for a long time. But now I don't know if they're my dreams," she explained quietly. "That's the problem. I mean, it's so ridiculous that I might've lived the last ten years doing something that wasn't mine—or at least not my passion. How could I have fooled myself so badly?"

"Because you wanted security. Because you didn't want to depend on a man," he told her.

She nudged his shoulder, but she was smiling. "True. But I didn't have to throw myself into my work and cut everyone off in the process. I did just what I grew up with, just what my dad taught me. I didn't realize that it was possible to be really good at something . . . even if I didn't love doing it, or even like it very much. I thought the two went hand in hand. Did you ever fool yourself like that?"

How did he explain that he never had the luxury of fooling himself? That reality hit him like a plank to the head on a daily basis from the time he could understand the life his parents led. He'd thought Tenn was okay with it, though—for a while, at least, but later Tenn admitted he was pretending in hopes that would make it easier. He'd also admitted it never had. "I've seen too much, Maddie. That's not always a bad thing. But it makes me try to have fun when I can, more than most people do."

"I think a part of me knew about my mom, that she was probably a lot like me. I guess that's why my dad didn't spend a lot of time with me."

"But your dad loved her," Tals pointed out. "He picked her over anyone. Even though your grandmother didn't approve."

"And it didn't work out."

"They had you, so something worked." Tals stared up at the stars. "He wasn't strong enough to stand up for your mom. You didn't make the same mistake. Sounds like something your mom would be proud of."

"It's amazing how I can miss someone I barely remember."

"Means she's still with you. I wish mine were around to see what me and Tenn have done. We could've put her on easy street a long time ago."

She knew the basics, but she'd also known not to ask too much about it. He hadn't wanted to talk about it, despite the initial confessions, but she'd known he'd grown up rough, but with a good deal of love from his mom.

He continued without any prodding from her, like he knew what she was thinking, "We were seventeen when she died. Same age she was when she had us. At times she was more like our sister than our mom, but man, she was tough. She didn't take any shit at all. She was strict with us, and she always made sure we were taken care of. Although she never worried about taking care of herself."

"And your dad?"

"He was around until we were about twelve. So when he went to jail, she left Tallahassee. Because she told us later that she'd been promised to some other Viper in that charter. Vipers was really fucked-up back then, and Tenn and I ran away to Skulls, because we heard that a new guy took over."

"Preacher."

"Yeah. Eventually, as the founding charter, he was able to make all of them clean up their acts."

"So you're really legacy MC, then."

"Born into it."

She frowned, trying to wrap her mind around it. "But your mom . . ."

"She was in love. She stuck by him until it looked like the MC could hurt her. That would translate to hurting us, so she'd never tolerate that. She wasn't happy we went to Preacher behind her back, but she knew we'd be safe, and we'd have our legacy."

"She sounds a little like Holly. Calla told me a little bit about her past with the No'Ones. I mean, she almost got out, but . . ."

"When this is what you know, you know the good and the bad. And if this family lets you be yourself . . ." He trailed off.

"I get it. The MC doesn't judge. They protect."

"And they tell you if you're fucking up too, but they never really tell you how to behave, as long as you have the club's best interests at heart. Club rules are really more about no drugs and keeping the law away. Have your fun but protect your family."

"I like the sound of that. I never really had any of it. Even looking back, the most I had were acquaintances. People who hung on because of who I was. Who I am."

"So you trusted no one."

She smiled ruefully. "Am I that transparent?"

"To me, yeah."

She supposed that was fair, since he'd always been transparent to her, at least where his happy act was concerned. "Some."

He didn't look surprised. Or upset. "Maybe that's what drew me to you. Because you saw what only Tenn could for a long time. And Preach and Cage. You saw what family saw."

Her throat tightened at how easily he said that. "You had so much good though."

"I did. But I couldn't help Mom—not the way I wanted to. Tenn and I tried to make enough money so she didn't have to work, but she refused to stop, no matter how bad things got. She wouldn't let us help her." He rubbed his forehead, and it was so obvious that this wasn't an easy conversation for him.

"Was it drugs?"

"It was everything. The sex was the drug for a long while. She was in demand. She made money. She wasn't ashamed of what she did. And it's not like she brought it home. We didn't know what she did until we were in high school, and even then . . ." He shrugged. "For a while Tenn got pulled in. He was trying to protect her. Figured he could bring home money and she'd quit. But she didn't."

"I'm so sorry, Tals."

"She always said she didn't want to be our burden." He gave a soft, humorless laugh. "She probably sounds like a nightmare parent, but she wasn't. She hid that side of her. She lived a double life in a lot of ways."

She didn't know what else to do but hug him. So she did, drew him close, and he didn't resist. His arms wrapped around her after a beat, and he murmured against her neck, "I'm here for you, Maddie."

"Me too."

Chapter 29

When Hugh was safely under protection and things seemed to have died down, Tals kept his promise. She hadn't been relegated to the clubhouse for the past couple of months—she'd spent time at the tattoo parlor and the bar and other Viper-run establishments, but she hadn't gone anywhere alone.

Typically, it was Tals who was with her, and she didn't mind that at all. Tenn had gone back home to run his businesses, had made her promise to come visit when things were all clear.

He also told Tals that he'd give her refuge, if needed, if things got complicated with the Albanians. But according to Holly's PI, who'd discovered those men in the first place, they'd vacated the area and they had bigger fish to fry.

"Let's go!" she called.

"I've never seen anyone this excited to do repo work."

"You told me it was time to explore and 'figure out my shit.' Find my passion again."

He shook his head. "You think you have a passion to be a repo man?"

"Repo woman," she corrected. "Can I drive when we go?"

He groaned. "Why do I feel like I'm creating a monster if I say yes?"

"Because you are."

It took an hour to get to their job, and she found it strangely anticlimactic. "I figured it would be more exciting," she said when they stopped to get gas for the flatbed.

He grinned ruefully. "Trust me, I'm really fucking glad it's not. I'd never get you to stay home."

"True."

"So why repo? Between your real estate and other stuff . . . I mean, you don't have to do this, right? So there must be a reason."

He shrugged, like it didn't matter, but she could see the pain etched on his face. "The club's history—it's not a pretty one all the time. A lot of guys who came in post-Preacher, they've heard the stories. They know it happens in other clubs, but they didn't live it. I was in it—me and Tenn. We were there for the worst, the struggle to make it better, and now we get to see the good from all the hard work Preacher did. From the work he had us do, from the real estate to the repo stuff. And we know how precarious it all is."

"And precious," she murmured, reaching out to brush his cheek with her palm. He tilted his head to rub his scruff against her palm, scratchy and comforting . . .

"Yeah." Then he pulled back from her touch. "We've got a lot of ground to cover tonight."

"I thought we were done."

"I wasn't talking about repo work." He smiled and went to pump the gas.

She sat back, the low hum of the radio the perfect complement to her contentment. Until she saw Tals walking toward her from the back of the truck.

She rolled down the window, called, "That was fast," but the word "fast" died in her throat when she saw he wasn't alone. Two men were walking with him, and she was pretty sure there was a gun or a knife in the vicinity of Tals's back. He walked, slow and sure, with his hands out in front of him, and he stopped at her open window.

He was looking past her.

Her breath caught as she looked next to her and saw a man, his forearm covered in tattoos, the ones Holly had shown her online so she knew what to look for.

"Just in case," Holly had said.

She glanced up from the man's arm and he smiled and said, "She understands."

"What the fuck do you want?" she growled.

"Maddie," Tals warned, but the man next to her smiled. Looked at Tals and said, "Can't control your woman? I could give it a try."

Shit. Shitshitshitshit. She kept her mouth shut, even though she wanted to tell this man to piss the hell off.

"Good girl," the man said, and she tried not to vomit on him.

"She doesn't know shit, Lee," Tals said.

"But you do?" Lee asked.

"Yeah, I do. Doesn't mean I'll tell you, but you let her go and I'll think about it."

"Really? Why don't I fucking believe that?"

"I don't have a stake in Hugh Montgomery. My job is to keep my woman safe. She knows nothing. She's not talking to the Feds."

Lee was staring at her, and she was staring at Tals,

who wouldn't look at her. She was sweating, trying not to panic.

"Fine. We know where we can get her anyway," Lee said. "Put him in the car." He went to take the keys out of the ignition of Tals's truck, but Tals said, "You leave her the fucking keys."

Lee turned to him. "You're not in the position to call the shots."

"I'm the one with the motherfucking information," Tals reminded him.

"That I'm sure we'll have to beat out of you. Even if we don't need to, that doesn't mean I won't." Lee's eyes glowed when she looked at him, but when she looked back at Tals's face, his expression remained impassive.

"You leave the keys. Leave her. Let her go back to Vipers. Until I hear she's back there, I don't say shit," Tals said.

"Again, you're not in charge, Tals. I'll let her go. But the second she pulls away, your nightmare begins," Lee warned, then said to her, "Get in this driver's seat. Now."

He slid out, and she slid over, turned the flatbed on.

"Give me your phone," he ordered, and she did. "Now say good-bye to your biker."

Oh God. She turned to Tals, who remained calm. "Tals . . ."

"Listen to me, Maddie. You drive as fast as you can back to Vipers. Don't stop anywhere—do you understand? I need you to listen to me and just go home."

Just go home. Her heart clenched.

I need you to do what I ask, for your safety . . . and for the safety of the club. "Okay, yes, Tals."

"Just in case you feel like not listening." Lee held up

what looked like a metal button. He leaned down and put it on the car. "I'll know where you go and when you stop, and if you stop, I'll kill Tals and come back for you. So if you stop before you get home . . ."

"I'll run out of gas," she blurted out. "You can't let me go like this."

Lee stared at her, eyes narrowed, and then motioned to one of the men. For several silent minutes, they all listened to the flow of the gas pump as she was given a quarter of a tank to go an hour.

Goddammit. They were looking for an excuse to . . .

No. She wouldn't think it

"Tell Preacher to call me if he'd like," Lee said. "It won't matter, but it might make Tals feel better. If he can still feel. Because there's a lot I can do in an hour."

With that he motioned for her to move. With a last glance at Tals, who'd stepped back from the truck and was giving her a reassuring nod, she heard his words "drive as fast as you can" echoing in the back of her mind.

She didn't remember much of the ride. It seemed like she passed more gas stations and rest stops, all of which taunted her with phones. But Tals hadn't wanted her to stop. He wanted her safe. The problem was, the faster she drove, the more gas she used . . . but she would push the car along with her bare hands if she had to. There was no way she was stopping.

When she burst into Vipers, having parked the truck at an odd angle in the lot and running past Rally, shouting, "Preacher, Lee has Tals!" over and over, Rocco caught her in his arms and sat her down.

"Maddie, take a breath. Come on now, honey . . . breathe."

She hadn't realized she'd been hyperventilating un-

til Bear brought her a brown paper bag to breathe
into. Finally she'd caught her breath enough to talk to
Preacher, who stood with his phone, waiting for her to
talk.

She explained what had happened. "If I stopped,
they'd kill him. Tals said he wouldn't tell them anything until you called Lee to say I'm here safely. He said
he might not pick up. He said he was going to torture
Tals until the call. And after. God."

She got up and raced for the bathroom. On her knees
in front of the bowl, she retched, but there wasn't much
in her stomach. When she was done, she realized Calla
was there, tying her hair back, wiping the sweat from
her face and neck. Handing her water and mouthwash
and helping her to her feet. She brought her to the rec
room and sat her on the couch.

"Preacher called Lee. Lee picked up . . . Preacher
heard Tals," Calla started.

"We all did," Bear said from the doorway. "He's
alive."

For how long? "I did what he asked. I didn't desert
him," she started, and Calla and Bear shook their heads
at her.

"Of course you didn't desert him," Calla said, and
Bear broke in, "You did what he asked. You had to,
Maddie. Tals couldn't do what he needs to if he's wor-
ried you're not safe."

"I was supposed to be safe—this was over," she'd
said, but the way Bear looked at her, it had probably
never been completely over.

While Preacher was muttering that he was going to
"kill Lee and feed him his own dick" as he got in touch
with his witsec contact, Rocco had the unenviable job
of calling Tenn.

Maddie had wanted to do it, but he'd convinced her that it would be better this way. Mainly because Tenn also had sources that it would be better for Maddie that she knew nothing about.

Tenn's sources made him privy to exactly where Hugh was being held until he was fully accepted into the program and officially erased and placed. Tals would want Maddie to be able to answer truthfully that she had no idea where Hugh was. Because basically, Rocco couldn't be sure Tenn wouldn't kill him.

"I'm going to turn him over," Tenn railed now. "Why the fuck are we protecting that douche bag?"

Preacher motioned for Rocco to put Tenn on speaker; then he covered his phone's mouthpiece and asked, "Can we trace a tracer?"

"Looking into it," Rocco answered above Tenn's ranting. "If it's a transponder, we might be able to back into the ISP."

"I'm in the car—on my way to Hugh's," Tenn said, then promptly hung up.

"That's going to go well," Rocco muttered, and Preacher shook his head, then said into his phone, "You need to start asking Hugh or your other contacts where these guys hang."

Then he hung up. "Holly!"

She was there in seconds, phone to her ear. "He's checking—he's never followed them to anyplace but the motel, but he might have a lead. Maddie and Tals were at a gas station an hour from here, half hour from the hotel they were staying at."

"They've got to be someplace in between," Rocco said. Maddie hadn't seen them in her rearview—she hadn't even known what car they'd put Tals into. She'd just driven away fast.

"I think we should get on the road, at least to their hotel and work from there," Preacher said. "I'll take Cage, Rally and Bear and . . ."

"Take them all—I'll stay here and deal with the intel," Rocco told them. "Holly, the second you get something—"

"You'll be the first to know." Then she walked over to Preacher, tilted her head up and kissed him on the cheek. Whispered something in his ear and then walked away.

Preacher touched his cheek like he'd been given something precious. Rocco looked down before Preacher caught him noticing.

Within twenty minutes, the clubhouse was vacated, save for two guys guarding the outside, Rocco, Holly, Maddie and Calla. Although Rocco loved going out on the road—hell, it's why he'd given up his practice and joined the MC in the first place—he understood that in times like this, his role was better served being left behind. He would be kept out of the action, and he'd have an alibi, which would allow him to serve as the other men's lawyers, if need be.

Judging by the venom in Tenn's voice, this could get really ugly. And if Hugh—or Hugh's temporary handler—didn't feel like giving out information, or worse, really didn't know . . .

Fuck. After a minute's deliberation, Rocco picked up the phone and called Lola. On her private line.

She picked up, obviously annoyed. "How did you get this—"

She'd been asleep—he could hear it in her voice. "Tals was kidnapped by the Albanians—they're looking for Hugh."

There was silence. Then, "Does Tals know where Hugh is?"

Rocco debated telling her. Finally, he said, "Yes."

"Will he tell them?"

"No."

"How can you be so sure, Rocco?"

"Because Tals is smart enough to know that the Albanians won't let him go—they're not exactly the fair-trade types."

"What do you need from me?"

"All the fucking help I can get looking for Tals. He doesn't have a lot of time."

"What makes you think I'm going to go out of my way for Tals?"

"Because your department is involved. Because the tracker the Albanians put on Tals's truck is standard police issue."

"You're assuming my office found the Albanians, planted this GPS and they found it?"

"That, or else someone from your department is working with the Albanians in hopes of taking down Vipers. I'm betting they approached your office, said we were framing them. Talked about Hugh."

"That's a stretch," Lola told him . . . but she didn't tell him it was completely implausible.

Twenty minutes later she was at the door of the club-house, wearing sweats and a T-shirt under an open black coat, her hair pinned up loosely. "Someone in the department is working with the Albanians, but for something unrelated to Hugh Montgomery. Something to do with a car-theft ring."

Rocco stilled inside at the mention of the car thefts, but she didn't seem to make any connections—or jump to any conclusions. She probably figured the Albanians just misused the tracker for their purposes. "Then you can track the GPS."

She shook her head. "That information I just gave you is the best I can do."

"I'll let Maddie know."

She looked pained. "If I can't stop women from getting into bed with Vipers, the least I can do is goddamned protect them from themselves. I couldn't help Calla—"

"You didn't know," he said gently.

"Don't, Rocco. Don't you dare be nice to me now after trying to play on my emotions."

"Guilty as charged."

"We're even after this. Even if I can't help you, the fact that I'm putting my ass on the line means we're officially even." With that she walked away, got back into her car and drove off. He watched the taillights on the car get smaller and smaller until they finally disappeared.

Only then did he go back inside, feeling like he'd lost something he'd never really had in the first place.

Chapter 30

Tals had ruthlessly shoved away the image of Maddie's face as she'd driven off. She'd been trying so hard not to cry, to be strong for him. The fact that it killed her to do so wouldn't help him now. The fact that she'd had the strength to do so would.

He'd been through worse than this—the Army had taught him that bitching and moaning about your situation wasted precious energy. Instead he sat still, and he watched and he waited. Collected information. Even though they'd threatened to begin torturing him, Tals figured they were worried enough about the Vipers' reach to wait until they got the call from Preacher. What they were doing now, by taking him, didn't go against what they'd promised, which was keeping Maddie out of their sights.

Really, taking Tals instead was smart. He wished he'd considered that angle, but fuck hindsight. What worried him was that Tenn also knew where Hugh was. It should worry Hugh more.

Lee and Co. wouldn't start trying to hurt him until they got him to wherever their home base was around here. In the meantime Tals would try to glean any intel he could to use against them.

They'd blindfolded and gagged him, cuffed his feet and tied his ankles, and he rode in the trunk. He'd found a paper clip on the floor. He could break the cuffs, but a paper clip was also a good weapon, and he debated the merits of popping out a taillight in hopes a cop would spot them and pull them over.

That was risky though. If they didn't run across any cops, Lee would see the damage and know Tals had done it. The guy was already going to hurt him, but Tals didn't need to give him any excuses to do his worst.

Rocco had taken to pacing. Pacing and cursing. Holly's PI had no leads. Preacher trashed Lee's hotel room and found nothing. Lola tried to trace back the GPS, but they'd bounced their ISP, so it showed they were somewhere in Japan.

But Tenn came through with flying fucking colors.

"I'm on my way there—have the guys meet me."

"They're on their way." Rocco had already texted them while they were talking and had received a confirmation from Preacher. "Are you going to need a lawyer? Or is Hugh going to need an ambulance?"

"Rocco, give me some credit—Hugh's fine." Tenn paused. "Although the marshal isn't too happy, so yeah, there might be an issue."

"Never doubted you for a minute," Tals rasped to his brother as he sat, propped against the wall of the basement, where Tenn had found him ten minutes ago.

Tenn glanced at the bodies of the men scattered around the room—four in all. "Couldn't have saved any for me?"

"Gotta . . . get here . . . more quickly." Fuck, his ribs hurt like a bitch. Everything was one big throb, now that the adrenaline rush of fighting for his life was over.

"Preacher's about ten minutes out," Tenn assured him. "Ambulance will be here soon too."

Tals already knew about Maddie—she was the first word out of his mouth when Tenn burst in. "How'd you get Hugh to spill?"

Tenn smiled. "I gave him a suitcase of money from Maddie's dad."

Tals frowned. "Why . . . would he pay . . . for me?"

"He wouldn't." Tenn put pressure on the deepest of Tals's wounds, and Tals grimaced, cursed him. "Sorry."

"Fucker." Tals closed his eyes for a second, then opened them. "You told Hugh that Lee had Maddie."

"Yep."

"And you lied to her dad too?"

"Nope." Tenn looked over his shoulder as he heard the sirens in the near distance. "They're on their way. Just hang on."

Tals swallowed hard. "So fucking tired."

"I know. But now that Maddie's father's willing to make sure she's happy—and he knows she's happiest with you—if you die now, he'll probably kill you."

"Fucker," Tals repeated.

The second Rocco got the call that Tals was heading to the hospital but that he was breathing and expected to recover, he'd come in to tell her. Maddie had been resting with her head against Calla's shoulder. Holly was like stone, standing to look out the window.

"He's hurt?" Maddie asked.

"He's hurt," Rocco confirmed. "Tenn's with him in the ambulance—he's a trained medic, so Tals had a good start before the EMTs got there. They're taking him to a hospital close to the scene."

"I need—"

"To go. I know—the truck's ready."

"Does she have to worry?" Holly asked, finally turning around.

"Lee and his men have been neutralized. I don't know who they're connected to, but this should send a pretty solid message. And Hugh got money to pay off his debt."

Maddie crossed her arms. "Do I even want to know?"

"No," Rocco told her. "Pack a bag if you want to stay with him—he's not coming out tonight."

Maddie's heart squeezed, but Calla took her firmly, guided her by the elbow to Tals's room, where she and Holly packed for both Maddie and Tals. Holly and Calla stayed behind, and Maddie rode with Rocco.

Surprisingly, the ride went fast. Probably because she was in a blind panic most of the way there. She didn't remember much about the walk inside . . . until she saw Tenn. He was standing outside the ICU, and he looked like he was sleeping standing up. As she got close, she noticed blood on his clothes.

As soon as she stood in front of him, his eyes opened. "He's going to be fine, Maddie," he said fiercely, and she wasn't sure which one of them he was trying to convince.

"Can I see him?" she asked.

Just then one of the nurses was walking out, and she glanced at Tenn and pointed at Maddie. "Is this her?"

"Yes."

"Maddie, honey, come on in for a few minutes. I told this one to grab some food and coffee before he keels over and I have another patient on my hands." She looked at Tenn with a mixture of stern disapproval and concern.

"I'll take care of that," Rocco assured the nurse.

Maddie gave Tenn a sudden hug, and after a second he wrapped his arms around her, then said, "Go wake him up."

"Now, he looks worse than he is. They all do in the hospital," the nurse told her. "He lost a lot of blood, so he's a little pale. But he's breathing on his own. He's a strong one."

"He is," Maddie said quietly as she walked past the curtain and saw Tals lying on the bed. His head was slightly raised, and there was an oxygen cannula in his nose. There were IVs in both arms, and monitors, with their low, oppressive hums, surrounded the bed.

And yes, he looked pale. She walked right up to the bed, curled her fingers in his. "Tals, it's me. I'm here. And I'm not leaving."

"Good," he rasped. "Finally listening."

"You're awake?"

He opened his eyes a little. "In and out. Lotta good drugs happening." He glanced at the nurse. "Tell her to feed me."

The nurse wagged a finger at him. "Nice try. Ice chips."

Tals grumbled. She ran a hand along his bruised cheek. "Are you really okay?"

He nodded. "I've got . . . an infection. That's what they're worried about. But Tenn started antibiotics right away, and that helped."

"He's worried."

"I know. He's . . ." Tals closed his eyes and took a breath that looked painful. "He's hovering. Make him . . . stop."

"Sorry. No can do." Then she leaned close, brushed some hair from his forehead. "It killed me to let you go like that."

"It killed me . . . to force you to . . . leave . . . like that," he echoed. "But you knew . . . it was right."

Later she'd learn just how extensive his injuries were. He had been sliced six times, beyond generally being hit. And he'd taken it . . . because during that time, he'd been interrogating Lee, who was only too happy to talk. Mainly because he figured Tals would never survive.

At least that's what Tenn told her when he came back into the ICU. (Although both of them weren't supposed to be in the room at the same time, the nurse looked the other way.) Tals was sleeping, and Maddie refused to remove her hand from inside of his.

"He really picked the wrong man," Tenn continued. "That's all Tals and I know—we cut our teeth on survival. But we also knew we never wanted to end up in jail like our old man. The bastard."

She noticed Tals's eyes were opened. "Is he still . . . ?"

"He got out when we were just seventeen. Came to visit us," Tenn said, with a glance over at Tals.

"Right," she echoed hollowly.

Tals's eyes were on the ceiling. "Yeah. He was pissed that our mom had left Tallahassee. By the time we got home from school, it was too late. And he went after . . . me." Tals took his hand from hers and then twisted his forearm so she could see the long scar. "Slashed me . . . but Tenn stopped him."

She blinked at "stopped him," but she got it. She ran two fingers across the knotted scar.

"Never saw him again after that," Tals said carefully.

She looked at Tenn, who shrugged, then met Tals's eyes. "Yeah, me neither."

It was like the two of them had a routine, to help keep them in practice. She supposed it kept them from forgetting, from letting their guard down.

It was only then that she noticed that Tenn had the

same exact scar . . . in the same exact place, mainly because he was rubbing it like it was habit. A reminder.

He noticed her staring. So did Tals, because he told her, "Afterward, Tenn slashed his own arm and pressed it to mine. Sounds so fucking dramatic now, but fuck, it meant so much. Still does."

"One for all," she whispered.

"One for all," Tenn agreed. "Someone's got to take care of him."

She smiled. "Like you rescued him tonight?"

"Fuck that," Tals bit out.

Tenn gave a small laugh. "He didn't need rescuing, Maddie. By the time I got there, it was all over and he was looking for a first-aid kit."

She glanced over at Tals and back at Tenn. "He . . ."

"He got loose. I wish I'd been there to help."

And what Tals had learned would be enough to keep that part of the Albanian mob away from her—and from Vipers. Preacher told her that later that night, when she'd gone into the hallway during rounds. It looked like a biker convention in the hallway, but at least there was good news.

And during those quiet moments, she made a call . . . to her father. Once she'd discovered that he'd actually given Hugh money on Tals's behalf, she couldn't believe it.

"Maddie . . . there's a lot of making up I have to do. Things I'm just learning about." Her father sighed. "If you can change, then maybe I can too."

"You know where to find me, Dad."

"I'd like to come see Tals when he's out of the hospital."

"I think he'd really like that," she whispered. "I know I would."

Chapter 31

"I'm worried—Tals is really pushing himself. I'm thinking it's too much, too soon," Maddie confessed. She
didn't want to tell on Tals, but he wasn't listening to
reason. "The doctor said he needed to rest so he didn't
reopen his wounds."

Preacher's eyes sparked with anger and concern. "I
thought he was upstairs sleeping. Looks like he borrowed Holly's car."

"So I can ask her where he is?"

"She won't tell you. She's not supposed to do stuff
like that without consulting with me, but for Tals . . .
they've always been close."

"What does that mean?"

Preacher's lips twisted ruefully. "Never wanted to
ask."

"But you . . ." She couldn't bring herself to use the
word "claimed." "I mean, Tals wouldn't . . ."

"No, nothing like that, Maddie," Preacher said evenly.
"It's just that Holly doesn't even typically like men."

"She's in the wrong place for that," Maddie noted.

"We provide the best protection," he said wistfully,

and in that moment she saw what she hadn't before that moment. Preacher had claimed Holly for reasons above and beyond protection.

He loved her.

She didn't want to push it—not on that front, anyway. "Tals told me how you protected him and Tenn."

Preacher nodded. "I raised Tals and Tenn. Cage too, and all at a time when I wasn't even raised myself."

"Where is he?" Maddie had demanded of Tenn over the phone that evening. He hadn't answered her, but two days later, an hour after Tals pulled his magic disappearing act—again—Tenn picked her up and drove her to a big building with a mainly empty parking lot.

There was Holly's borrowed car, and another one.

She followed Tenn up to the building and they went inside quietly. There were several closed doors along a hallway, and Tenn stopped at the third one. Pointed.

Maddie peered through the glass at the top of the door.

Tals was with a woman—she was half under him, and for a brief moment her heart nearly stopped with the shock of being so completely wrong.

They were moving, the woman pushing up against him with her entire body, and Maddie almost turned and walked away.

But she didn't. And then she saw the woman attack Tals and realized there was a self-defense class happening.

"He's done this for a while. It took him time before he even told me. I got into my business because I couldn't save Mom, so I get to save her in spirit, over and over. Now Tals gets to too, every time he trains another woman to fight back." Tenn sighed. "It's amazing—we've never blamed each other for not getting her out of the game, for not showing her how to defend herself, just in case. She was used to men doing it for her. But we've never forgiven ourselves. Not sure we ever will. Or can."

"She shouldn't have put that on you."

"Maybe not. But she did the best she could. It's all she knew." Tenn shrugged. "Just know it's his penance, okay? He does it willingly, but a big part of him hates having to do it."

"Because he revisits what happened to her every time," she said quietly.

"Vipers has some old-fashioned rules, but they're mainly about protection—keeping the members, and their women, safe."

"It's a strange world for someone who didn't grow up inside of it."

Tenn gave an understanding smile. "And for Tals and me, it's all we know. We all try to prove our success to our parents. Always trying to please, even if we don't consciously realize it."

"How'd you get so smart?"

"Lots of sex." Tenn moved away from the door and she followed.

And then she backtracked, but she didn't make it all the way to the door before Tenn caught her. "I think I want to see him."

"He's going to hate that you're here," Tenn told her bluntly.

"Yes, Tals wants some fucking privacy."

Tals's voice. Angry. She turned to see the door open and him behind her, sweating in a T-shirt with the sleeves cut off. The woman was nowhere to be found.

"Told you," Tenn said.

Tals pointed at him. "Shit list."

"Used to it, brother." Then, "I'll give you two some space."

When he walked away, Maddie said, "I think it's . . ."

Tals held up a hand. "Don't."

"Tals—"

"I don't want to hear what you think it is."

"You don't even know what I was going to say."

"You're going to say it's great that I'm giving my time to help these women, et cetera."

"Is that so wrong?"

He just shook his head. Muttered, "I'm not a motherfucking saint, Maddie. You've got to know that."

"Thin line between sinners and saints," she said quietly. "I know that now."

"Ah, babe. I'm not who you think I am."

"You're exactly who I think you are. I know what you've been doing."

"Teaching self-defense?"

"Trying to put space between us because of what happened. Because you can't stop thinking about the fact that I was almost hurt, just the way I can't stop thinking about the fact that you did get hurt—for me."

"It's something that's hard to get past. You think that by staying with me, you'll be in less danger?" he demanded.

"Yes. You said you protect people."

"At a cost. Don't romanticize it."

She crossed her arms, jutted her chin defiantly. "Calla seems to be doing fine," she pointed out. "And Holly—"

"Ah, fuck. Don't even go there. Don't try to put *Holly* and *fine* in the same sentence." Tals pressed his palms to his temples. "I know you so well, Maddie. And you know me. What I have to adjust to is letting you have some freedom."

"We both have adjusting to do, Tals. But we've done the hard part. We're here, together. Right?"

"Right," he murmured. "Fucking finally."

"I guess good things really do come to those who wait."

He picked her up, and she wrapped herself around him. "Not waiting any longer," he growled.

"Tals," she protested, but he was taking her into the room, pulling the curtain on the door and locking it before carrying her over to the mats. "Is this part of self-defense training?"

"Only with you, Maddie. Only with you."

Chapter 32

Preacher stood at the doorway of Holly's room and knew she was gone. He gripped the doorjamb so hard his fingers would ache for days afterward. And he couldn't bring himself to walk inside her room. He knew most of her clothes would be there—probably a bit of her jewelry too, some of which he'd gotten her. But he'd bet that her ring—her wedding ring from Mickey—would be gone.

He'd bet that if he ran the guy's number again—the one he'd found in her pocket—he'd see calls to him tonight. Probably several of them, just like the several he'd found over the course of the last two weeks. And probably one of the calls would be right before she left to go "shopping" before work.

She never showed for work. None of her usual haunts reported seeing her over the last few days, never mind tonight.

Her bank account stood untouched. "She's got no money," he said to Cage, who'd come up behind him.

"She was storing cash," Cage told him now. "Had to be."

Preacher didn't doubt it, had thought so himself, but it was still a knife through his gut. And heart. A betrayal he'd seen coming.

Then again, maybe it was wish fulfillment. Holly lived up to what he'd always expected her to do. So he shouldn't be surprised she'd done so.

You can only trust your own.

He thought about Maddie and Tals, hating to be like that. Maddie was a Skulls girl, so he took some comfort in her town ties.

But Holly . . .

He'd never get her over the ghost of that bastard husband of hers. He couldn't even lie to himself and say she didn't know what he'd done. She knew. She'd been involved . . . but then again, so had Preacher.

That was something he doubted she knew. He'd had no idea that Mickey was married, or that Holly would be implicated or involved.

If he were honest with himself, he probably would've gone ahead and done it anyway. Hindsight was fucking blind.

Guilt made him give her refuge. He'd never expected to fall for her, despite all the odds. He'd always expected that he'd push her away like this. It'd taken longer than he'd expected, and it'd killed him slowly every step of the way.

Yeah, he was a completely selfish prick. As long as he could keep proving it over and over, he didn't have to admit he might not've been.

"You going after her?" Cage asked.

Preacher glanced at him. "Is that club business?"

"Actually, yes," Cage said. "The second you brought her here and gave her refuge, you crossed the No'Ones, and now we just *forget it*?"

Preacher turned to Cage, attempting to remain calm

and failing. The anger in his tone was at himself more than Holly, but he pretended differently. "She left our protection. Thinks she's queen of the fucking universe, can do whatever she wants and we're gonna be there to protect her. She knew what the goddamned risks were if she cut ties with us. The agreement to keep her safe never entailed me chasing her to the ends of the earth. I don't run after any bitch."

Yeah, saying it like that almost had him believing it.

Cage frowned. Stared at Preacher like he was seeing him for the first time. And Preacher didn't like that look at all. "What?" he barked.

Cage shook his head. "Nothing left to say."

Cage was right—there wasn't. "Clear out the rest of her shit and paint the room. I don't want any trace of her left here come morning."

Acknowledgments

Writing a book is never a solitary venture. I have to thank my editor, Danielle Perez, for her patience and help. For Kara Welsh and Claire Zion, for their support. For the art department and their simply amazing cover.

For the wonderful readers who buy my books, chat about them on Facebook and Twitter, and send me terrific e-mails. I couldn't do this job without your support.

And as always, I have to thank my family for their constant, unwavering faith in me. Thank you.

Don't miss this novel in the Section 8 series
by Stephanie Tyler

FRAGMENTED

Available now from Signet Eclipse.

Chapter 1

"What are you so afraid of, Andrea?" her school counselor probed.

Fifteen-year-old Drea Timmons shifted in her seat, wanting nothing to do with this. But at least the woman sitting across from her with the smooth bob and placid expression hadn't tried to call her by her nickname. That, Drea reserved only for friends, and these days, that pool was small. "I'm not afraid. Where do you get this shit from?"

That last part was one of Danny's favorite expressions and was usually a conversation ender with most adults.

Not with this counselor, trying to bore into her brain by pulling the "we're all very worried about you" card. "Your grandmother is concerned that you're hanging out with dangerous people. I've heard the same thing from your teachers. They're particularly concerned with your boyfriend . . . I believe his name is Danny Roberts?"

Drea shrugged. It was all the truth, yes, but what was the counselor going to do?

Continue to push, that was what. "Andrea, do *you* consider the people you're hanging out with dangerous?"

Drea hadn't bothered to learn the counselor's name, because she was simply another in a long line of seemingly well-minded people trying to help. She wanted to ask where they'd been when her mother was doing drugs in front of her, when her mother's boyfriends touched her in her bed at night, but she'd learned from Danny that showing weakness was to be avoided at all costs. As was the truth. "Why does it matter? I mean, they're not dangerous to me."

"Not yet," the counselor countered. "But eventually, you'll get caught up in it. There's no way around that."

"He'll keep me safe."

"Who's *he*? Danny?"

Drea clamped her mouth shut—she'd said enough already. Danny didn't like her talking about him to anyone in authority.

"Andrea, listen to me. I understand how you're feeling."

"No you don't. How could you? You're not me. You're not in my mind. You have no idea how I'm feeling," she challenged. "Danger isn't always a bad thing. Sometimes his kind of danger makes me feel alive."

"And the other times? Does it scare you?"

"Sometimes. But being afraid is part of life."

"Not to the extreme to which you're taking it, honey." The counselor shook her head. "To you, danger has somehow come to mean safety, and that's completely wrong."

"Who says?" Drea demanded.

*   *   *

Seventeen years later

"You're angry."

Drea stared back at Dr. Siegel, the casually dressed older man who sat across from her, alternating his gaze between her and the open laptop in front of him. He and his wife, who was a doctor as well, made a formidable team. Some days they tag-teamed her, but today it was one-on-one. "Wouldn't you be angry if you were me?"

He wagged a finger at her. "Spoken like a true medical professional. You've got to open up to me if you want this to be of any help."

She threw up her arms. "Hypnosis didn't even work—so how is just talking going to do it?"

He turned the laptop to face her, and there was a picture of a dark-haired, dark-eyed man wearing a black leather jacket. He'd been caught off guard by the picture, but he still looked easy and relaxed as he stared at her through the screen. "Tell me about him."

She looked at that picture an awful lot these days, and for a guy she had zero memories of, the man called Jem certainly consumed a lot of her thoughts. But she hated having to admit that, and tried even more not to show it. She forced herself not to grit her teeth as she answered, "I can't."

"Tell me what you know. Tell me what you've heard. Tell me what you're feeling when you look at him."

She frowned and sat back in the chair like a petulant child. "He's the reason I'm here. He's part of the reason I don't have a memory, although he didn't do anything to me himself. He rescued me."

"So he's a white knight?"

Drea snorted softly, blurted out, "I wouldn't say that," without thinking.

"So what would you say, Drea?"

She crossed her arms for a second, but once she realized she'd done so, she uncrossed them, going for a more relaxed, neutral position, telling Dr. Siegel in a reasonable tone of voice, "I'm not sure what he is. Maybe it's not black or white. Because he rescued me, but according to Carolina, he's also the reason I was in the position to need rescuing in the first place."

"So this man, he got you into trouble. He put you in danger."

"From what I've been told." It should've been painful to hear about all this, but whenever this topic was broached, a part of her went numb, like her mind was still trying to protect her from whatever horrors she'd endured. Some days she thought that maybe she was better off not remembering the hell she'd gone through. But that would mean not remembering Jem, and she'd been clawing at that memory desperately. "But I wanted to go with him."

"In spite of the danger?"

"That. And maybe because of it too."

"Because you didn't have enough in your life already?"

"I didn't say it made sense," she muttered. "You're very judgmental."

"It bothers you?"

"I thought you people were supposed to stay neutral."

He wrote down some notes, then glanced at her casually. "I thought you wanted to figure your missing memories out."

She sighed, stared around the sitting room in the grand old house that had become her touchstone.

Both Dr. Siegel and his wife had been working with her for just over two months—longer than any of the others, but her tolerance was running low. Especially for him, because he was more fond of telling her what she was doing was wrong instead of waiting her answers out. Probably because he knew he'd get none. "I just want you to realize that you're repeating old patterns. Over and over again, it appears. And you have a chance to finally break them."

"How? Because of my amnesia?"

"In spite of that. Because the one thing you didn't lose is your feeling that somehow danger equals security. And that's wrong."

From everything she'd heard about Jem from Carolina, Drea knew this therapist was the one who was wrong and she'd finally found something so right she wasn't about to let logic ruin it. Jem's picture did something to her insides, made her stomach flip, and she leaned forward and pushed the laptop screen back toward the therapist so she didn't have to see Jem staring back at her. "Okay, that's not exactly true, about the kidnapping-me-the-second-time part. Apparently I volunteered. More than once. He took me up on it both times. The second time is when it went bad."

"You volunteered to put yourself in danger?"

"Yes."

"This is the first time you've done something like that in your life?"

"I've always been attracted to danger. I guess I feel like the more dangerous a man is, the more he can protect me from the danger I'm running from." Even so, she knew that Danny's kind of dangerous had never been good. But Jem? He was a whole other story.

Dr. Siegel steepled his fingers as he stared at her. She felt she'd had some kind of breakthrough, but of course it didn't make her recognize the man in the picture any more than she had before. Truthfully, she didn't even want to look at the picture.

"Are you?" Dr. Siegel asked.

"Am I what?"

"Running."

That she could answer truthfully and without reservation. "Every single day of my life."

Chapter 2

Six months later

When Drea first arrived at Carolina's a year earlier, she hadn't realized she'd been running from an outside danger . . . and running just as hard from her missing memories. She'd also thought she was only seventeen, that Danny was still her savior, the only man who stood between her and her grandmother, who treated Drea like she was the devil incarnate. Truthfully, after just escaping her mom and her mom's never-ending series of boyfriends, living with her grandmother should've been a dream come true for Drea.

Instead, her grandmother had been a nightmare, and Danny, the son of the president of a very danger-ous motorcycle club, was the only person in Drea's life who'd ever stood up for her.

She believed she owed him loyalty . . . She believed she owed him everything.

Slowly, she'd begun to discover that, despite these feelings otherwise, something inside *her* was off, and that Danny wasn't the right man to love.

Now she kicked the treadmill into high speed, ran until her mind was settled and her muscles were jelly, all the better to give the trapped memories a chance to surface. This was part of her daily routine, since she couldn't run outside. At times she resented it, yes. However, it was one thing to be a prisoner in Carolina's house—and she had no doubt she was a prisoner—but there were many worse places she could be.

Like with Danny—or the FBI, who was apparently looking for her because of Danny. Or so she'd been told. Carolina was careful in doling out information, and while Drea hated being treated like something fragile, she was also smart enough to know Carolina was right.

And if Carolina didn't trust her, it never showed. There were no interior key locks on the door, just a bolt that slid easily. But the house was like a fortress, with alarm systems, cameras in every room and an unending supply of ammunition everywhere Drea looked. The alarm bells chimed whenever a door or window opened, but that was so they could keep track of who entered, like the grocery delivery or Drea's therapists.

The newest of those were a married couple—the Drs. Siegel were a formidable team. They didn't let her get away with anything. They probed her mind until she wanted to scream, but they didn't use drugs or any invasive methods . . . unless you counted what she'd started to deem as "the mind fuck."

And yes, over the past six months with them, she'd made tremendous progress. As it happened, this very treadmill was where her first memories, post "happy Daniel time," had come back to her.

It'd been a brief flashback, and even though she'd known logically that Danny wasn't there with her, hitting her, threatening her with a knife, she still hadn't been able to hold back her screams. When Carolina found her, Drea had been huddled on the floor in the corner, tears running freely down her face.

It'd taken a while for her to reassure Carolina that she was truly okay, that at least a crucial part of her memory had returned . . . everything, it seemed, except her time with the mysterious Jem.

Now she upped both the speed and the incline, pushing her muscles harder, the same way she'd continued to push forward from that breakthrough.

Discovering Danny was a violent criminal, and now the head of the upstate New York Outlaw Angels MC, like his father before him, made her even more certain that she was with good people. These days, the face she saw in the mirror, while by no means old, was not seventeen.

You're a doctor.

You're in trouble because of Danny.

Jem's been helping you.

Carolina had kept her from mirrors in the beginning, and that hadn't been hard. Drea had been in a fog, thanks to the antianxiety medicine she'd slowly been weaned from. Even after she'd realized her real age, she continued to actively avoid looking in the mirror for several more weeks, until Carolina forced her hand.

"You're thirty-two, not ancient," Carolina would tell her. "What do you think you're going to see?"

Carolina had to be fifty, but she was ageless. Steely. Beautiful. Her hair was a beautiful white-blond sheen and she had the complexion to pull it off. She looked natural. She had laugh lines in her smooth skin. Her face had character.

And when she'd walked Drea to the mirror and forced her to confront her present, Drea saw a fierce amber-eyed woman with long, tawny hair that was wild and loose past her shoulders, staring back at her, one who didn't look nearly as weary or exhausted as she felt inside at times.

"Beautiful, child." Carolina had pulled some of Drea's hair off her shoulders as they stared at their reflections together. "Trust me. Your memories are all here." She pointed to Drea's forehead, and then to her heart. "And here."

"What happened to me?"

"You've gone through more than most, Drea," Carolina said gently. "The most important thing you need to know is that you're safe with me. And you're safe because of Jem."

Drea believed that, which was why she sat with Carolina nightly since learning that she'd been kidnapped when she was with Jem, that she'd been helping him and things had gone terribly wrong. It was at that point when she'd asked Carolina to tell her about Jem, wanting to know more beyond his physical appearance. Only then did Carolina begin to show her pictures and tell her stories until Drea began to feel as if the man were an old friend.

But somehow she knew Jem was far more than simply a friend.

It was all so much more complicated than it had seemed at first, and she wasn't at the bottom of it yet. There was so much more to learn, and Drea was determined to make sure she did so.

Carolina had quietly slipped into the gym toward the end of Drea's workout, knowing that the treadmill tended to fill her with more questions than answers. And she carried the file folder that contained pictures of various Section 8 members, including—especially— Jem.

Drea shut the treadmill down, patted her face with a towel and grabbed for her water bottle, and Carolina motioned for her to follow.

They sat at the kitchen table, and Drea asked, "Did you know any of them—the old Section 8?"

"I'd heard of them, sure. They were part legend and myth, but anyone who worked for the CIA during that time knew that a team like that could be far too real. There were so few rules then. It was . . . lovely."

"So if you'd been asked . . ."

"I'd have joined that team in a second," Carolina confirmed. "These days, I'm much better as backup."

They'd had this discussion before. So many times Drea hadn't recalled it the next day. Now she did, but they still started this way. It comforted Drea that she could retain information. And this information was important—she could feel it.

To her credit, Carolina was very good at pretending this wasn't the nine millionth time they'd done this. It happened mostly every night, except for those times when Drea was too frustrated to try.

Tonight wasn't one of those nights.

They went over the background easily, with Drea recalling, "The old Section 8 was disbanded. Most of the members were killed, except for Darius and Adele. But then Darius disappeared, Adele was killed and Darius's son, Dare, and his half sister, Avery, found each other. And realized they were in trouble, because they were the kids of Section 8 members."

"That's right."

"So Dare and Avery are part of this new Section 8, right? Along with Jem and Key, who are brothers, and Gunner."

"Yes."

"And this new Section 8 started unofficially when Dare kidnapped a woman named Grace but ultimately ended up helping her."

Carolina pointed to a heavily tattooed man with spiky white-blond hair. He stood outside a tattoo shop, his arm wound around the shoulders of a shorter blond woman. "This is Gunner—he's a tattoo artist, and a pretty famous one at that. His father was a former CIA guy and a pretty nasty terrorist. Gunner hid from him for years, until Dare and Avery came along, looking for their father. Turns out that Darius was kidnapped and killed by Gunner's father."

Drea frowned. This part was always tricky. "But Gunner's father was Grace's stepfather—she calls him Rip. And Grace didn't meet Gunner until last year. Together, all of them helped to capture and kill Rip."

"Exactly. And then Gunner tried to leave S8 to keep them safe, once he'd been exposed as Rip's son, and they'd ended up having to help him get rid of some old, dangerous enemies," Carolina added.

As always, Drea muttered, "I swear, if I didn't know better—which I don't—I'd think you were making this up. It's like a soap opera." More so especially because Drea couldn't recall ever meeting any of the players involved.

"I did not make this up . . . but I could always write this up and sell the script. Do you think anyone would watch it?" Carolina mused, then frowned. "I'd have to redact several classified points, though. Perhaps if I changed the names and dates . . ."

Drea sighed and motioned for her to go on with the picture viewing.

"Oh yes. Where were we? Right. So this man right here is Key. He's Jem's brother—younger."

"You haven't said much about Key yet," Drea pointed out.

"Key was in the Army, until he rescued Dare and got court-martialed."

"I thought rescuing someone was a good thing."

"You'd think, wouldn't you? Anyway, that's how they all met. Key and Jem went looking for Dare."

"To thank him?"

"To kill him," Carolina corrected. "And that's when they all realized that they had Gunner in common, and that Grace's stepfather was trying to kill them."

"That would be Gunner's father too."

"Right. But none of them knew that at the time, except for Gunner." Carolina sat back and nodded.

Drea traced her fingers over the tablet where the picture of the team, sitting together on some steps, was looking out at her. The photo had been taken of them especially for her so she could get to know them, that maybe something in their faces would jog her memory.

And then there was Jem. He was in her dreams an awful lot, and before she'd learned anything at all about Jem, she'd assumed the dreams were about Danny. In those dreams that she still had, she'd never see his face, and even though she'd call out to him for help, he'd never turn around.

The first time he did turn around was the night before she saw his picture.

And she still hadn't told any of that to anyone—not Carolina, not the therapist—and she certainly wasn't going to tell Jem, if and when she ever met him. Instead she held on to the dream for dear life, because that was what it was to her—a complete and utter lifesaving moment. And every day and every night she scratched and scrabbled to try to regain another scrap of memory, of him and her time together with Section 8.

Tonight, she didn't ask Carolina any questions about the parts that involved her kidnapping. She repeated those facts over and over in her mind often enough, anyway, and that's all they were to her: facts, with no feelings behind them.

Jem had kidnapped her because he needed a doctor to save Avery, who was dying. Drea had saved her, but spending time with Jem had gotten her in trouble with Danny and the OA. S8 helped her get away from the OA, and she'd gone on the run with them, willingly. And when they had a job to do, one that involved a human trafficker who was after Gunner, she'd gotten involved as a decoy. Unfortunately, from what she'd been told, it'd gone wrong, and she'd been kidnapped.

By the time Jem found her, she'd gone into shock and was close to death. Physically, she'd recovered fine. The memories were coming slowly but surely, but those last months were more like listening to the plot of an action movie as opposed to having anything to do with her life.

Carolina assured her it was no movie plot. That she hadn't done anything wrong during her part of the operation. That S8—Jem especially—felt horribly guilty, and hadn't so much abandoned her as left her with Carolina for her own safety while they continued their attack on human traffickers and other criminals.

"Is this the kind of work you do?" Drea asked Carolina.

"When I retired, I swore I was done with this kind of work. But what am I supposed to do—sit around, read magazines and garden? Those are all fine things, but

I'm trained to kill. Frankly, I'm finding retirement boring. I told Jem I'd be more than willing to help them out, but I'm not going up in planes or crossing the country for jobs. That's the beauty of being old and crotchety—you get to make them come to you."

"Well, I'm very grateful that you took me in."

Carolina patted Drea's hand. "Obviously in my line of work it's hard to have family. I think of Jem as family. Anyone he's close to is my family by default."

Drea's head was swimming with all the information. It was starting to integrate, but still in that frustrating way because it didn't seem like her story.

It was always, however, a hell of a bedtime story. "So I know that Gunner is with Avery. And Key is with . . . ?"

"Many different people," Carolina finished. "Apparently, he's still hung up on some girl from the bayou. That's what Jem says."

Carolina looked as though she didn't believe what Jem said in that regard. All Drea could do was shake her head and mutter, "Old loves," disapprovingly.

"Not all old loves are necessarily bad." Carolina paused. "Granted, right now I can't think of any good ones. But I'd have to say that second loves are better. You're through all that infatuation bullshit and you know what's real. And there's nothing more real than these men and women you're learning about. They've made lots of sacrifices for one another. That's the way you build a successful team."

"And they sacrificed for me too," Drea said thoughtfully.

"Well, honey, they did almost get you killed. Twice," Carolina pointed out.

Drea rolled her eyes. "That's so not helpful."

"Just keeping it real, dear. Isn't that what you all say these days? In my time, it was 'Honesty's the best policy.' But come to think of it, that's total bullshit."

"You and Jem got along well as partners, then?"

Carolina flashed a brief smile. "Quite."

Also available from
New York Times bestselling author

Stephanie Tyler

VIPERS RUN
A Skulls Creek Novel

Former Army Ranger Christian Cage Owens joined the
Vipers Motorcycle Club for its sense of brotherhood. In
return, he pledged to live outside the law, protecting club
members and their families, as well as keeping other MCs
out of Skulls Creek. But when Cage discovers that a rival
MC plans to push meth into his town, he calls an old
Army buddy turned private investigator who's helped the
Vipers in the past. By doing so, Cage endangers both his
friend and Calla Benson, a woman who works in the
PI's office.

Calla knows she's formed a deep connection to a
dangerous man. She quickly discovers that although he
may live by a different set of rules, Cage is an honorable
man who wants to be more than her protector—if only
she can accept his dangerous lifestyle. But Calla comes to
Skulls Creek with her own set of secrets. As she and Cage
put their newfound love to the ultimate test, Cage will
risk everything he cares about to save her...

stephanietyler.com

s0595

Also available from
New York Times bestselling author

Stephanie Tyler

SURRENDER
A Section 8 Novel

For former Navy SEAL Dare O'Rourke, Section 8 was
legendary. The son of one of its missing members, he
grew up in the shadow of its secrets. All he knew was that
it was a cabal of operatives discharged from branches of
the military and reassigned to dangerous, off-the-books
missions. And that their handler was as shrouded in
mystery as the missions themselves. Now the handler of
Section 8 has given orders to kill any remaining
members—along with their families. Dare must save his
long-lost half-sister, whom he was never meant to meet.
They must come together for one last mission to avenge
their families and to survive.

"No one writes a bad-boy hero like Tyler."
—*New York Times* bestselling author Larissa Ione

stephanietyler.com

Available wherever books are sold or at
penguin.com

facebook.com/LoveAlwaysBooks

Also available from
New York Times bestselling author

Stephanie Tyler

UNBREAKABLE
A Section 8 Novel

When Gunner agreed to help Section 8, he didn't realize
his past with international smuggler Drew Landon would
threaten the other mercenaries, and most important,
Avery. In order to protect the mercenaries and Avery, he
makes an impossible choice…and disappears.

Avery's not willing to give up on Gunner. She knows
there's only one way to keep him safe: fake his death and
take him off the grid. But when she finally locates him,
Gunner is harder, more desperate, and on the edge of
self-destruction. Only Avery can find a way to free him
from Landon—and from the demons of his past—before
it's too late.

**"A page turner full of action and secrets."
—Fresh Fiction**

stephanietyler.com

Available wherever books are sold or at
penguin.com

Also available from
New York Times bestselling author

Stephanie Tyler

FRAGMENTED
A Section 8 Novel

When Dr. Drea Timmons was kidnapped during Section 8's last mission, Jem did everything in his power to rescue the woman he'd fallen for—a woman unwillingly recruited for one of S8's most personal and dangerous covert operations. Drea survived, but at a price. The trauma of her capture has rendered her without a single memory of her ordeal—or any recollection of how violently unpredictable her ex-boyfriend, Danny, an Outlaw Angel, had become, or why she had left him.

When Danny threatens to turn Drea over to the feds, Drea has no choice but to trust Jem, the only man who can help her, the only man whose electrifying touch brings back memories—piece by piece—too stirring to forget.

"Prepare yourself for one hot ride."
—Joyfully Reviewed

stephanietyler.com

Available wherever books are sold or at
penguin.com

s0596